UNTRUE BLUE

UNTRUE BLUE

LORD & LADY HETHERIDGE MYSTERY SERIES #7

EMMA JAMESON

For Jim and Barbara, who recently celebrated twenty-five years of marriage

CHAPTER 1

*H*ow to begin, wondered Anthony Hetheridge, private detective, occasional consultant to Scotland Yard, and ninth baron of Wellegrave.

Over the past couple of years, his well-ordered life had spiraled out of control, collapsing in some zones, exploding in others, until the old picture he'd painted—from the start of his police career to exactly three weeks before his sixtieth birthday—burst into bloom like jeweled flowers inside a kaleidoscope. In times past, he'd regarded Wellegrave House, a Grade II-listed building in the heart of Mayfair, as mostly a place to sleep. The only person waiting for him at home had been Harvey, his old-fashioned manservant, a person who could be counted upon to do everything and do it well. In those days, Tony had no wife, no children, no pets, no hobbies, and not even an interesting vice. Now he really only lacked for the vice, and once the baby came, various vices were likely to suggest themselves, or so other parents warned.

The birth of his child was only four weeks away,

according to the reckoning of his wife Kate's obstetrician, Dr. Laidslaw. Just four more weeks of keeping her on bedrest, which she loathed, and keeping her calm and happy, which for her was a tall order when confined to bed. The fact it had been a very wet April, raining almost every day, made her less mutinous about being stuck indoors. But she'd already been in bed for ten days, and she was cranky and frustrated over the prospect of twenty-eight more. Making the question all the more urgent: How to begin?

He parked his new vehicle, a Mercedes EQC 400, in the mews-styled garage, also new, but constructed to look as if it had been beamed in from the Georgian era. Practically everything in and around Wellegrave House was new, but since the dwelling was listed, the proper term was "repaired like-for-like." Living in a Grade II-listed home came with ironclad responsibilities that did not change because of mere circumstances. In his case, those circumstances included a house fire that gutted the ground floor, a serial killer's attack, and occasional threats to him and his family by the now-deceased killer's deranged fans.

Tony had kept the Bentley—it had been in his family for a dog's age, and Harvey loved it—but sold his silver Lexus coupe; various security concerns regarding it had been identified while he and his family were, for lack of a better term, in hiding. Now with the attack a year distant, his injuries only a memory, and Kate's rehab complete, he suspected giving the Lexus the push might have been unnecessary. But it was done, and he rather enjoyed driving the new SUV. It could travel two hundred miles on a single charge and ownership entitled him a one hundred percent discount on London's congestion charge. Moreover, it had various info-tainment options. However much he loathed the Franken-term "infotainment," it served to keep his adopted son, Henry, and his brother-in-law, Ritchie, quietly content whilst riding in the back. Both seemed a bit rattled by the imminent prospect of a new baby Hetheridge, so little luxuries didn't go amiss.

From the exterior, Wellegrave House looked precisely as it had pre-fire, but the moment Tony stepped over the threshold, the newness washed over him like that April's ever-present rain. Under Harvey's precise direction, the floors had been replaced with like-for-like materials (at a dizzying cost) and the walls were repapered with a vintage pattern from 1910, similar to the irreplaceable wallpaper that had gone up in smoke. The ruined light fixtures had been swapped out, including the foyer chandelier and all of the ground floor wall sconces. But the total effect was still new as far as Tony was concerned, because all the disapproving pictures of Hetheridges past were gone. Now the crated portraits occupied a mini-storage unit in South London, where they would frighten no one but the occasional rat. Harvey had been shocked by the disrespect shown to the stony visages of past Anthonys and Millicents and Leonards and Lucilles, but Tony had whistled while he packed them away. He very much looked forward to never seeing them again.

Post-fire, the living room had also been transformed. The mantle and hearth were the same, but all the old furniture was gone, even those pieces that had been rescued from the fire. Goodbye to fringed brocade curtains better suited to a house of horrors; farewell to the bulky walnut canterbury that only gathered dust; sayonara to the green velvet sofa with lumpy horsehair stuffing. He and Kate had agreed on what Harvey called "stylized Contemporary-Georgian fusion," which meant they'd bought new furniture that was classic, well-proportioned, and highly fire resistant, just in case.

Now that Wellegrave House's living room offered comfy

places to sit and pleasant photos to look at—Kate, Henry, Ritchie, Maura, and Jules, plus Paul Bhar, his wife Emmeline, and their newborn daughter Evvy—Tony could now be induced to spend an hour there without manufacturing an escape.

"Good evening, Mrs. Snell," he greeted the woman sitting on the sleek new sofa. Though he'd known her for over thirty years, they still addressed one another formally during working hours. After his retirement from the Yard, she'd followed him into his second career as a private detective. In the early days, there'd been so little for her to do, she'd frequently resorted to light housekeeping to earn her pay; she was the sort of person who couldn't bear to be less than completely busy. It was rare to see her sitting down before six o'clock, especially empty-handed as she was now—no book or smartphone, no teacup, but just sitting on the sofa with a blank expression on her face. That meant one thing. She knew.

"Oh, Tony." Her voice didn't tremble, but the use of his given name said it all. "How dreadful. Perfectly dreadful."

"I know." He searched for something profound to say, or at least useful, but nothing came to him. "I don't suppose—that is to say, I certainly hope no one—"

"No. She hasn't been told," Mrs. Snell broke in, reading his mind as she often did. After so many years as his administrative assistant, and now his personal assistant, she frequently understood his needs before he did. "I rang key people around the Yard and absolutely forbid anyone to call or text Mrs. Hetheridge. I made each person give me their word. They did."

He wasn't surprised. Although Mrs. Snell had tendered her resignation on the very day he was forced out, she was still something of a living legend among her fellow secretaries, and held sway over many of the senior homicide detectives, too. Few men or women, including battle-hardened Met veterans, possessed the intestinal fortitude to defy Mrs. Snell. Even Kate was still rather edgy around her, and she was not only the lady of the house, but Lady Kate, if one wanted to be precise about it.

"Where's Henry?"

"Finishing his homework. Is it possible for a ten-year-old to suffer from teenage moodiness?"

"Maybe. He's always been ahead of the curve." Tony didn't request explication; he knew why the boy was going through a rough patch. "And Ritchie?"

"Upstairs watching a movie."

"Good day?"

"So-so. I think he feeds off Henry's moods. He must've said it fifty times today."

Tony nodded. No need to ask what "it" was. Ritchie's modes of communication varied, but when he hit upon a word or phrase he liked, he wasn't shy about repeating it. For a time, he'd pointed at his sister Kate's burgeoning belly and said, "Fat." She hadn't minded in the slightest, but Henry, who'd found it exasperating, had taken it upon himself to teach Ritchie the difference between a midriff that was pregnant vs. one that was merely plump. Once the boy had successfully convinced his uncle that Kate would soon give birth, Ritchie discovered a new phrase to express his feelings: "No baby."

Tony asked, "How's supper coming along?"

Mrs. Snell frowned. "I can't vouch for this new cook's ability. Lunch was positively briny."

"Missing Harvey?" He tried not to sound smug.

"I suppose." She blinked behind her thick magnifying lenses. "But if you repeat that to him, I'll deny it."

"Silent as the grave. Oh, and perhaps now I'd better break the news—he's taking two more weeks in the south of France. He rang this morning to ask permission and I said yes."

Mrs. Snell's eyes flashed in a way that had terrified many a junior officer. "But that will be ten consecutive weeks' holiday. It's outrageous."

"It's well-earned. He moved heaven and earth to get this house fully restored ahead of schedule," Tony said firmly. "Moreover, should you ever want the same amount of paid time off, my dear Vera, you have only to ask."

"Nonsense. You couldn't do without me." She sighed. "Now that you've mentioned dinner, I'd better pop in the kitchen and reassure myself she isn't cooking with ghost peppers. Have you delayed long enough?"

"Perhaps." He started for Wellegrave House's antique lift.

The old rattletrap monstrosity was now in better working order than it had been in decades. This delighted Henry and Ritchie, who never missed a chance to ride in it. Even Tony found it more tempting now that the brass grille latched firmly in place and the car ascended smoothly without jerks and creaks. Nevertheless, at the lift he thought better of it and redirected himself toward the stairs. Although tired after an emotionally draining day, he climbed them at his usual moderate jog, ignoring the twinge in his arthritic left knee. "Twinge" was probably too kind a word. These days, it flat-out ached by midafternoon. Sometimes, especially when he was working out, the joint got his attention with a sudden sharp pain, like a nail driven through his kneecap. It didn't matter. He refused to change how he customarily did things, from his exercise routine to always taking the stairs. Some problems were best faced, and others were best denied. His aging joints fell in the latter category.

Although the master bedroom he shared with Kate had

received only mild smoke damage, they'd taken the opportunity to do over its furnishings, too. Now the bed was a California king, the color scheme was Kate's favorite—cobalt and silver—and since Dr. Laidslaw placed her on bedrest, the television had been upgraded, too. In the first year of their marriage, they'd hardly had time or interest in watching telly, apart from occasional news broadcasts. But now that Kate was home all day and abstaining from work on doctor's orders, she kept the TV switched on from the moment Tony kissed her goodbye to the moment he reappeared to ask how her day had been.

The door was open. Pausing by the jamb, he peeked around the corner to catch a glimpse of his wife unawares. This long-wished-for, completely unexpected pregnancy had been hard on her, but Kate was bearing up with the sort of grit he'd come to expect of her. Presently she was nesting with the duvet cast aside—overheated again, no doubt. Her lower back was supported by two pillows and her bare feet were propped up on a third. Apparently she'd spent part of the day on YouTube tutorials again, because her typically untidy blonde hair was arranged in neat spiral curls. Judging from the open makeup kit beside her and the amount of kohl around her eyes, she'd done a beauty tutorial, too.

On television, a woman shrieked. Not a regular TV yelp, but a full-throated scream of unadulterated terror.

"Still on your Hammer horror movies, I see," he said, strolling into the room.

"*Taste the Blood of Dracula*," Kate agreed. "A ripping yarn if there ever was one."

"Mrs. Snell is convinced our child will come into the world permanently petrified."

"She's barmy. Nipper will come into the world with a stake in one hand and a silver bullet in the other." Since they'd declined to be told the sex of the baby, and repeatedly saying "him or her" was tiresome, the next Hetheridge was called Nipper for the time being.

"Barmy? I'd like to see you call her that to her face."

"Please. I'm up the duff, not clinically insane. Mrs. Snell is holding this operation together now that I'm laid up and Harvey has swanned off to Saint-Tropez."

"Yes, well, I'm afraid he's in for another two weeks of olive groves and azure seas. But he promises to be back in time for Nipper's arrival."

"He'd better. I miss him terribly." Kate smiled up at Tony. "What do you think of my makeup? Henry said I should join the vampire circus."

"Henry is out of sorts," Tony said, sidestepping what he thought of the exaggerated eyeliner. "Mind if I sit?"

Kate blinked her over-mascaraed eyes at him. "Of course not, guv."

He sighed. There was no fooling her. When delivering bad news, a task for which he had several lifetimes' experience, he always reverted to gentle formality. And Kate never missed a thing.

"Does it have to do with your case? The blackmailer?"

"What? Oh, no, that's sewn up. Sorry, I should've told you. It was the son's ex-girlfriend sending the letters, as I suspected."

"Is it something to do with the Yard, then?"

"Yes." He eased down beside her, careful not to upset her mattress kingdom: lipsticks, bottles of nail varnish, fancy brushes, tissues, and a curling iron. "I'm afraid I have bad news. Very bad news, as a matter of fact."

He paused, not for effect, but to allow her a moment to prepare herself. Long ago he'd learned to break it in stages, much slower than necessary, allowing the recipient's mind to leap ahead. Somehow the psyche absorbed the shock better that way. The worst approach was to drop the facts on the receiving party like an anvil to the head. Even with a fellow homicide detective, that way was needlessly traumatic.

"All right, Tony." Kate was more emotional these days thanks to pregnancy hormones, but her voice was steady. "Fire away."

"This morning, one of your colleagues—not Paul, of course," Tony said hastily. "This morning, one of your other colleagues was found by a neighbor. She was lying unresponsive on the floor of her flat. The front door was unlatched and some items were taken." He paused again, letting Kate's mind leap ahead.

"Don't say Gulls," she pleaded.

He sighed again. "I'm so very sorry, my love."

Kate let out a wail he'd heard countless times. The most typical response to news of sudden death was some kind of cry. But to hear it from her lips was excruciating.

"Amelia can't be dead. Wasn't she only thirty? If that! She can't—" Kate broke off, too shocked to weep, hazel eyes searching his face. "How?"

Tony's eyes stung. Blinking rapidly to clear them, he thought of lost colleagues from years past. Some died under tragic circumstances, but none of them had been as young or as full of promise as DC Amelia Gulls. Watching Kate reflect his own emotions back to him threatened to override his control. He took a moment, then said,

"Kate, the only thing that matters is, she's gone. I don't think the details are relevant. You shouldn't go out of your way to upset yourself. You have to think of your health, and the baby's."

"Oh, my God." Kate stared at him at horror. "You mean you can't even tell me what happened to her? Did she—was she—"

He waved a hand to forestall speculation. Imaginings

from an experienced copper like Kate could be more appalling than the plain facts.

"Very well. Paul rang me and asked me to come to the scene. He's engaged me to consult on the matter. Shall I report what I observed?"

"Yes!" She was getting angry, her go-to emotional state, as he grew colder, which was his.

"Kate. Can you at least try to remain calm?"

She closed her eyes and took a few deep breaths. When she opened then again, she seemed more composed, though her cheeks were pink and the well of her throat was blood red. "Tell me everything. I won't interrupt."

"Very well. Around nine o'clock this morning, DC Gulls was discovered by a neighbor who immediately rang 999. She had been dead for some time. Our friend Trevor Stepp was the medical examiner on call. I asked him for his preliminary conclusions. He estimated the time of death as sometime between nine p.m. and midnight, at least twelve hours before discovery.

"As to the body, DC Gulls was found fully dressed in the clothes she'd worn to the office. There was no evidence of sexual assault or a protracted struggle. Dr. Stepp believes the intruder broke into her flat and waited for her behind her door. When she entered, he sprang out and struck her down with a heavy object, probably the base of a lamp. Once she was down and either stunned or unconscious, he wrapped the lamp cord around her neck and killed her via ligature. That was how she was found, with the cord still in place."

Although Tony described the death in the flattest, most professionally neutral words possible, the action nevertheless unfolded in his mind's eye. DC Gulls had been very petite, both in size and stature, with springy red-gold curls and an exuberance that never flagged, no matter how hard the job or how long the hours. From the moment he'd met her, bullied relentlessly at the Yard for her diminutive size and bubbly demeanor, he'd recognized in her all the ingredients for an exceptional detective: dedication, attention to detail, good instincts, and a sense of humor. He'd expected to soon see Gulls recognized within the MPS as a rising star. Instead, she lay silently in a cool steel locker, waiting to be claimed by her next-of-kin.

"Garroted," Kate breathed. "I can't bear to think of her dying that way."

Tony, who could still see Gulls's distorted features, was grateful Kate had at least been spared that. He could think of only one truthful detail he could offer to make her feel any better, and after a moment's hesitation, he did.

"I should add there were no self-inflicted fingernail marks on her face or neck. Dr. Stepp thinks that after stunning her with a blow to the head, the attacker pulled the cord very tight, compressing both carotids as well as the airway. In which case, she probably had little or no idea what hit her. It may have been over quite soon."

Kate said nothing. Tony sat quietly at her side, wishing he could weather the storm for her, or at least share it in some way. On the television, another woman let out a terrified shriek as Christopher Lee's Dracula went for her throat. Annoyed, Tony snapped, "Power off TV."

"Powering off TV," agreed the female-sounding voice that controlled such things.

Kate looked startled. "Was it still on? Sorry. Miles away."

"You might do better with something a bit less violent."

"Maybe." She sounded doubtful. "But I like Hammer horror movies. When you watch them, it's impossible to feel sorry for yourself. Yes, I'm stuck on bedrest and I hate it, but the people in those films have real problems. Vampires and werewolves and Dr. Frankenstein creating monsters every other year..." Her voice wavered. "Amelia had her whole life ahead of her. She was lovely. Just lovely. A good copper and a good detective and..." Kate's face crumpled and the rest was only gasping sobs.

"I know," Tony murmured, pulling her to him and holding her tight. "It's bloody awful. That's all."

And obscene. And downright evil, he thought, but there was no point saying it aloud.

Kate tried to pull away, though her tears still flowed freely. "My makeup...I'm staining your shirt..."

"Damn my shirt." When he held her tighter, she gave up resisting and cried herself out. As she did, Tony once again wished it had been possible to conceal DC Gulls's death until after the baby's safe delivery.

He'd read over the risks associated with preterm births many times—almost to the point of obsession—and knew them by heart. In the modern era, it didn't sound so bad, a child arriving three or four weeks early, but even late preterm infants were at risk for myriad complications, including breathing issues and brain problems. There was Kate's health to consider, too. According to Dr. Laidslaw, her preeclampsia was mild and her most recent bloodwork was satisfactory. But while Tony could tolerate risk when it came to her chosen career—after all, she'd been a dedicated copper when he fell in love with her—he was determined to make her pregnancy as safe as possible. Even if it meant lying through his teeth to spare her unnecessary anguish.

"I know what you're thinking," she sniffed, pulling away from him to blow her nose into a tissue. "You're thinking you should have sworn Paul, Mrs. Snell, and every single person at the Yard to secrecy."

"Alas, I was told a conspiracy so large can get a bit bothersome."

"Probably true." She wadded up the tissue, flung it in the bin's general direction, and traced a finger down his shirt front, smiling weakly. "There's gobs of mascara and eyeshadow all over you. Is that a silk tie?"

"They're all silk. And I have more than I'll ever need." To prove it, he unknotted the tie with a practiced motion, rolled it into a ball, and pitched it toward the bin. It missed the target even more spectacularly than Kate's wadded-up tissue.

"Oh, I wish I had video of that. No one will ever believe it." From her cosmetic arsenal, Kate selected a pop-up container of pre-moistened wipes, pulled out a handful, and began working on her face.

Taking the wipes away, he said, "Let me. Close your eyes so I can do it properly." Getting to work, he continued, "My first notion, when I got over the initial shock of Gulls's death, was to devise a way to keep you in the dark forever. That being impossible, I started thinking of ways to distract you. Nothing seemed likely to suffice, short of horse tranquilizers."

"Elephant tranquilizers. How could I possibly—"

He silenced her with a vigorous swipe to the lips. "Then I came on an inescapable conclusion. The only way to calm you down after upsetting you so deeply is to put you to work."

Kate caught her breath. "You mean it, guv?"

"I'm no one's guv except Mrs. Snell's, and I'd never dare say so. But it already seems clear that DC Gulls's death was no chance robbery gone wrong. It reeks of premeditation."

"Was anything taken from her flat?"

"Paul is trying to create an inventory, but since she had no flatmate, it may be hard to determine. Certainly her handbag was gone and a framed picture had been pulled off the wall. And yet."

"What?"

"The doorknobs were wiped. The lamp was wiped. And in the corridor where her flat is located, there's one CCTV camera. Its lens had been blocked with an acrylic resin— Super Glue or similar. Paul checked with the building's security monitoring company. The footage is reviewed only if there's a complaint. When that particular feed was looked at, they found the lens to have been blocked for almost thirty-six hours. So not a spur-of-the-moment operation."

"Exterior cameras?"

"One. Rather the worse for wear and discovered to be non-functioning. Either negligence on the building's part, or another precaution taken by the killer." Done with scrubbing Kate's face, he balled up the dirty wipes and tossed them in the bin—this time hitting the target dead-on while her eyes were closed. "Much better. Now tell me, DI Hetheridge. Impressions?"

"It sounds like a hit. Do any of her neighbors recall seeing or hearing something that seems odd in retrospect?"

"Paul's team was still checking around when I left. I don't think it's likely. Most of the people who live in that building are single young professionals with busy lives. From a policing standpoint, it ought to be against the law to have a multi-unit residence unless at least two of the tenants are old busybodies."

"Sexist."

"Not at all. I said busybodies. You're the one who assumed they'd be female. I asked the landlady what she could tell us about DC Gulls's social life. She said Gulls had small, informal parties in her flat at least once a week. No sinister types reported. The landlady called them clean-cut, polite, and soberly dressed."

"She's describing a load of coppers." Kate sighed. "Once people finally started accepting her at the Yard, Amelia was determined to keep them sweet. Reinvented herself as a social butterfly. I should've done that myself, back when Jackson was making my life hell, only I was too prickly and stubborn. Maybe too afraid of rejection, too. But Amelia was fearless. She invited over virtually anyone of her rank or below—Paul's been over, and I popped in once to make an appearance. It was fun, the booze flowing and everyone talking shop. And now it'll be a bloody nuisance. Three dozen unique hair samples and bits of DNA, all of it leading to the Met's active duty roster."

"Paul and DC Kincaid share your opinion."

"Oh. Poor Sean, he worked closely with her on lots of cases. How's he taking it?"

"Not well. Turns out he was seeing her. I had no idea, did you?"

"No. Lord, that makes this even worse. They would've been so good together. Was it serious?"

"I'm not sure. I can only tell you he was white as a sheet. Stuttering a bit, and he only does that when he's badly shaken. He may need a leave of absence in order to function properly."

"Poor sod. It's a hit, Tony, it has to be," Kate insisted. "Amelia was a total straight arrow. No skeletons in her closet. We need to look at the cases she was working on. Were any of them controversial? Touching on Interpol or Europol stuff?"

"Don't know yet. I'm merely a consultant." Cupping her face with both hands, he kissed her mouth, pleased by her righteous indignation. The grief would linger, of course, but as long as she was on fire to catch a killer, he didn't fear for her state of mind.

She said, "I want to discuss it with Paul. Can we ring him?"

He withdrew his mobile from an inner jacket pocket, displaying it tantalizingly. "If we call him, can I count on you to stay calm?"

Kate's eyes flashed. "Sure," she said sweetly. "But remember. I won't be on bedrest forever. And once I'm up and about, I'll get revenge on you for smothering me like a—oh! A kick." She pressed a hand to her belly and grinned. "That's Nipper's way of agreeing with me."

"I think you'll find Nipper is very much on my side," he said, and rang Paul.

CHAPTER 2

*D*I Deepal "Paul" Bhar had temporarily given up on three things many considered essential: sleep, sex, and peace of mind. Sex had gone in the eighth month of pregnancy, on that fateful Saturday "date" night when his wife Emmeline told him if he tried to get a leg over, she'd snip off his dangly bits and feed them to a ferret.

"Haven't you done enough? And why would you even want to mess about with me?" she'd demanded, draped miserably across the futon with her belly pointing straight up. "For heaven's sake, I'm gargantuan. Do you realize people ask me *every day* if I'm sure there's just one in there?"

"I think you're beautiful."

"Stuff your *I think*," she'd snapped. "Too right I'm beautiful. There's nothing wrong with my face. It's my body that's blown up like a Slitheen."

Paul suspected she meant an Adipose, a race of generously-proportioned *Dr. Who* aliens that were cuter than the Slitheen, despite being literal blobs of fat. But he hadn't said so, because it never paid to correct Emmeline's pop culture references, especially when she was in a mood.

As for sleep, it had gone three and a half weeks ago, on the day his flawless, delicate, superlative daughter Evangeline Sharada Bhar came home. Before her arrival, he'd been a great enthusiast for sleep, and although policemen frequently worked long hours, he'd always managed to make up the loss. Not anymore. Evvy, as they called her, spelling it like that to discourage people from pronouncing it E-V, had her own priorities: to sleep at least forty minutes straight, to feed every two hours, and to fill up nappies. She also cried at least two hours out of every twenty-four, which Paul's mum Sharada breezily assured him was nothing to worry about.

"You cried far more. Morning, noon, and night. You were such a crier," she told him, leaning over the crib to smile down at Evvy.

"I wasn't," Paul had said lamely, wondering if it were true.

"He was," Sharada said, aiming at glance at Emmeline, and they'd exchanged a knowing sort of laugh.

"I'm beginning to regret the day you two buried the hatchet," he'd said, and skedaddled.

Regarding his peace of mind, Paul had never even realized he enjoyed such a thing—what with his many qualms, misgivings, bugaboos, and deep-seated fears—until that peace was suddenly and perhaps irrevocably gone. On the ride home from St. Thomas's Hospital, it occurred to him in a horrific burst of clarity that if the cabbie blew through a stop sign or executed a reckless turn, the darling little creature in Emmeline's arms might be hurt. Unthinkable—yet absolutely possible. And almost entirely beyond his control.

As the cab ride went on, he'd become more and more worried. Long ago, he'd accepted his own mortality—working on a murder squad will do that for you—and as much as he loved Emmeline, she was her own person and never his to control. But his daughter Evvy, this brand-new, perfect little being? Her welfare was in the hands of a cabbie who'd started their ride by mentioning that since York City F.C. had decided to lose every match, he should probably just hook his cab into oncoming traffic and be done with it. Paul could've hit the panic button, demanded the cabbie pull over and let them hoof it home, but who said the streets of London were one hundred percent safe? What about muggers? Machete-wielding terrorists? Frozen loo contents dropped by a passing plane?

So his peace of mind was out the window and might never come back. But there was so much joy in cuddling Evvy, singing to her as she curled her hand around his finger, that he was learning to do without. His mum assured him a day would come when Evvy slept through the night, graciously allowing her parents to do the same, and he hoped that around the same time, Emmeline might become a tad more receptive to his advances. Pre-baby, they'd never had any problems in the bedroom; on the contrary, that part of their relationship had always worked, even when every other aspect threatened total collapse.

In the meantime, there was work to sustain him. He'd been riding high professionally for months. Ever since helping to rescue numerous hostages from Sir Duncan Godington, risking his own life many times in the process, Paul's old reputation as a bungler was forgotten. It had never been a fair or accurate representation, as Tony had reminded him time and again; it was perhaps only because Paul had internalized that label so completely that he'd often seemed to stumble and bumble his way through Toff Squad investigations. Receiving a promotion and the AHS Silver Medal had done much to exorcise that false perception.

Kate's being on leave made it easier, too, he thought, discomfited by his own disloyalty. But it was true. Kate's absence during her long post-Sir Duncan recuperation had been lonely for Paul, who was still adjusting to having DCI Vic

Jackson for a guv instead of Tony. But without DI Kate Hetheridge around to cast a shadow, Paul's own abilities had shone clearly for the first time in ages.

When she exited for maternity leave, he'd again found himself in great demand. Now he was routinely looped into executive meetings and invited to superiors' private homes for drinks. Even his old enemy Vic Jackson, who'd surprised everyone by sobering up, installing a filter on his mighty gob, and making a go of running the Toff Squad, now seemed to trust Paul completely. One day he'd awakened to realize he wasn't a "diversity hire," as he'd been called, or Tony Hetheridge's pet project, or any other infuriating trope. He was actually popular with the Powers That Be, as Kate called them, or the old boys' network, as Tony called them. He was in the club.

What if she hates me for it? Paul thought, emerging from Green Park's tube station and walking briskly toward Euston Place. His feet knew the way to Wellegrave House, and would take him there without troubling his brain.

If I'm really one of the boys, there's only one thing for it. I'll have to make Kate one of them, too.

It wouldn't be easy. For years, Paul had believed his dark complexion, South Asian surname, and aura of "otherness"— alleged otherness, as he'd grown up in Clerkenwell and was English down to his tea-infused marrow—was a greater stumbling block that anything his female colleagues faced. Now he wasn't so sure.

With Kate, they used to say she was East End and slutty. Then they said she was competent but overaggressive. Then they said she was lazy and slept her way to a promotion, Paul thought. *Now they say she has no ambition, that she's more interested in having babies than doing a job. But didn't they used to say she was an odd duck, and any normal woman in her mid-thirties would have a family?*

It seemed that "they," the aggregate of public opinion around the Yard regarding Kate Hetheridge, disliked something about her, something amorphous that could twist or expand to fit any new development. True, the Powers that Be admitted, she always got the job done, and they counted on her. But it was evident that, given the choice, they much preferred a man like Paul. Over drinks at his home the previous week, AC Deaver had actually put it that way: "You know, Paul, it's just easier with a man like you."

And I thought he was Tony and Kate's personal friend.

The memory rankled. It wasn't because Deaver's confession surprised him. Years ago, Deaver had been one of those "standing athwart history," or more accurately athwart the promotional ladder at Scotland Yard, yelling "Stop!" at the incursion of women detectives in their midst. What bothered Paul was his own reaction. What had he done? Smiled and murmured his thanks, that's what. How could he do that to Kate when she was the best friend he'd ever had, not counting Tony? Moreover, as a DI, he had a responsibility to the up-and-coming women under his command. Of those young officers, the sharpest by far was DC Gulls...

That unguarded thought, from a mind not yet accustomed to thinking of Gulls in the past tense, made his throat tighten. Maybe Sharada was right about him being a crier; he'd already broken down once, and might do it again before the day was out. Gulls hadn't looked the part of a detective constable—she'd been more like your favorite kindergarten teacher, the one who led the class in "Frère Jacques" and coaxed even the shyest kids out of their shells. The sight of her garroted corpse, with its bulging eyes and swollen tongue, had been almost unendurable. He tried to tell himself everything that ever made her Amelia Gulls had gone. That what remained on the floor of her flat was only a placeholder, desanctified and discarded.

Did we ever fully appreciate her? I didn't at first, and neither did Kate, until the chief jerked us up short. He saw her potential right away. And now some bastard has stolen it forever.

Still guided by his feet, Paul crossed over to the cul-de-sac where Wellegrave House sat. The restored facade looked happy and rested, much like the chief himself these days. Although Tony Hetheridge had retired from his post as Chief Superintendent over a year ago, Paul had never made the transition from honorific to Christian name. Desisting with "guv" or "boss" had been tough enough. Calling him "Chief" was as informal as he could stand. Simply calling him "Tony" would feel as disrespectful as calling his mum "Sharada," and Tony wouldn't stand for friends addressing him as "Lord Hetheridge" in his own house. So "Chief" he was, and probably always would be.

Funny how whatever the Powers That Be has against Kate, they seemed to have against Gulls, too, Paul thought. He resolved to wait and see if Corinne Baker, the Yard's newest female DC, found herself facing the same pressures. He'd already heard her criticized as aggressive. Someone else called her cold. Without DC Gulls around to absorb some flak, would DC Baker suddenly be regarded as coarse, stuck-up, overambitious, and terminally lazy, all at the same time?

He arrived at Wellegrave House's front gate. Once upon a time it had been nine feet high, with a common three digit electronic lock. Now it was twelve feet high and made of reinforced pillars that could withstand a vehicular ramming attack. As for the new security system, it generated a different alphanumeric passcode every hour. To gain entry, Paul had to text someone inside, usually Harvey, and wait for the magic sequence.

Though he knew Mrs. Snell had moved out of her house in Muswell Hill and settled permanently inside Wellegrave House—an arrangement that suited everyone—he nevertheless texted Tony instead. When it came to Mrs. Snell (whom he no longer called ghastly except in the secret recesses of his heart), he gave her nearly as wide a berth as he had in the old days at Scotland Yard. Though Paul thought of himself as charming, witty, and not bad to look at, his best antics always fell flat with Mrs. Snell. Like Queen Victoria, she was not amused.

In a few seconds, his mobile beeped, signaling the passcode's arrival. Paul punched in the numbers and entered, pausing to turn and make sure the automatic gate latched properly behind him. Security concerns had done to Tony Hetheridge what shiny gadgets and enticing phone apps could not; it had made him turn on his mobile and leave it on, night and day. The man who once gloried in being incommunicado whenever he felt like it had bowed to his family's new normal: safety first.

Such layers of added security were, of course, the unfortunate legacy of the Sir Duncan Godington affair. He was dead, but his small band of worshipful followers—a group currently under surveillance by the Met and known as the Fan Club—was very much alive, and had created a sort of religion around Sir Duncan.

The least dangerous members of the Fan Club insisted Sir Duncan was still alive. They were lost in what Paul thought of as serial killer fanfic, posting long dissertations online about how Sir Duncan had faked his death, or had his brain transplanted into a cloned body, or uploaded his consciousness into cyberspace. It wasn't that Paul considered them harmless—he believed there was something intrinsically dangerous about people who idolized psychopathic killers, even if they never committed violent acts themselves. At the very least, they were morally repugnant—more so, in his opinion, than Sir Duncan himself. He, at least, was a freak of nature, born with abnormalities that drove him to commit his crimes. According to the Met's report on the Fan Club, fully half of its members were categorized as typical citizens, with no history of anti-social behavior. Probably they simply enjoyed morbid fantasies, but their fixation on Sir Duncan's supposed return repelled him.

The most dangerous Fan Clubbers are the ones who understand that Sir Duncan's dead, and the chief killed him, Paul thought. *One day there might have to be a reckoning.*

As he approached the front steps, the door opened slowly, as if by magic. Inside the foyer, lights burned brightly and the restored black and white marble tiles gleamed. But no one, it seemed, was there to greet him.

"Well, now. Isn't this mysterious?" Paul remarked to thin air. "Didn't reckon they'd put in an automatic door." After a moment's pretended hesitation, he advanced.

"Boo!" cried Henry, leaping into view.

"No baby!" cried Ritchie, landing beside Henry and grinning at Paul. He loved the "scare Paul" routine.

Paul said, "Ritchie, the word is boo. Remember? I wasn't nearly so frightened this time because only Henry shouted boo."

"No baby," Ritchie said.

"He's hopeless." Henry sounded surprisingly bitter. "There's no point explaining. He won't listen."

Paul regarded the boy sympathetically. He was usually quite good with his uncle Ritchie, who lived by his own lights and was occasionally too much for anyone but Kate or a paid carer to handle. Today, however, Henry seemed close to his limit. "On my last and not very good nerve," as Sharada Bhar put it.

"Yeah, I get it. Nobody listens to me, either." Paul shut the door behind him, again turning to verify that the electronic lock flipped from green to red. "How's school?"

The boy groaned.

"That good, huh? Oh—your specs are a bit askew, did you know that?"

"Of course I know it," Henry erupted, throwing his arms in the air. "Some tosser pushed me down in the lunch queue and bent my frames. Mrs. Snell will take me to the optician next week. Until then I just have to live with it. Typical."

"You know, kiddo, it might be easier to run around shouting 'No baby.'"

He only meant to lighten the mood, but the boy's cheeks went scarlet. "That's not it!" he roared. Usually he liked talking to Paul, arguing over thorny intellectual puzzles like whether the Mandalorian could win a fight with Iron Man, but apparently not tonight. Like a child half his age, he simply ran away, darting into the living room and out of sight.

Ritchie, unperturbed, was still smiling at Paul. His specs were askew, too, but in his case, it was par for the course. Those heavy duty plastic frames took a lot of abuse. Under the foyer's brilliant new lights, Paul saw how scratched up the lenses were. He also noticed for the first time that there was plenty of gray in Ritchie's curly mop.

We must be about the same age, he thought, surprised by the realization. *My hair would be that gray if I didn't color it.*

"No baby," Ritchie said.

"Understood. You do you, mate," Paul agreed, and headed for the lift.

* * *

AT THE MASTER bedroom's threshold, he stopped and bellowed, "Everybody decent?"

"Get in here," Kate barked from the bed. Propped up on pillows, she had swollen eyes and a red nose but wasn't crying. That came as a relief; if she started, he'd start. As for the chief, Paul honestly didn't know if he was capable of tears, but the idea was jarring. Bad enough that the world had lost Detective Constable Amelia Gulls. If the old man broke down, time and space might crack asunder.

"You have fancy hair," he announced, scrutinizing Kate's spiral curls. "It's weird. I don't like it. Also, your son Henry just had meltdown for no reason, and your big brother has come out against you having a baby."

"Never fear. We have a plan for that, when the time comes. As for Henry, he's having a bit of a moment. It's not easy being ten years old. Especially when things keep changing."

"Yes, well, I suppose in ten years Evvy may be having a moment," Paul said, though he didn't actually believe it. At ten his daughter would be exceptionally smart, wise, and emotionally mature. She would achieve this in spite of her parents' manifold flaws—his bouts of neuroticism, Emme-line's fits of temper, and her grandmother Sharada's control-ling tendencies. He didn't know *how* she would sidestep such flaws, especially if they continued to be acted out in front of her on a daily basis, but she would. Because she was the most perfect little girl in the world.

"What's with the mooncalf look? Oh, is it because you mentioned Evvy?" Kate smiled, looking a touch mooncalfy herself. "I'll allow it. Think Ems might bring the baby round tomorrow? I'd love some cheering up."

"I reckon that can be arranged. Where's Tony?"

"Getting changed. I cried all over his shirt."

Paul nodded. He didn't have to babble about how Gulls's murder was terrible, or unfair, or atrocious; they could communicate all that just by looking into each other's eyes. Instead, he skipped ahead to what really mattered now: what they could do about it.

"The investigation's already well underway. I don't care

how many extra officers I have to put on it or how long it takes. We'll nail the killer. See if we don't."

"That's the spirit," Tony said, emerging from the master bedroom's deep walk-in closet. It had been a separate room until 1910, when one of his Edwardian forebears had knocked down a wall to make room for the essentials of that opulent age: morning coats, frock coats, Derbies, damask gowns, chiffon skirts, cartwheel hats, and heaven knew what else. Paul would've gloried in such a fashion repository—most his own bachelor wardrobe was currently stashed at his mum's house to make room for the baby—but Kate's side of the closet was less than half full. For the last month he'd seen her in nothing but ill-fitting pajamas, and while he was tempted to tease her about it, he didn't dare. Instead he gave Tony a sweeping glance from head to toe.

"It's half-seven. You're in your own home. Are wingtips really necessary?"

"I'm in the habit of going shod."

"And the tie under your jumper? Is that for me?"

"It's good to have standards. Keeps the rot at bay."

"When I'm home, I go about in a t-shirt and boxers. Sometimes just the t-shirt."

"A mental image I did not request, and could have done without," Tony said equitably, pulling an armchair up to Kate's bedside and gesturing for Paul to do the same. "Have you eaten?"

He shook his head. "I forgot all about it. That might be a first."

"I don't think I'll ever eat again," Kate said.

"Nonsense. I've asked the cook to bring up a light meal. Soup, fresh bread and butter, and cut fruit," Tony said.

"I can't eat it."

"You can if you try."

"Paul, do you order Ems about this way?" Kate demanded.

He let out a slightly hysterical giggle. "No."

"I'm not ordering anyone about. I'm suggesting. Quite reasonably," Tony said. "Now. While we wait, let's discuss the matter at hand."

"Yes, guv," Paul and Kate said in unison, and for a moment it felt just like old times.

CHAPTER 3

When Kate Hetheridge said she might never eat again, she meant it. The news about Gulls's murder turned her stomach, which had been disrupted throughout her pregnancy. Contrary to popular belief, morning sickness wasn't just for mornings, nor was it restricted to the first trimester. She'd been intermittently ravenous or nauseous, and prone to bouts of indigestion, too. Paul would've let her forgo dinner as she brooded over Gulls's death, but Tony wouldn't have it. Fetching her a cyclizine tablet and bottle of water, he'd simply returned to his seat, handed her the medicine, and waited for her to take it. Cyclizine usually did the trick.

He *was* ordering her about, but sometimes she secretly enjoyed it. At moments like this, it was nice to feel looked after.

Tony told Paul, "Before you arrived, I reported to Kate the salient facts as I understood them. I don't suppose anything new has come to your attention since I left the scene?"

"No. Dr. Stepp will have an unsigned preliminary report

for me tomorrow morning, but the head of CWC Labs—they're the ones we're using this month—already rang to say they're completely backed up. I—"

"Then tell them to expedite it," Tony cut in. "The Ministry of Justice now categorizes the murder of a police officer as a crime of exceptionally high—"

Kate touched her husband's hand. "Paul knows that."

"I'm sure he does. My point being, if the lab is already bleating to you about how slow they expect turnaround to be, they need a short, sharp lesson in priorities." Tony sounded calm, but his clipped speech betrayed the depth of his emotions. "I know all about CWC—their history and where the bodies are buried. Give me a name and one phone call will clear things up."

"Yeah, no, I'm not doing that." Paul sounded amused. "But maybe I should, just so Kate and I can listen in. Hearing you give them the full Retired Chief Peer of the Realm would probably cheer us both up. But no. I may still be a newly-minted DI, but I'm not that new. I complained to Jackson, and he said AC Deaver already rang them up and told them he'd engage the services of a different lab."

"Which one?"

"Queen's Scientific, I think. Whoever it is, the director has promised to put Amelia at the top of the queue. We should have some data by this time tomorrow."

"Tony told me Amelia and DC Kincaid were dating," Kate said. "I realize he's gutted, but if he was able to comment on the scene as a detective, I'd love to hear it."

"I have it right here," Paul said, and proceeded to pat himself down in search of his leatherbound notebook. It took a moment. Discovering it stuffed in his trousers' hip pocket, he asked himself, "Why did I put it there?"

"Why are you still in your coat? That's what I'd like to know," Kate countered.

"Because it's freezing in here, just like it's freezing at home. You and Ems prefer it positively arctic."

"That's because we're great sweaty lumps. Though she started slimming the day she brought Evvy home. And you've lost weight, too, you lucky bastard."

It was true; his cheekbones were more prominent, and his usually well-fitted suit hung loosely. "Isn't Sharada feeding you?"

"She's too busy spoiling Evvy. I've been demoted to second place, thank God. But I'll thank you not to make personal comments. And I'd like Parliament to pass a law forbidding any and all whinging about weight."

"Amen," Tony said.

With effort, Kate stifled further complaint. She knew Tony was tired of hearing her go on about her widening backside and tree trunk legs, but the transmogrification was a shock. She felt like the girl in Willy Wonka's factory who turned into a blueberry and had to be rolled away. She also felt useless, forbidden from rising except for trips to the loo, while Paul was wasting away, probably from the strain of doing his job and hers, too.

She was grateful to him, of course, but also a bit jealous. She couldn't shake the suspicion that the Powers that Be had finally cottoned on to what she'd long known—Paul Bhar was a damn fine detective and brother-in-arms. During her long recuperation after the Sir Duncan affair, it had been pleasant to imagine Paul at last receiving his due. But she also hoped she wouldn't return to find her career back at square one.

"My notes on observations by DC Kincaid," Paul said, having flipped through his notebook to the correct entry. Though he carried both a personal mobile and an MPS secure smartphone, both of which were equipped for digital note-taking, he preferred pen and paper.

"He states that Amelia was not seeing anyone else romantically, to the best of his knowledge. He doesn't believe she would've permitted a stranger to enter her home, so the hypothesis that her killer broke in and waited behind the door seems almost certain. She hadn't mentioned any red flags to him, like a potential stalker or a stranger hanging about. She had no enemies in the building and was on cordial terms with her neighbors and landlady."

He flipped a page. "DC Kincaid noted and will swear an affidavit to the effect that her handbag, described as black faux leather with a long strap, brand unknown, was missing from its usual place on the coat tree by the door. Her bracelet, a gold and diamond item of moderate value, was left on her body, as were the approximately half-carat diamond studs in her ears."

"Not a robbery. Got it," Kate said gruffly. Despite her promise to Tony to remain calm, if she didn't stay at least a little angry, the discussion would become unbearable.

"Not a robbery for trinkets to swap for rails, woollies and whatnot," he agreed, meaning cocaine and dope-laced cigarettes. "But Kincaid also will swear that Amelia's personal computer, a MacBook Pro, was missing. So was her personal mobile and her MPS mobile."

Tony asked, "What can you tell us about the cases she was working on?"

"Hang on." Paul flipped more pages. "Here we go. First one was a cold case—Lin Wu Chen, age twenty-two. He was the uni student apparently abducted from the Westminster area and pulled out of the Thames by a tugboat captain two days later. His mum works at Downing Street and is keeping the pressure up, but the case is static. The trail petered out after Mr. Chen's boyfriend—a cocky little git that the mum all but accused of murder—produced an invincible alibi.

"Second one, also a cold case. Geoffrey Marquand, thirty-one years old. No job, no spouse or children, in and out of rehab, basically a troubled soul. Found dead in the Epping Forest. Though the presumed cause of death was a combination of overdose and exposure—it happened on a cold day, January before last—there are still some unanswered questions."

"Did DI Marquand take early retirement?" Tony asked, referring to the victim's father, who'd spent most of his career at Scotland Yard.

"No, he transferred to a teaching post at Peel." The Peel Center in North London was the MPS's police academy.

"Ah. So he buggered off to Hendon." Like many coppers of his generation, Tony still referred to the college by its old name. "A common threat in my day, but few of us actually went through with it. Remind me, what was the sticking point with that case? It was first reported in the press as passive suicide."

"Two things," Paul said. "First, the M.E. found a fresh injection site in young Marquand's neck. His forearms were heavily scarred and it was evident he routinely shot up in his feet. It isn't impossible that he sat down in Epping Forest, decided it was a nice place to die, skipped the foot and jabbed his carotid instead. But given that he was an experienced user who understood how risky heroin injections in the neck can be, that was suspicious.

"Second, a few days after his death was widely reported as suicide, the Met received an anonymous tip claiming Geoffrey was afraid of his father. The tipster also claimed DI Marquand frequently threatened his son's life. An investigation was opened to talk to Geoffrey's friends and check his online activity, and to some extent those allegations were corroborated. Geoffrey was quite open and public about his stormy relationship with dear old dad."

"I remember when the investigation began, DI Marquand

was furious," Kate said. "Never been so insulted, this was the thanks he got for thirty years of blood, sweat, and tears, etc."

"Yes, well, I'm not sure I blame him. He was a good officer," Tony said.

"Praise indeed, coming from you," Kate said. When it came to his critique of others' work performances, her husband never pulled his punches or erred on the side of good manners. He also refused to rush to judgment when his fellow lawmen were suspected of wrongdoing. He preferred to give them the benefit of the doubt, especially when they were distinguished veterans like DI Leland Marquand. Over the years, Tony himself had occasionally been accused of misconduct—during the first case he worked on with Kate, he had been sidelined over false accusations of brutality. He knew how easily things could get twisted.

"I know he was a good officer, and for what it's worth, I've heard his students at the academy idolize him," Kate said. "But his reaction to the second investigation was over the top. That happened about six weeks ago, didn't it?"

"Thereabouts," Paul agreed.

"Right, so he burst into Jackson's office looking for a fight. I don't mean Marquand had a red face or shed a single manly tear. He went off like a bomb. Called Jackson everything from a stonking plonker to a plonking stonker."

That made Tony brighten up a bit. "Don't tell me you were put in the position of defending Vic Jackson against the charge of being a plonker in the first degree?"

"I was. And I did. He's reformed, sort of." She shrugged. "More importantly, he took your job, so Paul and I are stuck with him. He's our plonker, right or wrong."

"What happened six weeks ago to reopen the case?" Tony asked Paul.

"Another tipster. The identity of which is shrouded in

mystery, at least from mere mortals like me. It seems like someone complained to the IOPC."

"The IOPC?" Kate goggled at him. The Independent Office for Police Conduct investigated serious and sensitive claims of police wrongdoing. To be the target of their scrutiny could become extremely uncomfortable for a copper—and extremely public. "A fellow officer probably complained on Marquand and you decided to sit on it? You didn't think a *huge* piece of gossip like that was worth passing along?"

Paul looked guilty. "I didn't mean to sit on it. Fatherhood's doing something to my brain. I'm like a computer with too many tabs open. And too many programs running in the background."

"It will get better," Tony said. "Evvy's only three and a half weeks old. Before long you'll—"

"Nope. No advice from you, Chief, till your baby comes." Paul waved his hands in a slightly unhinged manner. "I know you've been reading and researching and asking around, but take it from me—it's all bollocks till you're up all night praying to God for the crying to stop."

Tony's eyes sparkled. "I beg your pardon. I withdraw the statement. May I offer an observation on a topic on which I have greater experience?"

Paul nodded. He seemed a bit taken aback by his own outburst.

"If Vic's unit was asked to reopen a case that old, with such delicate implications," Tony said, "then the request was issued from an unimpeachable source. And the only way it could've fallen out of the sky, shocking Marquand into making a spectacle of himself, is if someone like AC Deaver was the instigator."

"Oh. Well. Maybe he was. But if so, why Michael didn't mention it?" Paul asked. "Off the record, of course."

Kate gaped at him. "Is this for real? Are we shooting an

episode of *Punk'd UK*? Since when does *Michael* chat with you off the record?"

Paul cringed.

She turned to Tony, expecting astonishment to rival her own, but got only his poker face.

"Come on, Kate, you know better than to pay attention to the stupid things I say." Paul gave her an unconvincing smile. "I wouldn't dare call the AC anything but sir to his face. In a professional setting, I'm all business. Down the pub or at a party, it's a bit freer, obviously, of course. That's not, erm, every day. That sort of after hours, erm, fraternizing is, well, rare, isn't it?"

Hugh Grant couldn't have done a better job comprehensively stammering his way through that one. Rather than toss a life preserver to a drowning man, Kate simply waited.

"It started at Christmas!" Paul cried, waving his hands again. "You were out. Vic was in hospital for that prostate thingy he doesn't like mentioned. Kincaid and I were practically the only representatives of the unit left, so we were invited to Mi—to the AC's home for his annual Christmas gala. After that—"

"What do you mean the only ones left? How about Amelia? She had seniority over Kincaid as a detective, at least by a few weeks. Was she invited?"

Paul looked to Tony for assistance. All he got was the poker face.

"I'll refrain from speaking on matters I know nothing about."

After a sort of suppressed groan, like a man holding back a geyser of profanities by force of will, Paul said, "Gulls didn't make the guest list. And no, she wasn't best pleased. Kincaid offered to bring her along as his plus-one, but she thought that was insulting."

"Which it was," Kate said.

"And she had a quiet word with me as well. But the sticking point was, for the last twenty years AC Deaver and his wife have always thrown a personal party—family, friends, neighbors and so on. Representatives from the Yard are invited, but in an unofficial capacity."

Kate's cheeks grew hot, but for once she didn't fight it. She welcomed the rage. "So you and Sean caught the AC's eye. After everything Amelia did for the Met, all her dedication and crack detective work, it wasn't enough to get her invited to Michael and Monique's bloody party. All my dedication and hard work wasn't enough to get me invited, either, but I'll admit it, I come with some baggage. Put me to one side. But *Amelia* should've—"

Tony made a discreet noise.

"What?"

"Sorry, my love. Only there was an invitation last Christmas. But we'd just got the news of your pregnancy, and were already having a lovely holiday at Strange Mews, so I..." He cleared his throat. "Strategically misplaced it."

Kate was momentarily startled out of her righteous indignation. Then she cottoned on to her husband's slippery phrasing. "Wait. You're saying I was invited? DI Kate Hetheridge?"

"It was understood."

She took a deep breath. The nerve of these two. The sheer, inexhaustible, never ending nerve. "So what you really mean is, the invitation was addressed to Lord Anthony Hetheridge and *guest*?"

"It's a standard mode of—"

"Oh, please. No. Stop. Don't defend it. In the grand scheme of things, I'm glad you binned the invite. Really I am. It's Amelia's exclusion that sticks in my craw. Just couldn't manage to catch the assistant commissioner's eye, could she?

I reckon she has it now. All she had to do was be strangled to death."

Someone knocked timidly on the open bedroom door. The temporary cook had brought up their food on a trolley. She'd done it up right, with a white tablecloth, covered dishes, and rolled silverware. Kate, who still occasionally felt more like a long-term guest in Wellegrave House than a resident, and had certainly never taken a full inventory of its kitchen supplies, zeroed in on the trolley. It was standard hotel size. Large enough for an armed man to conceal himself beneath the floor-length white cloth, as killers so often did in movies.

Rubbish. We did a thorough background check on that woman before she set foot in this house, Kate reminded herself. The shock of Gulls's murder had reignited her PTSD, which she'd been working on for months. Currently her therapist wanted her to recognize when she was irrationally fixating on million-to-one hazards and say to herself, *This house is safe. I am safe. We are safe.*

"Perfect timing." Sounding almost indecently relieved, Tony made for the trolley. "Thanks very much. I'll take it from here."

CHAPTER 4

*B*ecause Kate was obliged to take all her meals in bed, Tony had obtained an overbed table, which he now wheeled into place. On it he placed her bowl of soup, a plate of bread and butter, and some cut strawberries. She gave the soup an experimental taste and frowned—tomato bisque wasn't her favorite—but broke off a chunk of dry bread and chewed slowly. She was making an effort, and he wouldn't ask for more.

As for himself and Paul, they put the trolley between them and ate from there. The soup wasn't completely inedible, although for this meal (perhaps due to Mrs. Snell's earlier scolding) the temporary cook had forgone all the usual seasoning. The result tasted like hot tomato juice. Trying not to think of Harvey's superlative tomato bisque soup, which was one of his many specialties, Tony reflected that over the years he'd become rather spoiled. He'd fallen into the trap of taking his expertly prepared meals and perfectly run household for granted. When Harvey returned, he would receive a pay rise.

The meal played out in silence, more out of respect for

DC Gulls than because of any lingering pique. Rows and blowups never lasted long between the three of them. They were a team. They'd faced almost everything under the sun together, from public humiliation and death to a mechanized specter and a woman who believed she was a horse. Kate and Paul were habitual bickerers, anyway, and the bond between Tony and Kate had always been electric. That was how he preferred it.

Over the course of his long bachelorhood, he'd met many soft-voiced, deferential ladies. They'd viewed him chiefly as Lord Hetheridge, or Chief Superintendent Hetheridge, or the ninth Baron Wellegrave—at the least, a walking title, and at the extreme, some kind of paragon. But Kate saw him as a man first. Everything else—his title, his generational wealth, his brilliant career—were mere attachments. And it was the man beneath the attachments she wanted.

At the end of the meal, he caught her looking at him and smiled at her. She pushed the overbed table aside. Her bread and strawberries had been eaten, at least.

"Top marks. Shall I start clearing up?"

"I'll help. It was good. Good enough, anyway," said Paul, who'd hoovered up his portion. "Who am I kidding? I'll eat anything if someone gives me a plate and five minutes' peace."

Having pushed the trolley into the hall, Tony looked both ways before closing the bedroom door. Henry's ongoing moodiness didn't preclude him from eavesdropping on privileged conversations about murder, and Ritchie was still prone to wandering into rooms whenever the mood took him. Besides, they both had a remarkable sixth sense when it came to what he was going to do next.

"I believe it's time," he announced solemnly, heading to the hand-painted Sevres vase in the corner, "to break out something I've been saving." Removing the lid, he reached inside and pulled out a brand-new Cadbury Milk Tray. It was the big one: three hundred and sixty grams of pure delight.

Kate saw the purple box and sat up straight. "Tony! You know I'm trying to cut down."

Deaf to her objections, he handed the box to Paul, who was already reaching with both hands. "Get cracking. Convince Kate to have a piece. Surely you can quote a bit of pop culture nonsense to get her on board?"

"Too right. Dementors, Kate. Give it a think." Ripping off the shrink wrap, Paul lifted the box's lid, flung away its inside liner, and took a long, deep sniff. "Oh, yeah. That's the stuff. C'mon, Kate. The only cure for being exposed to a Dementor is chocolate. Today has been a soul-eating, dark apparition kind of day. If medicinal chocolate is good enough for Harry Potter, it's good enough for us."

Groaning, Kate reached for a Perfect Praline. "Fine. It's on your head. And on my backside, quite likely, but I'll deal with that later." Popping the bonbon in her mouth, she pointed at his selection and said, very garbled: "Watch out, that's an Apple Crunch."

"So? I quite like an Apple Crunch," Paul said, or something to that effect. It was hard to be sure with all the chewing.

Tony, who had never quite got over the loss of Turkish Delight, sincerely hoped that if Paul actually enjoyed those apple abominations, he would eat every last one of them. Selecting a Caramel Softy, he settled back in his chair to watch Kate and Paul's rising delight as they attacked the chocolates. It was cheap magic; the spell wouldn't last long. Still, a few minutes' pleasure was better than none. He had the feeling they ought to savor what enjoyment they could. He wasn't one for presentiments or premonitions, but something about the Gulls case sent a shiver up his spine. Old coppers had good instincts. Of course they did—otherwise, they never grew old.

He started them off by asking, "So what do we know? When DC Gulls died, she was concerned with two cold cases. One, Mr. Chen, is a suspicious death wherein the usual prime suspect, his romantic partner, had an airtight alibi. But the mother, who works in the government, keeps pressing for action," he began, speaking the details aloud to fix them in memory. "I don't suppose either of you have any personal opinions regarding Mr. Chen?"

Kate, in the process of swallowing a chocolate, shook her head.

"I never rule out suicide in a case like his," Paul announced, going for his third Apple Crunch. "No one knows what goes on behind closed doors, much less inside someone's skull. All we know is, he went out alone one evening and wound up in the river. He had a small insurance policy, which has never paid out because the case is unresolved, and left his boyfriend a bit of cash. The mum deeply resents that and considers it proof of wrongdoing. Meanwhile, the boyfriend says Mr. Chen got depressed sometimes. Maybe he had a bad night and decided to end it all."

"Maybe someone mugged him and tossed him alive into the Thames. Could he swim?" Kate asked.

"According to his mum, quite well. According to his boyfriend, he could barely dog paddle. I re-read the key statements this afternoon. The mum and the boyfriend didn't get on, so whatever one said, the other contradicted."

"Yes, well, on the face of it, it hardly sounds like the kind of case that would lead to a Scotland Yard detective's murder," Tony said. "Have you asked Vic's opinion?"

"Not yet. He's in a rage over Gulls. Once he knew the AC was expediting the forensics processing, he pulled Kincaid into his office—alone—and kept him in there for an hour.

Poor kid stumbled out looking like he'd been through an old school grilling. The kind with a Kleig light in your face and three beefy coppers taking turns giving you a slap."

"I would've questioned Sean, too. Right away," Tony said. He'd always liked Kincaid and had great confidence in him, but in a case like this, the romantic partner always received intense initial scrutiny. Gulls's manner of death was slickly professional. DC Kincaid had been a policeman for almost ten years and his deep knowledge of criminal evidence-gathering far exceeded that of the average hit man.

"Second case. DI Leland Marquand and his son, Gregory," Tony said. "I have no opinion as yet, though I've already mentioned Leland's professional record was irreproachable."

"Except for when he pitched that wobbly," Kate said. Tony was pleased to note her cheeks were blooming again and her voice was calm and steady. Cadbury Milk Tray—it never failed.

"Indeed. To be fair, Marquand's exemplary record might be the very reason he went to pieces. Perhaps he felt owed the benefit of the doubt."

"Seems to me he'd put up with the insult if it meant resolving the questions about his son's death," Paul said. "Then again, there's no point pretending the situation was all hearts and flowers. Gregory and his father obviously despised each other. But that doesn't mean DI Marquand stuck a needle in his throat and left him to overdose alone in Epping Forest."

"Yet Michael Deaver, or someone else high up the food chain, wanted the case reopened," Tony said thoughtfully, eyeing the purple box's scanty leftovers. If there were no more Caramel Softies or Perfect Pralines, why bother?

"Paul. While I'm sure it goes without saying, I'll say it anyway. Don't mention what I said about the AC reopening the case to anyone. Not Vic, not a subordinate, not anyone. Is that understood?"

"Yes, sir."

The playful "sir" reminded him that he'd unconsciously slipped into CS Hetheridge mode. He flashed Paul a smile. "Sorry. Only that's the sort of indiscretion that can trigger monumental blowback. And I don't mean being sent off to patrol the Celtic Sea in an inflatable boat, like that poor bugger from Exeter, as you might recall. I mean a frame-up. Drugs planted in your workspace. An accusation of bribe-taking levied by a seemingly impeccable source."

"So one rung down from Amelia's fate," Kate said. That gave everyone pause.

Tony took his time forming a reply. Of course, he no longer spoke as carefully to Kate and Paul as he had when they were his subordinates. But his lengthy association with the MPS had shown him more than either of them could imagine. Much of it had happened long ago, before key reforms. No institution was corruption-free, and sometimes —rarely, but sometimes—coppers committed homicide. Sometimes they fitted up other coppers for serious crimes as a form of professional retaliation. And sometimes they conspired to bury crimes committed by fellow officers for "the good of the institution." The lure of that last transgression wasn't impossible to understand. Kate and Paul were still somewhat idealistic, far more than he'd been around their age; he didn't want to erode their belief with a lot of old war stories.

"Let me be clear," he said at last. "I've known Michael Deaver for twenty-five years. If you somehow spilled what you know, I absolutely do not believe he would ever retaliate against you in an underhanded or illegal way. *But,*" he added, holding Paul's gaze, since he had often been guilty of letting his mouth run away with him, "these internal investigations are always tricky. There are others at the Yard who might do literally anything, even to a fellow officer, if they felt betrayed. Or if they thought the Met itself was endangered."

"You've convinced me," Paul said. "As far as I know, the Marquand case was reopened due to an anonymous tip. If anyone ever told me more, I've forgotten it." He shook his head when Kate tried to pass him the purple box. "Nope. If I eat one more piece, I'll explode. Oh—I meant to say this earlier, but the food arrived. Gulls wasn't only handling cold cases. She was helping me with Valeria Chakrabarti."

"Refresh my memory," Tony said. He'd been too concerned with his own PI workload, not to mention Kate, Henry, and the impending birth, to keep up with much in the press, even murder cases.

"Come on, you've heard of her. Thrown out a window." Kate replaced the lid on the almost-empty Milk Tray box and tossed it aside. "Like I'll do to the next person who offers me sweets. I'm off them forever. I mean it this time," she told Tony, who was a good husband and tried to look as if he believed her.

Paul said, "As for the case—Chief, you know Parth Chakrabarti, right?"

"Slightly."

"Valeria was his eldest child. I call him Darth Chakrabarti, as in Darth Vader, because he's terrifying. Burly and deep-voiced. Sort of smoldering with eternal rage."

"A human volcano," Tony agreed. "He's served on the board of various charities and hosted some of the usual benefits. Children With Cancer UK, the Vision Foundation, etc. Go on."

"Of course, if you'll agree to consult on it. Already got the greenlight from Jackson, since there's reason to believe it may intersect with the Gulls case. Besides, we need the help."

"Excellent. Proceed."

Paul patted himself down again, discovered his notebook stashed in the same pocket, muttered something about losing his mind, and found the right section. He read,

"Valeria Chakrabarti. Twenty-nine years old. I'll send you some photos, but for now, take my word for it: gorgeous. Big dark eyes, long black hair, soulful look. Did some modeling. Not married, no children. Sporadically employed at the time of her death, which occurred ten weeks ago. Around two a.m. on a Saturday night. She was living on the top floor of an old converted townhouse in Shepherd's Bush—a very elegant building with four tall casement windows facing the street. Someone picked her up and flung her out of one. Defenestrated her, if you want to get technical."

"I don't recommend using that term around Mr. Chakrabarti."

"It's best to use no terms around him whatsoever. Be seen but not heard. Don't be seen, if you can manage it."

"Witnesses?" Kate asked.

"Of a sort. Valeria was in the habit of strolling around her living room with the lights blazing and the windows uncovered. Sometimes fully dressed, sometimes not. Her neighbors across the way couldn't help but take in the show. Apparently it was either very pleasant or completely infuriating, depending on how you feel about long-legged, half-naked models."

"From all this, I take it you're going to say someone saw the murder in the real time. How was the killer described?" Tony asked.

"Ah, but wait. The Valeria show didn't happen every night," Paul said. "At least three times a week, according to the neighbors, her blinds went down and didn't come up again till morning. On Saturday nights her windows were almost always covered, though the lights were on.

"That particular night, the neighborhood watch, as it

were, reported that her blinds stayed down all evening. But some American tourists on a pub crawl passed underneath her flat just before two a.m. and reported the blinds were up. They couldn't agree on whether or not they saw one person inside or two. A few even remembered all the rooms as empty." Paul shrugged. "Pissed and tired doesn't make for good witnesses."

"Sober and well-rested ones aren't much better," Tony said.

"Cynical. Accurate, but cynical. Anyway, a little while later, a Black cab stopped at the curb to let another tourist out. He was probably on a solo pub crawl, though he denies it, and had just exited the cab when he heard a scream. The cab driver was occupied processing the fare, but the tourist saw it—a woman falling headfirst out a window. He said her arms and legs were flailing and there was a look of pure terror on her face."

"Can he describe the killer?" Kate asked.

"No. I checked the angle, and it's not great. Perpendicular to the pavement. He said he was so focused on watching Valeria fall, he barely saw the shape of the killer. Tall and big is how he put it. Mind you, a couple of days later, he rang to amend his sworn statement. Said he'd had a think, and he was no long sure that the killer was tall and big. Said maybe he was standing in the wrong place to judge proportions, and looking back, all he was certain about was how frightened she looked."

"How far did she fall?" Tony asked.

"Around forty-five feet."

Kate made a disapproving sound.

"Fine. Fourteen *meters*. Last week, a memo went round, sternly reminding us that Great Britain has been metric since 1965 and in the Metropolitan Police Service we support our government by—" He broke off. "Hang on.

Have you been checking your work emails again, Katie my love?"

"Just general ones. Like that one about the metric system. But Valeria—was she dead at the scene?"

"Yeah. Massive injuries. Police response was quick, but her killer was already out of the building and into the wind. I was called in the next morning, because Darth Chakrabarti demanded an experienced liaison and he's precisely the kind of citizen the Toff Squad was formed to placate."

"To serve," Tony corrected him, but without rancor. Unless somebody connected to the House of Windsor, the Prime Minister, or Sir Elton John was murdered, there was no better example of a wealthy and powerful Englishman than Parth Chakrabarti. Tony had specialized in dealing with such individuals, and although he didn't miss it, he certainly didn't fear it. Nor would he shrink from following the facts wherever they led—including Buckingham Palace, 10 Downing Street, or the L.A. mansion of the world's favorite rocket man.

He said, "The death of Valeria Chakrabarti sounds intriguing on many levels. I take it you have no prime suspect after eleven weeks of hard work?"

"No, and very hard work, thank you very much," Paul replied. "Of course I was out for part of it, just after Evvy was born. But Gulls and Kincaid did well in my absence. Still, we have nothing to show for the investigation, except one angry father who's threatening to sue the MPS generally and Cressida Dick personally for gross incompetence."

"Surely not every question leads to a dead end," Kate said eagerly. "You mentioned she was a part-time model. A flat like you described doesn't come cheap. Was her father giving her an allowance, or was she fully independent? What about—"

"What about the telling-off I'll get from Dr. Laidslaw,"

Tony broke in, "if I'm forced to admit I let this *verboten* and supposedly brief conference stretch on for hours? She's made it plain that if you don't take it easy, Nipper will be born too soon. Paul's given us plenty to think about. Time to call it a night."

He expected Kate to snap at him or stubbornly go on questioning Paul, but apparently her sugar high was fading. Instead of resisting, she put out a hand for him to help her up.

"Loo time. This child has a fiendish way of lounging on my bladder. Oh! Quick—get me there quick! Paul, get out of the way!"

CHAPTER 5

Whenever Tony returned to the Yard as a consultant, he expected it to go as smooth as silk, and it usually did. After all, there had been a time when he'd devoted his life to the institution. Even after a long night, or during a particularly brutal case when the desire to lay hands on the killer hung on him like a millstone, each day he'd awakened buzzing with purpose. As for his old routine, it had been a thing of beauty. Harvey always had the Bentley warmed up and ready. Tony arranged himself in the back with a newspaper, the better to keep his mind engaged if traffic was bad. When he arrived at the office, Mrs. Snell had already made certain the morning's catered repast was perfect. Ah, those breakfasts. The sheer indulgence of it—of his team eating together as they strategized for the coming day—would never fly at today's Scotland Yard, which had moved houses to Victoria Embankment. It was a new day there, and probably the better for it. But his old routine had been wonderful while it lasted.

Wondering what his morning commute would be like in

the new SUV—listening to Rachmaninov, at least, instead of the cacophonous rubbish Henry and Ritchie liked—Tony got out of bed and promptly fell down. He didn't cry out—the bolt of pure pain in his kneecap had stolen his breath away.

"What?" Kate, always a light sleeper, stirred. "What was that?"

"Lights," Tony commanded. The bedroom's recessed light panels came on full blast. "Lower fifty percent." They dimmed to something more bearable.

"I thought I heard—where are you? On the floor?"

"No," he said, standing up. "I'm quite all right."

"Your knee locked up, didn't it?"

"No, it's your knee that locks up. Mine gives me the occasional jolt. This one was a bit more robust than usual. Took me by surprise." Easing himself on the bed, he massaged his kneecap, flexing it experimentally. "Hell of a time for me to get old."

She touched his shoulder. "Too late for whinging about age and infirmity. Buy the ticket, take the ride." Hand on her belly, she added, "Wait till you start toting Nipper about. He'll be heavier every month. Maybe you should ring the surgeon about a knee replacement."

"Haven't I had enough surgery?"

"You've had two surgeries. Minor ones, compared to me. But if you won't even consider it, perhaps you should start using the lift? It's pretty seductive, once you give yourself permission."

"That's what I'm afraid of. Ready...steady...ta-da." He stood up, made a point of confidently crossing to her side of the bed, and gave her a kiss. "How's this for an offer? I'm off to the Yard to show that lot how it's done. If I successfully expose Ms. Chakrabarti's killer, you'll forget the phrase 'knee replacement surgery' entirely. If I don't, I'll put ice on my knee every evening and use the lift at least once a fortnight."

"Counteroffer. I'll obey Dr. Laidslaw and endure bedrest, and you'll consult with an orthopedic surgeon once Nipper's here and I'm fighting fit."

"Fine. With the understanding that should I experience a remarkable rejuvenation, the matter will be dropped."

"You really believe that, don't you? That you can ignore the problem until it goes away?"

"Hope springs eternal. What are your plans for today?"

"I'm going back to sleep. It's as if I'm always resting, yet I never rest," Kate said. "Then I thought I'd have a pair of gossipy old ladies over for tea."

Tony made an approving sound. "I hadn't realized Margaret and Vivian were back in London." The two had been jetting around Europe with special emphasis on Rome, Lady Vivian Callot's favorite place in the world. Her better half—or worse half, as everyone, including Lady Margaret Knolls herself, would say—had probably spent the trip complaining she was bored to death. London, and specifically the great families of London, were her passion. She could spend an afternoon admiring Renaissance statues or Greek pillars, but before long she'd be ringing up friends to hear the news from home. A little politics, a little financial forecasting, and a lot of interpersonal drama: the more divorces, affairs, scandals, and money disputes, the better.

"Lady Margaret insisted they come back early, in case Nipper is preterm," Kate said. "She's wild with excitement over the baby. If I'm being honest, I think she's curious about Evvy, too, though she tries to be clever about it. She's spent too long terrorizing Paul to warm up to him overnight."

"Ah, how I long to see Margaret treat Paul like a human being. If only in an attempt to cuddle his baby daughter. Can I trust you not to let them excite you too much?"

"Of course. I'll even drink decaf."

"And the topic will be...?"

"Lin Wu Chen's mum. If she's an up-and-comer in the government, she'll be on their radar. And Valeria Chakrabarti, of course. I'd like to know more about the family. The only thing I reckon they can't help with is DI Marquand."

"It's just as well, since that line of inquiry is radioactive. I ask again: Can I trust you not to excite yourself?"

"Can I trust you not to deliberately jog up and down stairs all day in a vain attempt to toughen yourself up?"

He kissed her a second time, with finality. "No. Give Margaret and Vivian my best regards."

* * *

WHEN TONY CAME in to brew coffee, Wellegrave House's cavernous Victorian kitchen was still dark. However, as he entered, he glimpsed a fleeting ball of illumination near the pantry door. A superstitious man would've frozen in place, thinking some Dickensian ghost was about to waft through. Tony, not superstitious, switched on the overhead lights expecting to find a thief. Which he did—Henry Hetheridge, still in his pajamas, with his mobile in one hand and a tin of biscuits in the other.

The boy blurted, "I'm being systematically starved! You can't expect me not to fight back. Seeking food is a survival instinct."

"It is at that." Tony relied on his poker face to save him; according to Kate, he wasn't supposed to laugh when Henry went into a ridiculous self-defense spiel, no matter how tempting. "You could make a better choice than sugary biscuits."

Henry gave a melodramatic sigh. "Bacon?"

"In the fridge you'll find turkey sausages. Do a fry-up

with those and some eggs. I'll do toast and coffee." To demonstrate his seriousness, Tony held out his hand for the biscuit tin.

"Same amount of calories," Henry muttered, relinquishing it.

"Empty calories. Protein will do a better job seeing you through till lunch."

Opening the fridge, Henry said, "I don't see why it matters that I've gained weight. They make trousers in boys' plus size. It's called generous fit. You could buy me some. You can afford it."

Locating the wheat bread and a serrated knife, Tony considered his words before replying. Henry's peevish and insolent tone would've been startling only a year ago; now it was almost standard. When dealing with subordinates—his chief frame of reference—Tony never permitted insolence to go unchallenged. To anyone who tested him on that point, he would grow very cold indeed. But Henry was a clever, keenly sensitive boy who—until Tony came on the scene—had never had the benefit of a lasting male role model. On the contrary, in many relationships, he was expected to give more than the average ten-year-old. With his uncle Ritchie, he was sometimes playmate, sometimes junior carer. With his biological mum it was also skewed; though the emotionally fragile Maura, currently at Briarshaw to further her recovery, was his senior in years, she often leaned on him for reassurance. It seemed likely that Henry was breaking rules, whinging, and smarting off like this because he finally felt secure enough to do so.

"How did your paper on the history of enclosure go over?" he asked, opting for a change of topic.

"Top marks. Mr. Wein said it was an advanced topic and an example of good research. He invited me to watch the

Year 9 debating team next week. He says enclosure is the perfect contentious issue and asked if I'd rather debate for or against."

"And you said...?"

"I haven't decided." Placing a stool by the cooker, Henry climbed on it, the better to poke his fry-up with a spatula. "It's hard to choose. Like I said in my paper, it probably led to the Industrial Revolution, which was a good thing. But it put so much land and money in the hands of just a few rich people. Which can seem like a bad thing."

"Go to the debate. Pay close attention to the techniques used. Clever as you are, it may be just your thing."

"How? I can't even decide how I feel about enclosure and I wrote a whole paper about it. I reckon when Nipper's old enough to talk, we'll have rows about it. He'll say enclosure was for the best. That it kept the land from being overdeveloped and gave England all her famous green spaces. Of course he'll take that position, because he'll be the next Lord Hetheridge, set to inherit Briarshaw. I'm just a boy from East London. My people were always on the wrong side of the fence."

There it was. Tony, though aware he'd been handed the moment on a silver platter, didn't leap to answer. Instead he asked, "Why do you always refer to Nipper as 'he'?"

"Because Nipper *will* be a boy. Has to be. It's just my luck." Henry heaved another sigh. "I'm doing the eggs scrambled, is that all right?"

"Perfect. With regard to debating clubs, you may be surprised to learn it isn't necessary to believe in the side for which you argue. In fact, your coach may deliberately assign you to argue against an issue he knows you passionately believe in."

"No shit?" Henry, who'd been working to cultivate a cleaner, infant-friendly vocabulary, occasionally backslid.

"Indeed."

"But why?"

"To help hone your skills. It's easy to construct a defense of something you've already decided on, and perhaps advocated for. It's quite another thing to build a careful defense of a position you dislike, or even find reprehensible."

"Rep-re-hen-sible," Henry murmured. "That's good. My mate Tommy drives me batty sometimes. Perhaps today I'll call him reprehensible. But really," he continued, flipping sausages, "if you argue for something you don't believe in, doesn't that make you insincere?"

"In real life, I suppose so." Tony's toast popped up, first one slot, then the others. "In debating club, it's part of the game. And I suspect you could do it rather well, should you put your mind to it. Now as far as Nipper being a boy—what if he is? How is that representative of your so-called bad luck?"

"Never mind."

Thinking he detected a yearning to be cajoled—and not wanting to encourage any manipulative tendencies— Tony set about buttering toast. He could feel Henry's eyes following every scrape of the knife, but continued placidly until the boy said,

"Kate says I should always pass up butter."

"I know. But I won't grass if you don't. You still haven't explained about—"

"I reckon it's buyer's remorse, isn't it?" Henry all but shouted, as if someone had stuck a gun in his ribs and demanded he tell the truth. "You and Kate adopted me because you couldn't have babies. Now you're having one and I won't be wanted! If Nipper's a girl it might not be so bad, because I'd still be the only boy. But he'll be a son, I know he will, and I'll—I'll—I'll just be in the way. And fat," he added, as if that were the *coup de grace*. "Fat and in the way!"

"Good God. Did I just call you clever? I never heard such rubbish. *Sit down.*"

Henry looked stricken. "But I need to..." he faltered, poking weakly with his spatula.

"Sit. I'll do it." Silently and without haste, Tony took two plates from the cupboard, portioning out the turkey sausages and scrambled eggs and crowning them with toast wedges. It wasn't a full breakfast without beans and tomatoes, but he was already running late, so it would have to do. After pouring coffee for himself and semi-skimmed milk for Henry, he sat down across from the boy, who was red-faced and wretched.

"Now. Eat up while I talk to you. First: I expect you to be gentler with Kate, and indeed more respectful to all of the adults in this house, from now on. She's perfectly miserable on bedrest, and yesterday she lost a friend. It came as a terrible shock. One of our colleagues at the Yard was killed."

Henry looked startled. He opened his mouth to ask questions, but Tony forestalled him with a gesture.

"I said eat. There's nothing anyone can do to make her feel better about what happened, but we can all try to refrain from actively making her feel worse. You've been in a beastly mood, stomping around and complaining about everything. Do try and be more considerate.

"Second: if you'll agree to resume fencing with me three times a week, I'll see to it that no one here pesters you about your weight. I don't like you feeling as though you have to creep into the pantry and nick food. But I also think there's more to life than playing Xbox and watching telly."

"I'll fence with you again," Henry said. He'd lost the habit during the past year's many upheavals; perhaps now he was ready to fall in love with the sport again.

"Splendid. Third: it's quite right that if Nipper should be a son, he'll inherit the barony. Should Nipper be a daughter, she won't, because of male primogeniture. Female offspring are precluded by the terms of hereditary peerage. So if Nipper is a girl, my nephew Roderick Hetheridge will inherit the title when I die, as he's long expected to. Unfortunately—and you know I would change this if I could—there is no scenario in which you would ever inherit. It's beyond my power. You've understood all this for some time, Henry."

"I know. I don't know why I said that. I don't even think I want to be a baron. You've always made it seem like a pain in the arse."

"There's my clever lad," he murmured, relenting in his sternness just a little.

"Anyway, I'm not like Ritchie, going around saying 'No baby' all the time because I hate change." Henry picked up a sausage and nibbled it. "It's just—you're going to have a real son. I wanted to be your real son."

"Henry. I chose you."

"I know that."

"Do you? Think about it. When a new baby comes, it's like spinning the roulette wheel. Wherever the ball stops, black or red, double zero or thirty-six, that's what you get. Do you think my father was happy with me? No. He thought I was mad to become a policeman. I was alien to him, and him to me, from the day I was born. He reared me and cared for me because it was his obligation.

"You and I have a different relationship. I knew you before I married Kate. I loved you and decided I wanted you to be my son. Adopting you was an action I undertook with my eyes wide open. And never for a moment have I regretted that choice, not even when you're swanning about like a great goose."

Henry's eyes shone, but he was beaming. "Swanning about? Like a great *goose*?" He giggled.

"You're not the only one on a quest to remove questionable words and phrases from his vocabulary. Now tuck in. I mean to finish with breakfast and be out the door in a quarter hour."

After his final mouthful of eggs, Henry said, "That colleague of Mum's. The one who was killed. Was it a young man?"

"A young woman."

"Murdered?"

"Yes."

"I thought you said Scotland Yard detectives are almost never killed in the line of duty."

"Strictly speaking, she was off-duty. It's unclear who murdered her or for what reason."

"Yes, well, there doesn't have to be a rational reason." Henry said absently. His tone and manner of expression were so strikingly familiar, Tony stared.

Me. He sounds exactly like me. Astonishing.

"Very well. I'm off," he announced, rising. He meant to do it smoothly, pushing back the chair and springing to his feet in one motion, but his left knee had other ideas. This time, however, the pain didn't come as a bolt from the blue, and he caught the back of the chair to brace himself.

"Steady on. Is it your knee?"

"Afraid so."

"You should take vitamin pills."

"Perhaps."

"Or you could get a knee replacement. Titanium would be wicked."

"Wicked." Tony contemplated the word. "I rather like the sound of that. Have a good day at school." As he spoke, he laid a hand on the boy's shoulder, but Henry wanted more. Throwing his arms around Tony's waist, he pressed his face against his shirt front.

"I love you, Dad," he said, slightly muffled.

"I love you, too, Henry." Smooth as silk or not, the day was already a success, whether he accomplished anything for the Yard or not.

CHAPTER 6

"Hiya, Joy. Late again. Talk soon," Paul called over his shoulder as he blazed into DCI Vic Jackson's office. As he did so, he expected the administrative assistant, a bubbly and ever-upbeat woman named Joy, to call friendly questions after him, as was her habit. Joy was the type who effortlessly remembered the names of spouses, children, and pets, and she was always up for the latest pics. Today, however, she only made a noncommittal sound. It surprised Paul so much, he paused to look back at the reception desk.

Bountifully built, with dark skin set off by her favorite color—sunny yellow—Joy didn't look under the weather. Her curls had bounce and her smile was at about eighty percent of its usual intensity, which was forty-five percent more than the average Londoner. But something was wrong.

Amelia, Paul thought. The impossibility of it washed over him again. Twice during his commute, he'd caught himself absorbed by something innocuous—a story in the *Independent*, or snatches of someone else's conversation—only to suddenly remember Gulls was dead all over again. Every time it hit him, it was a fresh shock—an affront to the very idea of an orderly universe. Despite being a copper who'd witnessed every sort of cruelty, from contract kills to long-plotted revenge murders, he still clung to the idea of a world where most things worked as they should. Where most hard work was rewarded and most good people enjoyed good lives. Probably it was a childish fantasy that ought to be packed away for good.

"He's already in there. Lord Hetheridge," Joy said, nodding toward DCI Jackson's closed door. "Glad you called him in."

"Yeah. Pulling out all the stops for this one. Have you seen Kincaid?"

"He's in there, too. Poor thing. I can hardly bear to look at him."

Paul was tempted to linger and ask Joy's perspective on the Kincaid-Gulls relationship. He had no firm opinion; some detective he was, he hadn't even noticed. He'd been fully consumed by his own personal life when he wasn't working murder cases. Of course, Sean Kincaid wasn't one to kiss and tell, and Amelia Gulls had been equally closed about her private life. Had they only dated casually, hooking up from time to time? Overworked coppers often fell into low-key affairs with each other, mostly for convenience. Getting out and meeting new people was hard, and building trust with a stranger was particularly thorny for homicide detectives. Turning to an attractive colleague offered sex and companionship without all the complications, like having to justify a crazy schedule or the all-consuming nature of one's work. Paul assumed that was how the Kincaid-Gulls liaison had been, but if he was wrong, Joy would know. She was particularly insightful about interpersonal relationships.

If Sean was in love with her, I don't know how I'll face him today. Or how I'll handle him as a suspect.

Because that was the thing—if there had been real emotion between his junior detectives, there was a higher chance it had ended in catastrophe. Paul couldn't quote the latest statistics on domestic violence among police officers, but he knew it was higher than anyone wanted to admit, and unlikely to ever be prosecuted. There was a host of reasons for that—not least because an abuser or killer who knew the system from the inside would have an easier time covering his tracks. Paul, who'd known and liked Kincaid for over a year, wanted to believe the young man wasn't capable of strangling anyone, much less Amelia Gulls. But in an investigation, what he wanted to believe was about as useful as Bluetooth on a Bakewell tart.

Easing open Jackson's office door to minimize the interruption, Paul slipped inside. To his relief, the guv gave him only a flick of the eyes; the other conferees didn't even look. They were giving their attention to the woman standing beside Jackson's desk, who was in mid-sentence.

"...because the media won't stop with conjectures and fear-mongering, I can promise you that. I subscribe to push notifications from all the tabloids, and just since breakfast, *Bright Star* has sent three."

The woman, who was about seventy, with a heavily lined face and large, pallid blue eyes, reached in her trouser pocket and withdrew an iPhone. Reading spectacles hung around her neck on a beaded chain. Shifting the specs to the bridge of her nose, she read aloud,

"'Brave Amelia was a rising star.' 'Brave Amelia fought for women's rights, says mum.' 'Was Brave Amelia dating a policeman? Neighbor says maybe.'" Removing the specs with a click of beads, she returned the phone to her pocket and said, "You see, DC Gulls is already being portrayed as the next national tragedy. Which is perfectly true, of course. But the tabloids have no interest in her as a human being. This first volley of stories is just to test the public appetite. By this time next week, the media will have settled on a preferred narrative, and they will pursue it relentlessly."

"With respect," Tony said, "that's entirely outside the Met's control."

She didn't bristle at the remark. She merely studied him for a moment, large pale eyes unblinking. Then she asked, "Are you aware that the British public's confidence in the police is dropping steadily, according to the most recent polls? That one in five victims of rape no longer report their assault to the police, because they don't believe the crime will be investigated?"

Tony nodded.

"I would submit," the woman continued, "that perception of the Met is not completely outside its control. What's wanted in a case like this is full transparency. If DC Gulls was romantically involved with a fellow officer—"

"I did say we're looking into it," Jackson cut across her. He added, "Dame Ingrid."

Paul, who'd dragged a chair to a spot near Tony and Kincaid, recognized the speaker at last. It was Dame Ingrid Hayhurst, a retired police commissioner turned victims' rights advocate. Because of her long and distinguished career in uniform, she'd earned the right to criticize the MPS without the usual kneejerk howls of outrage.

She's earned it, he amended, studying the other men's faces, *but I'm not sure she'll get it today. The room's against her.*

Tony wore his typically noncommittal expression, but Jackson's face was scarlet. A vein bulged at his temple. Kincaid, usually calm and upbeat, was staring at the floor, his lips compressed into a thin line. His fists were balled at his sides, the knuckles white.

"Lord Hetheridge. Who called you in to consult?" Dame Ingrid asked.

"That would be me," Paul said, taking it upon himself to answer. When she looked at him somewhat blankly, he added, "DI Paul Bhar."

"Why did you request his consultation before even twenty-four hours had passed?"

"Because Gulls is—was—a colleague. Because it's imperative that we solve this case as quickly as possible."

"Do you recognize how his presence will be perceived by pressure groups like Preserve and Protect?"

He blinked at her. It had been another night of fractured sleep, and not just because of Evvy's wails. Every time he lay back against the pillow, his mind replayed images from the Gulls crime scene. He didn't want to keep seeing her death mask, that frozen expression of agony, but his brain seemed determined to immortalize the image. It wasn't conducive to rest.

"Did I say something amusing?" Dame Ingrid asked.

"I—no. I'm sorry. Bit sleep deprived, if I'm being honest. Only—lots of alliteration in that question. Lots of *puh*-sounds. 'Perceived by pressure groups like Preserve and Protect' is right up there with Peter Piper picked a peck of—"

Tony broke in with a fit of noise. It wasn't exactly coughing, but was so booming and insistent, Paul shut up.

Thank God. His mouth had really run away that time. Jackson was glaring a hole through him.

"Dame Ingrid, though your query wasn't addressed to me, I'd like to reply, if you don't mind," Tony said. "First of all, Preserve and Protect is a nakedly anti-police organization and always has been. They cater to those segments of the British public who believe all police are corrupt, all prisoners should be released, and all prisons should be closed down and reopened as—well, I couldn't say. Asda superstores, perhaps.

"As for how the IOPC will interpret my involvement, I do

realize the Metropolitan Police Federation presently considers them somewhat hostile. Whenever there's a crisis, the IOPC's constant issuing of press releases can feel like a bit of a pile-on. It certainly brings down morale in the ranks," Tony continued. "However, you may be unaware that I've consulted with the IOPC quite recently, and have a cordial relationship with the general director. There's no reason for him to see my involvement in the Gulls case as something sinister. Even if you do," he added blandly.

"Lord Hetheridge." Her tone was the sort one might use to address a titled devil in hell's equivalent of Mayfair. "I realize you consider yourself indispensable to any murder investigation. Also utterly blameless when it comes to the public's rising distrust in our criminal justice system. But mere mortals perceive you quite differently. Which is to say, you have a reputation as an institutionalist. One who has spent the better part of his life in harness, working to improve, yes, but where he couldn't improve, helping to conceal and apologize. You're an insider who's never bucked the chain of command. You mentioned the Police Federation. As far as I'm concerned, you might as well be here as their official representative. How can you expect anyone to trust your impartiality in an investigation which may potentially implicate—"

"Bollocks, bollocks, nothing but bloody bollocks," Jackson exploded, springing out of his chair. "Dame Ingrid. I appreciate your input, I assure you, but it seems you've come here to do a post-mortem on an investigation that's barely begun. I can promise you, procedure will be followed. Hetheridge is a damn fine detective and we're lucky to have him."

Paul noticed that Dame Ingrid hadn't flinched during any part of the discussion. Not when sparring with Tony, not when Jackson erupted into vulgarities, not even when he started babbling nursery rhymes. She had thirty years on him; at least twenty on Jackson; close to a decade on Tony. Judging by the impassive lines of her well-worn face, it was no longer possible for a roomful of disapproving men to intimidate her—if, indeed, it ever had been.

"Ah. Incoming push notification," she said, withdrawing the mobile from her front trouser pocket. "*Bright Star* again. 'Brave Amelia threw all-copper parties. Sometimes all-male.' Well. They didn't wait long to partner 'Brave Amelia' with a whiff of 'Slutty Amelia,' now did they?"

"She wasn't a slut," Kincaid snapped. He glared at Dame Ingrid like he wanted to snatch the phone from her hand and was holding himself back by main force. "She *was* dating a cop. It was me. I'm the one."

"Sean," Jackson groaned.

Dame Ingrid's pale eyes slid to him. She didn't have to speak to make her point; his deepening blush proved it had already hit home. She'd come as a victim's advocate, determined to ensure the investigation remained laser-focused on justice for DC Gulls. Jackson, not surprisingly, had chosen to play dumb about the Kincaid-Gulls connection, calling it a rumor he'd look into. For Jackson, talking out of school was a cardinal sin; serving up a junior officer to a watchdog like Dame Ingrid was equivalent to tossing him to, well, the dogs. But Dame Ingrid clearly took this revelation as proof positive that Scotland Yard wasn't meeting her in good faith. From now on, everything Jackson and his team did would be tainted in her eyes.

"I appreciate your honesty," she told Kincaid, gaze still lingering on Jackson, "if not your promptness. Now your superior must dismiss you from the case."

"He's not on the case," Jackson said. He was as close to losing control as Paul had ever seen him—since he quit drinking, at any rate. "He's attending this meeting at my invitation because he worked with Gulls for a long time. He may have valuable insights and I for one want to hear them. There's nothing wrong with—"

"You've eliminated him as a suspect?" Dame Ingrid cut in.

"I won't discuss the particulars of an open investigation. You can't ask those sort of questions and you know it. You came to lodge a complaint about Tony Hetheridge's involvement. Noted," Jackson said grimly. "Then you launched into an impromptu speech about how the people who've always feared and loathed the police still loath and fear us. Noted. Now you want to take control, and that's where I draw the line. Thank you, Dame Ingrid." It was her turn to have her title thrown back at her. "If you find you have additional input, please direct it to AC Deaver."

Face still impassive, she said, "I won't be frightened off, you know."

"Bully for you. I don't want you frightened. Just off."

Paul located a spot on the carpet and stared at it until Dame Ingrid closed the door behind her. Then he let out his breath in a sigh.

Kincaid said, "Sorry, guv. She got under my skin."

"Should've kept your gob shut, like I told you. Now they'll bring in an outside unit to interview you and review your alibi. Plus you'll get your knuckles rapped for fraternization. Times have changed, haven't they, Tony?"

"Indeed they have."

Paul asked, "Why was she so hostile? Me, I'm used to it. Reckon there's something about my face. But she seemed—"

"Your mouth, more like," Jackson said. "One day I'll sew it shut."

Paul accepted that rebuke as his due. Turning to Tony, he said, "Was it my imagination, or did she have something personal against you, Chief?"

"About ten years ago, AC Deaver and I worked the murder of a detective sergeant's ex-wife," Tony replied.

"Kimberly Urquhart was her name. DS Urquhart had a shaky alibi—he claimed to have spent the entire night with his girl-friend, who corroborated his story, but the ex-wife's next door neighbor swore to seeing him just outside the crime scene around the time of the murder. If memory serves, the forensics were inconclusive—the Urquharts shared custody of a child, so his fingerprints and DNA had reason to be found throughout the house. In the end, there was nothing substantive against DS Urquhart but the testimony of the neighbor placing him near the scene, and CPS rejected any notion of putting the witness before a jury. She admitted to drinking on the night in question, and every other night, and had once appeared in Magistrates Court for drunk and disorderly. So the case went cold and remains unsolved to this day."

"How did Dame Ingrid become involved?" Paul asked.

"Ms. Urquhart's family was convinced she'd been killed by her ex-husband. Her parents claimed he'd been abusive to her, physically as well as mentally, and said Ms. Urquhart feared him too much to report it. They believed that because DS Urquhart was a police officer, the MPS was either actively covering up his guilt, or doing a slapdash investiga-tion to keep from learning of it," Tony said. "Dame Ingrid had only just retired from her post as commissioner. Her victims' advocacy began informally with that case. In the course of it, she met with me and went away unsatisfied. Nothing I said would convince her I'd worked hard enough to find the killer. Then she met with the AC and according to him, the meeting turned hostile. Thereafter, Dame Ingrid has never made any secret of her opinion that AC Deaver and I conspired to shield DS Urquhart from a murder charge."

"It was a bad business," Jackson sighed. Seeming to realize he was still on his feet, he dropped into his office chair, which creaked in protest. "You'd think a former police commissioner wouldn't be so quick to judge other officers. She knows what we're up against."

"But thirty years ago, Dame Ingrid's only daughter was murdered," Tony said. "The killer was never caught. She understands our position, yes. But her heart will always be with the victims, and the victims' families."

"You're awfully tolerant, aren't you, Tony?" Jackson sounded sour.

He shrugged. "I did everything within my power to solve the Kimberly Urquhart case. If I missed anything, it was an honest mistake, not a deliberate attempt to protect a colleague from justice. And while I don't know what caused the breach between AC Deaver and Dame Ingrid, I've always assumed the bulk of her hostility is directed toward Michael."

"Can we get back to talking about Amelia?" Kincaid burst out, then immediately looked mortified. "I'm sorry. I keep exploding. I don't know why."

"You're raw, son," Jackson said. He wasn't trying to be comforting, only stating a truth. "And you're right. Let's focus on DC Gulls. Our interview yesterday left me with some questions, but you were so torn up, I thought you needed a rest. Let's go over it again. From the top."

CHAPTER 7

"We'd been seeing each other for about six months," Kincaid began in a monotone, fists balled at his sides. "I'd fancied her for some time, but I didn't think she'd risk it, since it meant one of us would have to transfer out. Amelia's goal was always to work for the Toff Squad. A bomb blast couldn't dislodge her. And it was the same for me. So even though I liked to flirt with her, I reckoned it was hopeless. Then one night she threw one of her parties, all coppers, all shoptalk, and I was the last to leave. Only I didn't quite make it out the door until the next morning. That's how it started."

He paused, looking from face to face. Paul resisted the temptation to give him a sympathetic nod.

Tony asked, "How serious would you characterize the relationship?"

"Serious," Kincaid said hollowly. "She knew how I felt. I knew how she felt. If not for work, we would've moved in together. Maybe tied the knot."

"Any friction? Pressure points?" Jackson asked.

Kincaid shook his head.

"Her parents didn't know about you."

"No. We were discreet."

"Did your parents know about her?"

He shook his head.

Jackson said, "Dame Ingrid wasn't wrong about *Bright Star*. They seem to have dug up a neighbor in Gulls's building who observed you going in late and coming out early. Will there be more revelations?"

"Like what?"

"You know what. Raised voices? Public rows? Signs of trouble in paradise the tabloids might pay through the nose for?"

"No. I mean..." Kincaid tailed off. "We did have a row once over—over something stupid. I slammed the door on my way out, and she followed me right into the hall. You know how passionate she could be when she thought she was right. It happened around four in the morning—I'm sure at least one neighbor peeked out to see what all the fuss was about. Next day she told me she smoothed it over, but I expect anyone we disturbed will remember."

"Nothing else?" Jackson stared stonily at the younger man. "I'm not hearing certainty, and by God, this is a time for it. It's your last chance to come clean. If you've left out one shove, one slap, one threat uttered in the presence of witnesses..."

"It wasn't like that! I'm not like that," Kincaid roared, leaping out of his chair and surging toward Jackson's desk. Paul and Tony leapt up as well, ready to grapple Kincaid if he was mad enough to actually lay hands on his superior.

"Sean. Enough." The whip-crack of Tony's aristocratic tone made Kincaid sag. "Sit down and answer questions calmly. Histrionics won't help Gulls and they certainly won't help you. Answer me this: Detective Constable Kincaid, where were you Sunday night between the hours of nine p.m. and six a.m.?"

Kincaid sank down again. With exaggerated calm, he replied, "Until nine, I was at Kentish Town Police Station checking up on another tip regarding the Marquand case. It was brand new, anonymous, but full of privileged details that made it worth looking into. Do you want me to—"

"Not now. Your movements only."

"Right. When I finished up at the station, I took the tube to a pub called the Black Dove. In Hackney. I was there until close to one o'clock. I—"

"Sorry. You said Hackney?" Paul asked.

Kincaid nodded.

"You live in Camberwell, right?"

"That's right."

"And Gulls's flat is in Cricklewood."

"Yeah. So?"

"So. Hackney is a long way from Cricklewood, that's all. Did you say the pub is called the Black Dove?"

"Yes."

"Give me a sec."

Withdrawing his mobile, Paul used an app to locate the establishment. It looked like a sagging hole in the wall, and the patron reviews were decidedly mixed.

"Got it. Please continue."

"Right. Erm, the pub. I was there for a couple of hours. Until at least half-twelve. I started for home, then realized I didn't have my overcoat. I rang the station, and sure enough, I'd left it back there, hanging on the rack. I decided to go back straightaway—Kentish Town is open twenty-four hours —and by the time I retrieved my overcoat and made it home, it was past two o'clock. I went straight to bed and didn't get up until half-six."

"You would've got more sleep if you'd left the overcoat for the next day," Tony said.

"I had to get it," Kincaid said. "My flat keys were inside."

"I had a routine check run on the GPS of your MPS mobile," Jackson said. "It didn't go to Hackney. So I did a check on your personal mobile and—"

"They were both at Kentish Town," Kincaid said. "Inside my coat, along with my keys, until I retrieved it."

"Yet you had the cash to pay for pints at the Black Dove," Tony said.

"Yeah. My wallet stays in my front trouser pocket."

"I'd like to establish your whereabouts after nine o'clock beyond doubt," Jackson said. "But without the GPS of your mobiles, it's difficult. Did you take a cab to Hackney?"

"The tube."

"Top-up your Oyster card or make any credit card purchases along the way?"

"No."

No one spoke. Paul knew the other men's silence was calculated, but in his case it was genuine. Kincaid had dropped from the grid during the crucial time when Gulls was murdered. It was a fact. No getting around it.

He asked, "What about the bartender at the Black Dove? Any chance they'd remember you?"

"Maybe. But it was my first time there."

"Why that particular pub?" Tony asked.

"I don't know. Somebody mentioned it to me once, I reckon. I just wanted somewhere to sit quietly and think over the facts of the case. I told you I had a new tip about the death of Gregory Marquand. It was bogus, near as I could tell, and it bothered me. I was trying to decide if we were dealing with someone who knew Gregory was murdered, and kept trying to nudge us in the right direction, or someone who was toying with the police. Having a bit of fun at our expense."

Silence again. Finally, Paul took the plunge. "Can you see how this will look to outsiders? People who don't know you?"

"Of course."

Paul bit back a sigh. "All right. We'll send someone round to the Black Dove. If the barkeep remembers you—a quiet man alone who paid cash and then buggered off—it will help a little. Even then, as alibis go, it's thin. If the barkeep dummies up and won't swear you were present, we have nothing but your word."

"And nothing against my word. No one who places me at the scene. My DNA will be in Amelia's flat, of course, but that's only natural. Search my place," Kincaid flared. "Search it! You won't find her bag or mobiles or laptop there."

"Of course we won't," Jackson said, but his tone was not reassuring.

"You think I could do that to Amelia?" Kincaid looked around the room with dawning horror. "You actually think I could strangle—" His voice broke. Then his hands went up, covering his face.

"You know I'd never want to believe that," Paul said as gently as he could. "But help me. Please, help me. You're saying you worked after hours on the Marquand case. All right. Did you call in to anyone after you decided the tip was no good?"

Kincaid shook his head. "I was working with Amelia. I reckoned I'd catch her up the next day."

"Hackney's a jaunt from Kentish Town Station. I can't believe you traveled all that way without noticing you'd forgot your mobile."

"I knew I'd silenced it. And I had a lot on my mind. Didn't fancy mucking about on it."

"Did you silence your MPS mobile?" Jackson asked.

"No, of course not."

"So that might have buzzed."

"There are nights when it doesn't, thank God."

"Yet you went from just after nine until half-twelve without noticing either phone wasn't with you."

"Maybe I noticed sooner..."

"That's not what you said before." Tony sounded cool. "You said as you left the Black Dove, you realized you didn't have your overcoat. Probably because it was raining, as it's done every day this week. Then you returned to Kentish Town because your flat keys and mobiles were in the jacket. Do you wish to revise your statement?"

Kincaid swallowed. "No."

Paul said, "Only I've never heard of an officer your age who loses tracks of his phone for hours."

"We're not all millennial mobile addicts."

"Perhaps not," Tony said. "But you don't wear a wrist-watch. I've never seen you with one. It appears that if you want the time, you check your mobile. I observed you doing that twice while Dame Ingrid was speaking."

"Look. I know I should be better at this. But I'm losing it. Amelia's dead and I'm sorry, but I'm losing it." Voice shaking, Kincaid took his hands away from his face at last. He sounded distraught, but his breathing was steady and his eyes were dry. Had he truly been on the verge of breaking down? Paul wasn't sure.

"We know this is tough," Jackson said stonily. "But it's all for Amelia. Dame Ingrid wasn't wrong about the need to eliminate you as soon as possible. How many people have you put to the question? It's your turn in the hot seat, that's all."

"How many people?" Kincaid murmured, sitting on his hands, probably to stop them from shaking. "Yeah. Husbands and boyfriends and punters. Half of them guilty as sin, half of them innocent but scared witless over what a murder investigation will expose. All the dirty little secrets we hold so dear. I don't have any dirty secrets, I swear to you," he said, focusing on Paul, perhaps because they were closest in age.

"I never raised a hand to Amelia, or she to me. Did we bicker and argue? Yeah, sometimes, mostly because of the work. It was a strain to be secretive when we both wanted more. I loved her, all right?" he declared. "I loved her, and she loved me, and this is a bloody nightmare, that's what it is. The whole week. It's all just—I mean—forget it. It's a nightmare, and I keep praying I'll wake up."

On paper, the words would probably seem about right for a grieving lover. Yet Paul found something about the way Kincaid's eyes bulged disquieting. He flashed back to Amelia, dead on the floor, her face a mass of swollen tissue and broken capillaries. By rights, he ought to be consoling Kincaid, helping him process the tragedy. Instead he was dissecting the quality of the other man's voice, the appropriateness of his affect, the frequency of his blinks.

Jackson and Tony exchanged a glance. When Tony was still at the Yard and Jackson was still drinking, they'd mostly worked in opposition. It was strange to see them on the same side, communicating like old school coppers—the merest glance and they were telepathically connected.

"All right, Sean. That's all for now," Tony said.

"Get yourself home. Try and rest," Jackson said gruffly. "Tomorrow you'll receive a new slate of assignments. Your present workload, including the Marquand case, will be parceled out among your colleagues."

"Yes, sir. Thank you, sir." Rising, Kincaid added with a note of desperation, "DCI Jackson, I'd like to apologize. I was hasty and disrespectful. I regret—"

"Stuff all that. I'm not a snowflake. Call me a right bastard to my face, see if I care. I said the murder of Kimberly Urquhart was a bad business. Well, this is worse. Gulls was a good detective and I take her loss personally. We'll all need a bit of slack from time to time. I'm not pulling you off Marquand or the other cases to punish you, son. But you can't just go on like you aren't a suspect. Like it or not, you are. I wish to God it were different, but there it is. Go home, punch the wall, ring your mum, whatever gets you through the night."

Mumbling, "Thank you, sir," Kincaid started for the door. When he touched the handle, he looked back and said, "Can I add one thing about that Marquand tip?"

"Go ahead."

"Now that Amelia is dead, and I know when she was killed, I wonder if someone didn't call it in to keep me busy."

"What was the nature of the tip?" Tony asked.

"It came through the switchboard, but it was directed to me personally, sir." Kincaid held himself to attention, speaking with careful formality.

"The caller was a man. His voice was muffled—not electronically spoofed, just muffled. Like he was on speaker-phone and standing near a blender or fan of some kind. He said he had information on the Gregory Marquand murder. I tried to interrupt—first to say it had only been ruled a suspicious death, not a murder, and second to ask how he knew I was assigned to the case. But he didn't give me a chance.

"He said at Kentish Town there was a DI called Went-worth," Kincaid continued. "This Wentworth supposedly used to work alongside Marquand—Leland Marquand, Gregory's father. After Gregory was found dead, he caught Leland in some false statements. According to Wentworth, Leland had told his mates he was logged in at the station during his son's time of death, helping the borough chief with a difficult case, but it wasn't true. He'd confided in

Wentworth that he needed a squeaky-clean alibi, because the real one was a bit compromising—he had a bit of stuff on the side and couldn't let his wife find out. She's ill, you know, and rather delicate. Anyway—this is all from the tipster but attributed to Wentworth—during the first investigation into Gregory's death, Marquand used that helping-the-borough-chief story to cover himself. Wentworth didn't like it, but chose to keep quiet. He didn't want to be seen as grassing on a fellow officer, or sticking his nose into a Scotland Yard investigation. But when he heard Gregory's death was being looked into again, he had second thoughts and wanted to unburden himself."

"Now that's a hot tip," Paul said. "Almost too good to be true."

"Which is what I thought. I asked the caller straight out, 'Are you him? Wentworth?'" Kincaid said. "The line went dead. I thought it over. It was already half-seven, and I'd had a long day, but I rang Kentish Town and was told Wentworth had just gone into an interview room with a suspect and would probably head home when finished. I decided there was no time to lose and rushed over.

"I turned up at half-eight, just as Wentworth exited the interview room. He was polite enough, but had no idea what I was talking about."

"Do you think he was the man who phoned?" Tony asked.

"No. Wentworth is loud and boisterous. The tipster was intense. Sort of furtive. Could have even been a female, if she had a low voice."

"What did Wentworth say about the tip itself?" Jackson asked.

"He called it pure rubbish. Especially the idea that Leland Marquand had a bit of stuff on the side. Wentworth even took the time to try and pull the original files out of storage —Kentish Town is behind in their scanning—that proved

Leland Marquand really was logged in and helping the borough chief during the time Gregory Marquand probably died in Epping Forest. He couldn't locate them, but said he'd ring when he did.

"So you see, sirs," he ended, still formal, gazing at a spot on the wall, "it's rather like someone intended to get me away from Amelia's flat. If the killer had been watching her, and it seems that he had, he must've known I turned up on different nights, usually around eight or nine. I think he designed a tip I couldn't resist. If Wentworth had been willing to swear that Leland Marquand got his police mates to fabricate an alibi for him, the case would have been broken wide open. Instead, I went on a wild goose chase."

"Were you planning to go to DC Gulls's flat that night?" Tony asked.

"No," Kincaid said.

"Who among your colleagues knew for certain that you two were involved?"

"No one."

"You mean you told no one."

"That's right."

"Yet you believe someone did know, and used that knowledge against you," Tony said. "Do you think DC Gulls might have confided in someone?"

"No. I mean, it's not impossible, sir," Kincaid said. "But I can't imagine it. Unless..." He sighed, unable to keep up the mask of formality any longer. "It's hard to know what I believe. She thought—I mean, it could've been—I don't know. It's been a nightmare of a week."

"So you said before. Very well." Tony's gaze moved from Paul to Jackson, in case either of them had something to add. Then he said, "Thank you, Kincaid. Do go home and try to rest. We'll speak again when and if something changes."

CHAPTER 8

"Oh, dear." From the lips of Lady Margaret Knolls, those words landed with a vibrating thud, like a javelin hitting home. "And to think I've waited so long to see inside Tony's bedroom. It might as well be a room at the Comfort Inn."

"Yes, well, you quite enjoyed the Comfort Inn Hyde Park didn't you? When our house was overcome by toxic fumes and we had to flee headlong into the nearest safe harbor?" Lady Vivian Callot pointed out.

"I quite enjoyed breathing, yes, I shan't contradict you on that point. There's something to be said for a funk hole, as it were, with a locking door, a loo, and even a television. But I would've felt quite differently about my surroundings had I been forced to retire to them each and every night. What's the point of a bland, anodyne, one-size-fits-all room?"

As Lady Margaret continued scowling at the furniture, Kate turned to Lady Vivian and mouthed, "Toxic fumes?"

Lady Vivian nodded. "Another decorating debacle. Mags," she called. "Do stop stalking around. Come. Sit. You're distressing Kate."

"Am I?" Lady Margaret turned away from her inspection of the hand-painted Sevres vase. "Good heavens. Is the fetus leeching your fortitude?"

"No," Kate laughed. "Though Nipper might be stealing a bit of calcium from my bones. Tony's the one who reads all the baby manuals and pregnancy pamphlets. I can't bear so many could-bes and maybe-nots. Give me the facts or leave me in peace. Now what's this about toxic fumes?"

"Ancient history." Lady Margaret finally alighted in a chair, pausing to arrange her knee-length tunic and flowing vest. All her casual clothes were breathable, unstructured, and undyed. She never bothered with makeup; the few pieces of jewelry she wore were usually breathtaking. Today it was earrings: canary diamonds, cushion-cut and sparkling whenever she turned her head.

"Her nephew, Edmund, was redecorating yet again," Lady Vivian said. "Something went wrong with the VOCs. That means volatile organic compounds, and they're meant to be handled with great care. But Edmund—have you met him? No. Well, I can assure you, he flies by the seat of his pants. As anyone who's stepped inside our dining room can tell from a glance at the tartan wallpaper and the Sputnik chandelier."

"Rubbish. Don't blame Edmund for the fumes. It was the fault of those assistants he had in, the dodgy ones with full beards and neck tattoos." Lady Margaret shuddered. "I told him I won't permit him to redecorate again until he promises to hire presentable—not to say recognizably human—helpers who are both careful and conscientious."

As Lady Margaret spoke, Lady Vivian winked at Kate and pulled a face. A swan-necked beauty with white hair swept back from a regal brow, Lady Vivian had a mischievous sense of humor; she wasn't above crossing her eyes and sticking out her tongue when Lady Margaret's back was turned. Lady Margaret was acerbic by nature and confrontational by choice; she enjoyed poking at people to find out what they were made of. But Lady Vivian was cheerful and happy-go-lucky, with easy manners like Tony's—the mark of true breeding, as far as Kate was concerned.

"Well I, for one, think this old heap has never looked better," Lady Vivian declared, beaming at Kate. "And neither have you, my dear. No, I'm not blowing smoke. I know you must feel like a prisoner—"

"I feel like a hippo. A pregnant hippo."

Lady Margaret said, "If there's anything worth creating that doesn't come with a price, I'd like to know what it is. What will you call him?"

"We don't know the sex. We're choosing to be surprised."

"Nonsense. It's a boy. I sense a very masculine energy."

Kate bit her lip. Lady Margaret, who clearly expected Kate to argue with her, turned to Lady Vivian in triumph. "See! I'm right. I'm always right about babies."

"Do you sense the same energy, Kate?" Lady Vivian asked.

She placed a hand atop her belly, as she tended to do reflexively when someone asked her a question about Nipper. "Between you and me...yes. I can't explain it. It might be that I'm so used to Henry and Ritchie, it seems natural that Nipper will be a boy, too. But it's getting harder and harder to resist saying 'he.'"

"Tony will be over the moon. And the name?" Lady Margaret insisted.

"I wanted Anthony, but Tony put his foot down. Said a child should have his own name. So I suggested Alexander, and Tony suggested Nicholas. Now I'm leaning toward Nicholas Anthony, if I can get Tony on board."

It was rare indeed to find a gimlet-eyed raptor like Lady Margaret Knolls beaming at you, but there it was. Kate's cheeks warmed with a sudden rush of answering emotion. It was pregnancy hormones; once again they'd burst into her control room and taken over. When they started flipping switches and twisting dials, absolutely anything, from a throwaway remark to a nappies advert, could make her burst into tears. At least these were tears of joy.

Lady Vivian said, "And if Mags is wrong, which she frequently is, despite all claims to the contrary—"

"I'm never wrong about babies."

"—and it's a girl, what will you call her?"

"Admit that when I sense a particular energy about a baby, I'm never wrong."

"In your mind, Mags, you are never wrong. That I will always concede." Lady Vivian smiled at Kate. "I read that all the hottest names this year were inspired by *Bridgerton*. Have you watched it?"

"A bit," Kate lied. She wasn't sure how the news she'd watched *Vampire Circus* and *Twins of Evil* multiple times while skipping the newer streaming dramas would sound to them. Paul's mum thought an excess of Hammer horror movies might cause the baby to grow up to be a writer of pulp fiction—a possibility which Sharada, a successful romance novelist, found intriguing.

"The *Bridgerton*-inspired names are fun," Lady Vivian continued as Lady Margaret pursed her lips in disapproval. "There's Cressida. Euphemia. Hyacinth."

"Nope. I can't name a baby after *Keeping Up Appearances*. Tony wants Lydia, and I rather like Maisie. Of course, with Amelia dead, I've half a mind to name a girl after her. But it's so sad..."

"Speaking of your late colleague. Tony rang me this morning," Lady Margaret said when Kate tailed off. "He told me you're mad to help in some way, and to try and keep you hermetically sealed would do more harm than good, no matter what your doctor says. But," she added, wagging a finger, "he asked us to keep the discussion brief and to the point. Half an hour should do it. What would you like to know?"

Kate, who'd expected such husbandly meddling, was ready for it. Reaching for her iPad and stylus, she opened a note-taking app to consult the prompts she'd already jotted down.

"First question: Xiuying Chen. She's a civil servant who works in and around 10 Downing Street. I understand she's a bit of a social climber. Have either of you met her?"

"Not I," Lady Margaret said. "Of course, I avoid government toadies like the plague. The aristocracy's bad enough."

"I believe she was introduced to me during a holiday party last year," Lady Vivian said. "Deputy Director Chen, isn't that right? Tall, slender, elegant? Married to a sort of vortex—you know what I mean. Not only was he a crashing bore, he seemed to suck those around him into a zone of irrelevancy. I wondered what on earth such a woman saw in him."

"I don't recall any such person," Lady Margaret sniffed. "Perhaps you're thinking of Chloe Wu? She's whip-smart, very stylish, very now. Works with the government, not for it, which exonerates her in my book. Married to Peter Cartwright, the most useless Englishman to ever draw breath."

Lady Vivian looked uncertain. "But it must've been Xiuying Chen. Why else would the title 'deputy director' trip off my tongue like that?"

"A great many things trip off your tongue. Is this government toady a murder suspect?" Lady Margaret asked. "That would at least make her faintly interesting."

"No. I told you, she's the mother of a man who died under suspicious circumstances."

"What does that have to do with your deceased colleague?"

"DC Gulls was working on Lin Wu Chen's case when she died. He was a uni student, top marks, bright future. He lived with a man called Orrin Parker. The night Mr. Chen disappeared, Mr. Parker was at work, which gives him a firm alibi. Mr. Parker says their relationship was good. Ms. Chen, who is on record as disliking Mr. Parker, claims they were actually on the verge of splitting up and—"

"I did meet her!" Lady Vivian broke in, jubilant. "Chloe Wu, indeed. Deputy Director Chen was at that Christmas gala at the Connaught Rooms. She wore a sort of Art Deco gown that matched the venue very well. Her hair was up— oh, surely you remember, Mags. Statuesque woman in five-inch heels."

"Apparently, she made no impression."

"But don't you remember? When she said something like, 'Between my job and my son, I haven't any time,' and I asked after her son, thinking it would be a nice bit of small talk, and she said he was murdered. You could've heard a pin drop. Doesn't that ring a bell?"

"I must've wandered off by then. I'd remember murder."

To Kate, Lady Vivian said, "I'm afraid I can't offer much more. Her husband cleared his throat and I apologized for bringing up such a fraught topic. There was nothing left to discuss but the weather, and I slipped away as soon as possible."

"Really, Vivian, how disappointing. Kate expected a confession, or at the very least, a bit of key evidence Scotland Yard overlooked."

"She thinks she's a dab hand at assisting the police," Lady Vivian stage-whispered to Kate. "This is how she signals dominance. Like a boss mare kick-fighting the new mare to show her who runs the paddock."

Kate smiled. Lady Vivian was what people called "horsey"

—she'd been a champion equestrian in her youth, still bred horses, and rode several times a month.

"How did the son die?" Lady Margaret asked.

"He drowned. Mr. Chen was missing for four days, and then his body was discovered in the Thames by a tugboat captain. Forensics wasn't able to determine much from the corpse. Inconclusive for drugs and alcohol, and inconclusive for a minor wound, like a bump on the head. There are plenty of scenarios—too many, really," Kate said. "The boyfriend, Mr. Parker, said Mr. Chen occasionally used street drugs, mostly MDMA. That's also called molly, or ecstasy."

Eyes flicking to her notes, she continued, "Just before you came, I re-read Mr. Parker's sworn statement, given into evidence the day Mr. Chen's body was positively identified. Mr. Parker said there had been some infidelity, and he was of the opinion Mr. Chen used the opportunity—Mr. Parker working late—to go out in search of drugs and maybe more. Mr. Parker suggested Mr. Chen might have approached the wrong person and wound up dead."

"No wonder his mum doesn't care for him. What a hideous portrait to paint in remembrance," Lady Vivian said.

"Do think the government angle might lead back to Scotland Yard?" Lady Margaret asked.

"At a glance, nothing else presents itself," Kate said. "The original investigation was by the book. I won't say flawless, it's never flawless, mostly because interviewees always lie about something, usually embarrassing details no one actually cares about. And witnesses, even eyewitnesses, tend to get it wrong. But we know Lin Wu Chen took the Northern line to Battersea, walked in the direction of a club called Red Rain, and dropped out of space and time. As near as we can tell, he didn't actually enter the club. His mobile data stops out in the street. The phone and his wallet were never recovered. He just blinked out of existence, and turned up dead in the Thames four days later. Orrin Parker has moved on, but every few months his mum starts agitating for the Met to do something. So Amelia was asked to look into it."

"Very sad," Lady Margaret said in her brutally practical way. "You mentioned three cold cases. What about the other two?""

"The second is more in Tony's purview," Kate said. "The suspicious death of Gregory Marquand, son of retired DI Leland Marquand. No society connections. Gregory was a drug addict and he may have decided to end it all. But he had an antagonistic relationship with his father, and DI Marquand seems to believe the reopening of the case is pure harassment."

"I fear we have nothing to offer there. Unless there's an equine connection?" Lady Vivian asked hopefully.

Lady Margaret snorted in a way that did nothing to dispel the "boss mare" accusation.

"No dressage or show jumping in the Marquand family," Kate agreed. "But I saved the best for last. What does the name Parth Chakrabarti mean to you?"

Lady Margaret looked appalled. "Beastly man. Unbearable. A blot on Great Britain."

"I find him...a tad challenging to warm up to," Lady Vivian said.

"Viv is a diplomat's daughter. Can you tell?"

Kate continued, "But you've heard about the death of his daughter, haven't you? Valeria?"

"So shocking—out a window," Lady Vivian said. "Everyone has heard."

"*Everyone*," Lady Margaret agreed. "At the bottom of the Mariana Trench, ancient creatures who dwell all of their lives in unbroken darkness have heard of Valeria Chakrabarti. And what her father would like to do to the person who defenestrated her. And the ten million pounds he will pay the person who provides information leading to the arrest and conviction of her killer."

"Defenestrated," Lady Vivian breathed. "I don't like that word. It sounds obscene."

"I thought the reward was one million pounds," Kate said, swiping her finger across the tablet to backtrack through her notes.

"It was. But as of this morning, it's gone up to ten million. Someone in this room reads *Bright Star* every morning at the breakfast table."

Lady Vivian offered a sunny, unapologetic smile.

"Really? Every morning? I don't think I could digest my food," Kate admitted. She had many grudges against the tabloid, and didn't expect to forgive the newspaper's unprincipled editors anytime soon.

"Yes, well, I can barely digest my food sitting across from her, seeing the front page," Lady Margaret said. "I don't see the point of bothering with a paper that flagrantly makes things up. If one desires the hard, cold truth about Parth Chakrabarti, one must come to me."

CHAPTER 9

"*H*e was born in London, you know, though his parents emigrated from Mumbai. When they came, they were already millionaires, and did even better in the UK. He's on the *Sunday Times* Rich List every year—closer to the bottom than the top, but still," Lady Margaret said. Slipping into her role as the repository of London society gossip, she delivered the tale in a slow, wise, revelatory fashion that made Kate think of a female David Attenborough. If the BBC ever made a documentary called *Rich and Titled Planet*, Lady Margaret would be the ideal choice to narrate the footage of wealthy Britons as they mated, raised their young, and occasionally fought to the death.

"His portfolio is, as they say, diversified," Lady Margaret continued. "I believe the Chakrabartis started as hoteliers, moved into finance, and from there into everything else, including the requisite charities. I told you the parents arrived as millionaires. That doesn't mean they were accepted socially, of course."

"I had the impression they weren't interested in that sort of thing," Lady Vivian said.

"Perhaps not. But they wanted Parth to have every advantage. They sent him to Brighton College, and then to Oxford, and they got their money's worth, in that he made friends. The father was a numbers man and the mother was the chamber maid who married the boss—"

"Sometimes marrying the boss is dead brill," Kate cut in.

Lady Margaret's eyes sparkled. "True. At least in your case. Anyway, young Parth was a posh British brat. He got on well with others of his kind, and before long he had pretensions. Now. Tell me, Lady Kate, what does a young man with money and pretensions do to further his societal ambitions?"

"I suppose you want me to say marry."

"Marry, yes, but not just anyone. He must marry the right sort of woman."

"Or man, nowadays."

"This was thirty years ago. The right sort of woman, full stop," Lady Margaret said. "There was a rumor that Parth's parents had strongly desired for him to go the traditional route, an arranged marriage. They'd chosen the girl, a Londoner with impeccable education and breeding, parents also from Mumbai, aligning with the Chakrabartis in all areas. Except Parth wouldn't have it. He'd fallen for a would-be pop singer called Mandy Haystack."

"The word you meant is 'wannabe,'" Lady Vivian said.

"I said what I meant. I don't recognize the existence of *that* collection of sounds as belonging to the English language."

"Was her name really Haystack?" Kate asked.

"I have no idea. But I remember—oh, I can't describe it. Better that you see it. Google her," she ordered, pointing at Kate's phone, which lay beside her in bed. "She had one song that received a modest degree of attention—"

"The term is airplay," Lady Vivian cut in.

Lady Margaret affected not to hear. "Google Mandy Haystack and her single, 'Tumble Me.'"

Kate did as she was told and wasn't disappointed. The song, which had been released almost thirty years ago, was accompanied by an image of the record sleeve. Mandy Haystack, dressed in a red midriff-baring blouse and denim cutoffs, lay in a pile of hay with one long piece between her glossy red lips. She was a petite beauty with a snub nose, long yellow-blonde hair, and over-plucked eyebrows. Beside the photo and capsule biography, Google had thoughtfully included an excerpt of the lyrics to "Tumble Me:"

> *I like my man*
> *To guarantee*
> *He'll take control*
> *And tumble me*

> *A simple girl*
> *A simple plea*
> *One big man*
> *To tumble me*

"Ugh." Kate tossed her mobile aside. "I don't remember ever hearing that on the radio."

"I don't believe it set the world on fire," Lady Margaret said. "Except for Parth, apparently, who swept her off her feet and married her. In Las Vegas, no less."

"I wonder if Elvis officiated," Lady Vivian said. "But in all seriousness, though I've always been one to advocate for children choosing their own mates, without respect to their parents' wishes—they will have to live with the consequences, after all—I remember feeling sorry for the Chakrabartis. This was more than a beloved son bucking tradition and preference. He destroyed himself socially. Or so they believed at the time."

"The wrong woman," Lady Margaret agreed. "But times were beginning to change. As for Parth, he wasn't the least bit ashamed of the new Mrs. Chakrabarti, and that was half the battle. I remember her as pleasant. Rather like the lyrics of her song—deferring to him, keeping in his shadow, and so on. Parth is a large man in every sense—tall, big-boned, rather fat. When the children came, and Mandy shepherded them along in his wake, she could've been mistaken for one of them, at least at a distance."

"Where is Mandy now? There's an ominous sound to this. Did she die?" Kate asked, picking up her mobile again. She did that a hundred times a day—consulted her iPhone, threw it down in disgust, picked it up again. No matter how irritated she was by a text, post, or email, the ruddy thing always found its way back into her hand.

"Consult Google," Lady Margaret said. "I'll wait."

The phrase "whatever happened to Mandy Haystack" produced a number of stub articles, all with variations of the same information. After skimming three of them, Kate said, "Apparently, she retired from music, divorced her husband, and now leads a quiet life in Karpathos, a Greek island in the Aegean Sea. Well." Kate chuckled. "I didn't see that coming."

"Mustn't believe everything you find on the Internet," Lady Vivian said.

"There's a glaring mistake," Lady Margaret agreed. "She didn't divorce Parth. He divorced her—after she ran away with the pool boy. A nineteen-year-old Greek Adonis, slender and pretty as a maiden."

"Oh! I guess being tumbled by a big man got old after a while." Kate chuckled again. "But wait. How old was Valeria when Mandy did a runner?"

Lady Margaret considered. "Perhaps eight. She was the

eldest, and from what I saw, the favorite by far. Her brother is—let me think—Antonio. Yes, it's Shakespeare, that's the conceit."

"Valeria from *Coriolanus*. Antonio from—take your pick," Lady Vivian said. "*Much Ado About Nothing* seems about right. And Octavia from *Antony and Cleopatra*."

"I'm going to shock you," Kate said with a smile, "but I'm not what you'd call up on Shakespeare. I don't think I've seen any of those plays, or movies—if there are movies."

"*Coriolanus* isn't the Bard's best work. Anyone can be forgiven for giving it short shrift," Lady Vivian said. "Valeria wasn't a memorable character, except perhaps in one respect. She enjoyed watching a young man torture a butterfly."

"I cannot believe Parth and Mandy considered that scene while naming their firstborn," Lady Margaret said. "I expect they chose 'Valeria' just for the sound of it. Assuming Mandy got any say at all, existing in Parth's shadow as she did."

"Until she summoned the courage to run away with the pool boy forever."

"Correct. That was a bit shocking. But either she was tired of motherhood, or she was too afraid of Parth to return. Antonio couldn't have been more than six years old when she left, and Octavia perhaps four.

"As for Antonio being described as much ado about nothing," she continued, "I shan't disagree. He's of the age where if he possessed any mettle, it would have glinted by now. He's been to school, and to university, and to America for a while, doing who knows what. Now he works for his father, which is understood to mean nothing in particular. Parth has the golden touch. He'd be a billionaire by now, I expect, if not for the shock of Mandy leaving him. In a certain sense, he never recovered."

"What do you mean?" Kate asked.

Lady Margaret and Lady Vivian swapped glances.

"He's become a sort of activist. A masculinist, he calls it," Lady Vivian said, with that gentle daughter-of-a-diplomat smile.

"A what?" Kate asked.

"One of those tiresome people who go about bleating that the rights of men are being trampled," Lady Margaret clarified. "He started with custody disputes. Apparently while Parth rearranged his life as a newly single parent, he met divorced fathers who felt the family courts were biased in favor of women. That's all very well, and may even be true in some cases." She shrugged. "But once he settled into the masculinist movement, Parth started looking for new mountains to scale. He founded a group called GTFO."

Kate blinked at her. She was well acquainted with the acronym—coppers weren't known for their dainty speech patterns—but even hearing the letters coming from Lady Margaret's lips surprised her. "Beg pardon?"

"It stands for Gone Too Far Organization. Meaning women's rights and feminism have gone too far, in Parth's view." Lady Margaret regarded her better half quizzically. "Why are you smirking?"

"No reason." Lady Vivian winked at Kate. "For the record, I personally think it's horrid, especially when one considers the many physical and economic hardships women suffer around the world. But neither Parth nor his fellow travelers care what I think. And I expect he'll resume his work, once Valeria's murderer is caught and punished."

"Oh. Yeah." Kate shook herself. "I have pregnancy brain. I was so caught up in Parth and Mandy, I forget this was all background for Valeria's murder. You know what else I have? Pregnancy bladder. Let me visit the loo and then we'll resume."

With a hand up from Lady Margaret, Kate got out of bed, stretched, and made her way to the bathroom, trying not to limp too much. When it came to bedrest, her titanium knee wasn't a fan.

When she returned, Lady Vivian fussed over her, plumping pillows and arranging them behind her for maximum comfort. "I have three children, you know, but there were five pregnancies. Two ended in miscarriage around the fourth month, which was devastating. So I always found myself on bedrest toward the end. I know you'll think I'm mad to say it, but do try to rest up rather than fight it. The moment your child arrives, the world changes forever. Be selfish now, while you can."

"Rubbish. Kate's never been selfish," Lady Margaret announced. "She's cared for her brother Ritchie for years. And before she and Tony adopted Henry, he was her foster child. And she's working right now, despite being forbidden, because a colleague was killed."

"I stand corrected. Oh, Kate, love, don't cry." Lady Vivian passed her a tissue.

"Sorry. Only—what a lovely thing to say." Kate dabbed her eyes, regarding Lady Margaret with amazement.

"Lovely?" The old woman made a rude noise. "Plain truth and nothing more. Where were we? Oh, yes, Parth's obsession with getting justice for Valeria. He's been on telly, made personal appeals, hired private detectives. As far as I know, he's still where he started: someone, probably a man, threw her out a window and disappeared. I suppose it's possible that the same mystery man also killed your friend. How easy is it for the public to learn which detectives are assigned to a murder case?"

"Not terribly easy," Kate said. "You can't just ring the switchboard or do a search online. Parth would know the identity of the SIO—senior investigating officer—and there's probably an FLO, which is Family Liaison Officer. So anyone in Parth's inner circle would've know about DCI Jackson and

Paul. But Amelia was a junior officer. Her specialty was research. If working on Valeria's murder got her killed, maybe she dug up some fact or bit of evidence that touched a nerve. Made someone think she was getting too close."

"It all seems so tangled. I don't know how you'll manage," Lady Vivian said. "On telly there would be a man in white overalls who'd find you a smidge of DNA or a partial fingerprint and solve the whole business."

"Now there's a contribution," Lady Margaret said acidly. "Perhaps you'd like to suggest Kate examine the boyfriend?"

"My guv's team is doing all of the above," Kate assured them. "A major forensics find would be a godsend, of course, but don't forget it has to match with something already in the National DNA Database. Or dovetail with a past crime that was entered into HOLMES 2. As for the boyfriend, there is one, and he's a colleague. Bordering on a friend. So I hope to heaven nothing about him pans out."

"Will they even look?" Lady Margaret asked shrewdly.

"They must," Lady Vivian protested. "Surely they must..." She tailed off, and Kate realized it was a question.

"Paul and the guv won't give anyone a miss simply because that person's a copper." The words came out a bit more heated than she intended. "Sorry. I think DC Kincaid is a good man, and if it turns out he killed Amelia, I can't begin to tell you how betrayed I'll feel. Still, since I'm shaped like a giant meatball and not allowed to officially take part, all I can do is probe around the edges. Ask what sort of person Deputy Director Chen is, ask if DI Marquand has society connections, try to get the inside track on Valeria and her family."

"When you put it that way, we really haven't answered many of your questions," Lady Vivian said. "We hardly know Ms. Chen. DI Marquand exists in a completely different sphere. And Valeria had no stardom ambitions like her mother, and no global finance pursuits like her father. She led a relatively quiet life until she went out that window."

"You never know. You might have provided a key piece of the puzzle and we just haven't recognized it yet," Kate said.

"Wouldn't that be lovely? At the very least, it will give you something to think about this afternoon," Lady Vivian said brightly. "If the tea and cucumber sandwiches and the clucking of hens gets too much, that is."

Lady Margaret's hooded eyes went wide. She turned a look of recrimination on Lady Vivian that would've reduced a lesser being—say, Paul Bhar—to ashes.

"Oh, dear." Lady Vivian didn't look the least bit repentant. "Only since our dear Kate was on record about not wanting a baby shower, and since Emmeline and Sharada and so many of Tony's relations are insisting on it—"

"Half that pack of vultures just wants inside Wellegrave House to see how Tony and his new wife live," Lady Margaret cut in.

"I thought a hint to our mummy-to-be might be wise," Lady Vivian finished, smiling hopefully at Kate.

"A baby shower." Kate stared at them.

"Wretched American concept. Materialistic and in questionable taste," Lady Margaret sniffed.

"A baby shower here in my bedroom, since I can't even go downstairs." Kate was horrified by the intrusion. She'd come a long way from her pre-marriage self, when she'd had no female friends and found even the company of other women rather fraught. Still, she didn't want this, and had specifically told everyone not to bother.

"Emmeline and Sharada are the hosts," Lady Vivian said. "They assured the other guests that there's plenty of room up here, and even though you're on bedrest, it will come off fine. No need for your cook to get involved—Emmeline hired a caterer to set up a buffet."

"But who besides the four of you would even want to come?" Kate asked. With Maura still at Briarshaw doing an intensive rehab program after a second relapse, and her mum's whereabouts mercifully unclear, Kate couldn't think of anyone who might care to attend. Except Amelia Gulls, of course.

"Oh, Mags was right to say Tony's aunts and cousins and nieces are gagging for an invitation. They felt cheated when you and Tony married privately at Briarshaw," Lady Vivian said. "The fire was a shock, and now everyone's curious about the renovation. Two-thirds of them have never laid eyes on you, except in those wretched tabloid stories."

"If you're planning to fight them, I'll stick by you," Lady Margaret said. "I know Tony has fencing swords, but I'm a bit beyond my swashbuckling years. I don't suppose he keeps a gun?"

"He does. Ever since Sir Duncan made the first threat against my life, he's had one. It's locked away so Henry and Ritchie can't lay hands on it. How many women would I have to shoot?"

"If you want to eliminate them all, about twenty-five," Lady Margaret said. "Twenty-seven if you count me and Viv."

Kate sighed. Maybe it was the hormones working on her emotions, or maybe it was just hunger, but she was suddenly very curious about the catered buffet. Emmeline knew how to throw a party, and as a new mum, she was sympathetic to Kate's cravings.

"When does it start?"

"Around noon. A bit more than an hour from now."

"I don't suppose there'll be a chocolate fountain?"

"I have it on good authority there will be," Lady Vivian said.

"And you two promise to help me call an end to it when I've had enough?"

"Yes. We'll even tally up the gifts and help write your thank-you notes," Lady Margaret agreed.

"Right. Well. In that case, I'd better put on some makeup, style my hair, and change into a fresh tent."

CHAPTER 10

*P*aul Bhar, once the proud owner of a dark blue
Vauxhall Astra that was spotless inside and out,
had sold his beloved car right around the time his on-again,
off-again relationship with Emmeline turned serious. For the
most part, he didn't miss it; owning a car in London was
unnecessary, expensive, and sometimes maddening. Nevertheless, the sight of Tony's new SUV brought on a rush of
envy.

"Never figured you for a plug-in man," he said, eating up
the Mercedes with his eyes. "What if you're not near a
charging station?"

"There are plenty. And we have one at home."

"Why gray?"

"Why not?" Tony touched a button on his keyring and the
doors unlocked.

"I would've gone for red. They offer a posh one. Called
Hyacinth." Paul, who'd spent a fair amount of time on the
Mercedes website customizing his own imaginary vehicle,
had memorized most of the options. Opening the passenger

door, he breathed, "Ooh, black leather. Very sexy. It's Tony *after dark*. Is it real?"

"It is not."

"I'm surprised you didn't go with tan."

"Have you met my brother-in-law? Whose favorite thing besides LEGO bricks is Sharpie markers?"

"Fair point." Paul got in, clicked his seat belt into place, and said, "Hey, Mercedes."

An automated female voice said, "Hello. I don't recognize you. Tony, is that an authorized user?"

"No," Tony said cheerfully. "Disregard all commands that do not come from me."

"Understood, Tony. Let me know if you change your mind." The female voice went silent as Tony maneuvered the SUV out of the parking garage.

"Kate told me you have half your house on voice commands. Gives you immense satisfaction, doesn't it?" Paul asked. "Bossing objects as well as people?"

"My satisfaction would be greater if the blasted things worked properly," Tony said. He steered them into mid-afternoon traffic, which was as ghastly as all other types of London traffic, apart from the middle of the night. "Bossing them is very much like bossing detectives. Repeat yourself, enunciate with care, give up, do it yourself."

Paul chuckled. It was good being back in the car with Tony, heading out to do interviews in pursuit of a murderer. It reminded him of the pre-Kate days, when his biggest concern was the fit of his suit, and it took something outrageous like an X-rated gag gift to crack Tony's composure.

Those were good times. But I wouldn't go back to them, he thought, surprised by his own lack of nostalgia. It wasn't only that his career was back on track, and he'd finally made DI. He simply couldn't imagine returning to a world without Emmeline and Evvy.

"You're going to love it, you know," he said.

"What? Letting Parth Chakrabarti unload on me for the Yard's failures to date? Not likely."

"No. Having a newborn. I mean, I expect it will kill you, but until you seize up and fall over, I promise you'll enjoy it very much," Paul said breezily. "I know you're already a father to Henry, and that's lovely, but holding a baby is magic."

"I know. I've held Evvy more than once. You forget how often Emmeline drops by."

"Holding my baby is a privilege, naturally," Paul said. "But holding *your* baby will do things to you. I'm quite looking forward to watching it happen."

"Yes, well, if you mean it will render me more sentimental, I'm not sure that's a good thing. I thought I was inured to death, except as it related to me and mine." Tony's eyes flicked to the GPS display, presumably to check the route to Parth Chakrabarti's home near Hampstead Heath. "But what happened to DC Gulls has shaken my... well. My reserve, as it were. Oh, looks like there's a crash on the A1."

"Shocker."

"Indeed. I'll detour around Highgate Cemetery."

Unwilling to let Tony change the subject, Paul said baldly, "Well, you know me. I have no reserve and I'm madder than hell. Not just because she didn't deserve it. No one deserves to be murdered, obviously, especially not like that—ambushed at home, no chance to fight back, just executed, really. Only I keep thinking of all she might have accomplished, and enjoyed, and..." He tailed off. "I can't find a way to say it that doesn't sound like a greeting card. She should have lived another fifty years, that's all. She should have had her life, but someone took it. On the one hand I feel bloody awful for Sean, and on the other..."

"You think he's involved."

"I don't think it," Paul said. "I mean, I haven't deduced it. I just have a gut feeling that something about his story was off. I've tried to remember everything he ever said about her—and to her, of course, in my presence. I don't remember any red flags." Paul sighed. "But we all know what goes on behind closed doors is a mystery. I asked Dr. Stepp to let me know right away if she was pregnant. I know it's monstrous to think Sean might have killed her over an unwanted pregnancy, but—"

"But it happens," Tony cut in. "What did Stepp say?"

"Oh, sorry. There's nothing. Amelia wasn't pregnant, there was no sign of drugs in her system, and nothing weird showed up. She was perfectly healthy until she was strangled to death."

"But your gut feeling about Sean is...?"

"It isn't about him per se. It's just the idea someone well-versed in crime scenes did it. Think of Marquand at the Peel Center. Suppose her investigation into his son Gregory's death shook something loose? Something he was willing to kill to keep quiet?"

"I'd like to know what was on DC Gulls's computer and her mobiles. How much has IT retrieved from the cloud?"

"I don't know, but they claim they should get it all in the end. Which is good, because it may turn out to be our saving grace," Paul said. "Amelia wasn't like me—pages of longhand notes that most people couldn't decipher for a million pounds and half her conclusions in her head. At the end of each workday, she sat down and typed up a summary of her activities. Plus her tentative conclusions. Any fool could jump in where she left off based purely on her notes."

"Perhaps you'll be inspired to start doing things her way."

"Pull the other one. I don't want any fool to jump in. My cases are mine, full stop. Anyway, Jackson's hot to get his hands on it. He mentioned wanting to see her notes on Marquand specifically."

"Vic doesn't much care for Leland, and vice versa."

"Really? He never said. That was one thing about the old Vic Jackson. No need to wonder what he was thinking. He screamed it into your face just before he stuck your head in the karzi and flushed."

"True."

"What about you and DI Marquand? Besides the good copper stuff, I remember you had no problem with his work."

"I never wanted to have a pint with him down the pub, if that's what you're getting at. He had a mean streak. Kind of man who might kick a dog if he thought—"

Tony's mobile rang through the dashboard's Bluetooth link. The panel said DEAVER, M.

"Hello, AC," Tony said, formal as ever when a junior officer was present. "I'm in my car with Paul Bhar, on our way to an interview."

"Where?" Deaver, always to the point, didn't bother to greet said junior officer, but Paul wasn't offended. He knew Tony had only begun the speakerphone conversation by mentioning his name so Deaver understood someone else was listening.

"We're coming up on Hampstead Heath," Tony replied.

"You're focused on Chakrabarti, then?"

"Yes. Formally, that is. Informally, I'm looking into the Gulls murder as well."

"Stick with Chakrabarti. Vic has the Gulls inquiry well in hand."

"I've no doubt of that, but—"

"Consultation on the Chakrabarti case is both appropriate and welcome." Deaver's tone brooked no dissent. "Parth has been very unhappy with DI Bhar. He feels misunderstood and to some degree disrespected. Try and work your magic on him, Tony. If you can convince him the Met is working diligently on the case, perhaps he'll be more accepting of the process."

"Yes, sir." Tony sounded perfectly affable, but Paul suspected his old guv didn't appreciate being cut off in such a high-handed manner. Deaver was always firm and in control, but not usually so abrupt.

"With regards to the Gulls inquiry—" Tony began.

"I've only just said Jackson has it in hand. Good God, it's barely begun. Could you give us forty-eight hours to process forensic data before trying to seize control? We didn't all simultaneously lose our faculties the day you retired."

"Yes, sir."

"You said Paul is with you? That won't do. Get rid of him before you see Parth."

"I'm on Archway Street, not far from Highgate Hall. You don't mean chuck him out on the side of the road?"

Deaver didn't answer right away. Paul sat quietly, unsurprised by the assistant commissioner's attitude. Parth Chakrabarti was a truly important Englishman who really, truly, deeply despised him. Would he be flung out between the pet salon and the bicycle repair shop? Hopefully there would be a pub within easy walking distance.

"All right, Tony, you can let him accompany you," Deaver said at last. "Make it clear this is a handoff. Don't tell Parth it was Paul who brought you in. Say I did it. He doesn't care for me, either, but in my case it's more of a neutral dislike."

"Understood, sir."

"Good. Forgive me for being on edge. The Gulls situation is—" Deaver broke off. Paul, who'd never seen the assistant commissioner evince any emotional state besides impatient pessimism, wondered if the man was close to breaking down.

But when he spoke again, he sounded as dry and mordant as ever. "It's not ideal. Keep me informed." He rang off.

Tony took a deep breath, nostrils flaring. Then he swore in a way that would've delighted Henry and sent Ritchie running from the room. Paul's mouth fell open and stayed there.

"Wow. Erm, quite. I should write all that down."

"Your ears can take it. I'm no longer allowed the indulgence of profanity at home, so it's here in the car with you or nowhere, I suppose." Tony chuckled a little, apparently already over the worst of his anger. "Obviously Michael's shaken by Gulls's murder. Losing one of our own is always a bitter blow. Still. That was beneath him."

"You got in some choice licks. All the things you called him. *And* called on him to do. He'll be busy from now till— oh, sorry, I let you miss the turning," Paul said. "You'll have to double back. It was that little access road, the one that looked like a lane to nowhere—it's actually the way to the gatehouse. Once we're buzzed in, it's half a mile to Planet Parth. I'm glad you didn't chuck me by the side of the road. I want to see how you handle him."

"How did he get on with DC Gulls?"

"He didn't like her."

"Fine. What a complete rotter he must be. Still, it's good to know."

Tony used a roundabout to send them back the way they'd come. Within five minutes they'd been approved at the gatehouse. After being waved through a pair of beautiful redwood gates that opened with slow splendor, they rolled down the heavily wooded drive that led to Highgate Hall.

CHAPTER 11

"*I*'d begun to believe there was nothing left in ostentatious homes to surprise me," Tony told Paul as he followed the stone-flagged driveway toward the multilevel garage. "But monogramming your mansion is a new one."

"Notice how the letters P and C combine to make a sort of sunburst?" Paul asked, smiling at the absurdity of the symbol. "That's not only Parth's initials, it's his company logo. Priceless Commodities."

"I have a feeling every slot in that garage is taken. It looks like a collector's showroom. Let's park outside." After his earlier outburst, both profane and heartfelt, Tony kept his tone light. Like all the Met's top brass, Michael Deaver was accustomed to being obeyed without question; if he thought he was being second-guessed, he turned to stone. Brisk impatience was also a hallmark of the service's upper echelon, as they were all kept busy, responsible for far more than they could control, and perpetually under the microscope. Still, Deaver was rarely nasty. His attitude toward Tony's desire to assist with the Gulls inquiry was probably the result of strain, but it rankled nonetheless.

He doesn't owe me anything, Tony reminded himself. Though they'd been friends for many years, their relationship had never approached the emotional candor of his friendship with Paul. Because Paul wore his heart on his sleeve, freely accepting and admitting his human frailties, he was easy to confide in. Deaver was cut from the same cloth as Tony—chilly by default, determined not to be read, and prone to withdrawal if matters became too personal. Probably he was hit as hard as the rest of them by Amelia Gulls's murder and had no idea how to express himself.

"The house itself isn't the monstrosity I expected," Tony said as he exited his vehicle. "I rather like the glassed-in spiral staircase. The marble stripes are interesting, too."

"It looks like a toy house. Barbie's London Dreamhouse plunked down on two acres that could be put to better use," Paul said. "I despise so much manicured shrubbery. Gives it all an Astroturf look. Why didn't he just shape them into chess pieces and be done with it? It's how he sees the rest of the world—pawns."

The squared-off bushes and hedges *did* resemble board game pieces, Tony realized. Especially when combined with the ornamental terraces. Parth's architect had been a great one for juxtaposing arcs against straight lines. As a whole, he thought it worked quite well, but then he'd always nurtured a secret passion for the kind of homes in which he'd never live. He hoped the interior was as harmoniously up-to-the-minute as the exterior. If this meeting was due to be painful, and Tony didn't see how it could be anything but, he might at least get some pleasure in their surroundings.

The entrance to Highgate House resembled that of a boutique hotel—glass doors, brass accents, and a long glass canopy supported by brass poles. Even the topiaries in their cement pots looked commercial rather than domestic. Therefore, as Tony approached with Paul beside him, he wasn't surprised when a young man in a suit and tie emerged to greet them.

"Good afternoon," the man called, flashing white teeth. "Do I have the pleasure of meeting Lord Hetheridge?"

"Indeed. With DI Bhar, of course, to whom I expect you've already become acquainted."

"Yes, we're old friends," the man agreed with flagrant insincerity. Something about his game attitude, combined with his excellent hair, Hugo Boss suit, and diamond tiepin, marked him out as either an estate agent or a day trader. "I'm afraid the mood isn't good today, Paul."

"Thanks, Ken. Can't say I'm surprised." To Tony, Paul said, "Ken is Mr. Chakrabarti's confidential assistant. He always comes out to inform visitors of the current mood."

"Ken Hussy," Ken said, reaching for Tony's hand and shaking it excessively. "I realize it's a breach of etiquette, me introducing myself to you, Lord Hetheridge, but in my line it can't be helped. When it comes to Mr. Chakrabarti, I do it all. Greeter of guests, keeper of the gate, reporter of the mood. When the mood is rather dark, as it is today, I come out to warn visitors before they step inside. Also to go over the rules of Highgate House."

With some effort, Tony managed to retrieve his hand. "I'd appreciate hearing the rules."

"Yes. Right. First," said Ken, flashing those white teeth again. "Shoes. Either they are deposited in the foyer, and guests proceed in sock feet, or you will be asked to step onto the sole sanitizer. It's a two-minute process, completely safe, and will not damage your shoes or your person. It's also non-negotiable unless you prefer sock feet.

"Second," he continued, maintaining eye contact with Tony that was interrupted by only the barest blink, "there will be no refreshments offered. Some years ago there was a regrettable incident wherein Mr. Chakrabarti furnished snacks to a young person with an undisclosed peanut allergy. The guest survived, but it was a close thing. Thereafter, first-time guests at Highgate House are not offered food or drink. Repeated guests may be offered a legal waiver to sign, but we'll cross that bridge if we come to it."

"It's my dearest wish to be offered that waiver," Paul said. Ken pretended not to hear.

"Third, your interview with Mr. Chakrabarti will be videotaped in full and witnessed by me. I have you down for a thirty minute session, but if Mr. Chakrabarti is willing to go longer, he will let us know."

"I presume there's some form we must sign, consenting to be videotaped?" Tony asked.

"No form," Ken Hussy declared lightly. "Mr. Chakrabarti is a lawyer by training, if you didn't know, as well as a financier and an international humanitarian. He's well aware of his rights within the confines of his own home."

Heaven help me. This is shaping up to be one for the ages, Tony thought, wondering if he wouldn't have been better off chucking Paul by the side of the road. It was too late to tell him not to speak unless nudged. Moreover, Paul tended to forget such orders when he was nervous, and judging by the way he shifted from foot to foot, his adrenaline was surging.

"The rules are understood. Lead on, Mr. Hussy," Tony said. "If you'll permit me a bit of curiosity—you said Mr. Chakrabarti is a lawyer by training. Are you?"

"Me? No. Before I came into Mr. Chakrabarti's service, I was an estate agent, if you can believe it."

Still got it, Tony thought, nodding politely.

The sole sanitation process, located in an alcove just off the entrance, was as quick and easy as Ken described. After Tony and Paul's shoes had been declared 99% sterile by the device, Ken led them into Highgate House, pointing out features along the way. Everything was white or gold except the art, which tended toward blazing colors: fuchsia, cobalt, cathode green. Tony, whose knowledge of art was scant, had no idea if it was any good, but it certainly revolved around a theme: exotic flowers, opened wide.

"Mr. Chakrabarti is a great patron of emerging artists," Ken said with what appeared to be inexhaustible enthusiasm. "There's a woman in Shoreditch who paints nothing but *Gloriosa superba*. He's purchased all of her work, which you see currently on display. He also maintains a collection of Chihuly chandeliers, both in his hotels and here at home, which *ARTnews* was kind enough to call 'beyond compare.' In the great room, just on your right, you'll find—"

"You'll find Antonio," called a young man, half-hidden in the cushions of a big white sectional sofa. "Who's this? More policemen?"

Ken didn't glance his way or even slow down. "Forgive the intrusion, Antonio," he called over his shoulder. "These detectives are going upstairs to see your father."

"He's not there," Antonio returned in a sing-song voice.

Ken stopped. Withdrawing his mobile from a leather holster on his belt, he checked the screen and frowned. "One moment."

He rang someone, began with "Sir, I'm so sorry—" and stopped, listening. "Yes. I see. Of course. Won't happen again."

Returning the mobile to its holster, Ken called, "Thank you, Antonio," before turning back to face them. Virtually every white tooth in his head showed, which Tony was beginning to take as a fair barometer of Ken's internal discomfort.

"My phone was silenced. I'm afraid I missed Mr.

Chakrabarti's call. He's out on the patio and will see you there. It means we're going back the way we came."

"But our soles are sanitized," Paul objected. Tony gave him a look.

"I do apologize for the mix-up. Mr. Chakrabarti is nimble, so we must strive to be nimble, too." With that, Ken led them back the way they'd come, moving twice as fast as before.

"Hurry! Mustn't dawdle, Daddy's in a bad mood!" Antonio, sunken back into the cushions so he was just a disembodied voice, called after them. Tony glanced over his shoulder, hoping to make eye contact—the powerful man's son and heir might be someone worth talking to—but Antonio didn't lift his head, and soon they were outside again.

"This way. Not far," Ken said, highly polished shoes clicking on the flagstones. "Lovely sunny day, isn't it? Mild. And people say global warming's a bad thing."

Tony shot Paul a second, reinforcing look. Paul blew him a kiss. Cheeky bugger had grown an inch since he made DI.

The patio was glaringly white. *Bleached bones*, Tony thought, regarding it curiously. He'd expected a swimming pool. Even if he hadn't reviewed the Valeria Chakrabarti files before setting out, and of course he had, it was well-known that Parth's wife had run off with the pool boy. But instead of a white-tiled pool deck and blue water, there was only white concrete, white travertine pavers, white deck chairs, and a big white umbrella. Beneath that umbrella sat Parth Chakrabarti, nude apart from large black sunglasses and a minuscule Speedo.

Good thing Kate isn't here, since her tum's so dodgy, Tony thought. He didn't much care for the sight, either, but he'd been subjected to worse in steam rooms and at natural springs. Parth, fifty years old, was six-foot-three and weighed approximately twenty-nine stone. He was also remarkably hirsute, with curling black hair over most of his body and a virtual pelt on his upper chest. Kate like to say the baby made her look like she'd swallowed a planet, but if that were true, Parth looked like he'd eaten a solar system, and he had nothing like her excuse.

"You have some nerve, showing your face," Parth called from his deck chair. His voice, an ominous rumble, made his hairy belly shake. "Did they demote you yet? DI Bhar! You should be back in uniform, cautioning jaywalkers."

"Good afternoon, Mr. Chakrabarti," Paul replied, giving the man a smile to rival Ken's. "We're still hard at work on your daughter's case. AC Deaver wanted you to meet the newest member of the team. Our consultant, retired Chief Superintendent Anthony Hetheridge."

"Lord Hetheridge, ninth Baron of Wellegrave," Ken put in. Apparently when he was physically within in his employer's orbit, it became part of his job to reflect the big man's emotional state. No longer the energetic, upbeat, semi-manic guide, he now appeared dour, even disapproving.

"Ninth baron? When was the title created?" Parth demanded.

"Just after the Restoration."

"Reward for a loyal Cavalier, eh?"

"In part."

"In part? What else got you a barony in those days?" He seemed to communicate only in barks.

"The first Baron Hetheridge was a royal by-blow. Charles II was recognizing his half-brother."

"So you boast of royal blood."

"No more than anyone else in the Peerage. Less than many." Tony shrugged.

"I know why Deaver sent you." Parth wagged a finger at Tony. "You're here to finesse me. To sprinkle magic pixie dust and convince me Scotland Yard is giving its all in pursuit of justice for Valeria. That's it, isn't it, old boy?"

Tony looked around at the empty deck chairs. "May we sit down?"

"Yes. Heaven forbid you be uncomfortable for one minute. I've been in agony ever since my girl died, but do sit on your arse, please. Take a load off." Parth removed the sunglasses, revealing large, protuberant eyes that suggested thyroid disease. With the shades, his face had been barely acceptable, but without them, he was ugly. Every feature was exaggerated, twice the size it should have been.

Tony wasn't usually baited so easily, but something about Parth raised his ire. Probably it was just all the things simmering on his mind's back burner: Kate's health, the baby's imminent arrival, Gulls's murder. He didn't want to give Parth Chakrabarti the satisfaction of seeing him irritated, since the man clearly wanted that above all else. Receiving them in such a state, in all his glory, was aggressive in itself; a reminder that he had all the power, and if they didn't fancy looking at his mounds and rolls and curling black hairs, they could go make a killing in the financial markets and arrange their lives to suit them, as he'd arranged his.

As he and Paul sat down, Tony noticed a CCTV camera sticking up from the grass like an automatic sprinkler. Its red light glowed steadily.

"Smile, you're on camera. It's for the civil suit. At first I thought the MPS was merely incompetent. Now I'm convinced it's all a cover-up. For some reason"—Parth's finger was at it again—"there are forces at work inside the police that do not want Valeria's killer exposed. So I shall expose them. See if I don't." To Paul, he added, "Where's that useless little girl?"

Tony stiffened.

"If you're referring to DC Gulls," Paul began.

"Gulls. You know what it is to be gulled, don't you? It means to be fooled. To deceive. A perfect name for every policeman who's ever darkened my door." Parth glared from Paul to Tony. "How is she even fit for service? That's what I'd like to know. Too short, childish voice, not pretty, not clever, not charming, not—"

"Mr. Chakrabarti, that's quite enough." Tony spoke automatically, without conscious decision. Yet the moment he heard himself, he was determined to see it through, whether it torpedoed the interview or not. "DC Gulls was an exemplary detective. She deserved to be spoken of with the proper respect, as indeed do we all. As for her physical characteristics, why you give yourself license to judge them is beyond me. Perhaps Ken could fetch you a mirror."

Parth stared at him. Tony, realizing he was about to get tossed out on his barony, decided to say as much as possible before the man's shock gave way to action.

"Yesterday, DC Gulls was found dead in her flat. Someone disabled her building's CCTV cameras several hours in advance. When Gulls entered, the killer strangled her with the cord from her own lamp. He—or she, it's not out of the realm of possibility—then stole the computer and mobile phones Gulls used in her investigations. Including her work on your daughter's case."

Parth was still watching him, eyes wide, lips slightly parted.

"I realize you've been in a state of agony, as you put it, since your daughter's murder. That's only to be expected. However, it's worth noting that DC Gulls's violent death is every bit as upsetting to her family and friends as your child's is to you. So I'll thank you to keep a civil tongue in your mouth when you mention her. Otherwise, Paul and I will say goodbye right now and you can contact AC Deaver to ask what other detectives might be willing to take up the case."

"A civil tongue in my mouth," Parth said at last. "You know who you sound like?"

Tony shook his head.

"My father. He used to say things like that." The big man seemed a bit looser now, as if Tony's fit of pique had lubricated his joints in a way deference could not. "My son Antonio says it another way. 'Keep her name of out your mouth.' That's how he'd phrase it. Mind you, he's an idiot. Waste of sperm. My daughter Octavia, too. She's one of those whiny women. Takes after her mother. Valeria was the jewel in the crown, the best thing I ever created. And I mean to have vengeance on the man who stole her from me." He took a deep breath. "DI Paul Bhar, you're useless, but you have a baby daughter..." He glanced at Ken.

"Evangeline," the man supplied. He consulted no notes; evidently he memorized such details and spat them at Parth when called upon.

"Yes, Evangeline Bhar. A well-chosen name. How is she?"

"Fine, sir. Thriving."

"Good. And you, retired whatever Hetheridge. Lord Hetheridge. You've fathered sons and daughters for England, haven't you?"

"A daughter, long ago," Tony said. "A young son at home and a baby due before much longer."

"How's your relationship with that daughter?"

Tony shrugged. He disliked Parth too much to make any personal revelations. Jules, the child he'd never known until she was an adult, had recently moved to Slough with her boyfriend, Steve Zhao. Since then, calls had gone to voicemail and emails went unanswered. The man she'd known as her father was dead, and so was her mother. For a while Jules had seemed keen on forming a real connection with Tony, but then Kate became pregnant and all communication ceased. It was impossible for him to guess why, or to do anything but wait and see if Jules resurfaced.

"For a long time I tried to find a soul mate in the police. A detective who adored his daughter the way I adored Valeria," Parth said. "It was foolish, and I've given up. But I like the way you defended that Gulls girl. Even if I didn't care for the way her mind worked, or the things she insinuated about Valeria. Do you know about that? Surely just because her hardware was stolen, that doesn't mean all her work product was lost?"

"We're in the process of retrieving it," Tony said. "DCI Jackson has been assured by IT that he'll have it very soon. But you mentioned DC Gulls insinuating something. What?"

"She thought my Valeria was a kept woman. A mistress at a man's beck and call. And one night, after he'd grown tired of her, he killed her."

CHAPTER 12

Tony said, "I assure you, I'm familiar with all the key evidence of the case, though I haven't yet read DC Gulls's notes. Even so, I don't find the notion shocking. It's a reasonable hypothesis that Valeria was involved with a man who paid her bills—"

"What? Why?" Parth snapped. "Tell me. Tell me what you think you know, and I will refute your argument point by point."

"For one thing, Valeria lived on the top floor of a rather exclusive building, and she paid her first year's rent ahead of time, in cash. Rare enough in London for a young woman, just twenty-nine years old, to live in such a large, elegant home. To have her produce a year's rent, plus all fees and additional costs, in one lump sum is extraordinary."

"A year upfront was necessary to secure the flat. Otherwise some visiting prince from Dubai would've scooped it up."

"Yes, but—"

"You think I'm Ebenezer Scrooge? That I wouldn't give her the money?"

Tony sighed. "Please. Remember that I *am* familiar with the case. Two days after her death, you told DI Bhar that while you gave Valeria an allowance, it added up to only a quarter-million each year. You're on record saying you didn't pay for the flat, and you don't know who did. Considering she modeled only sporadically, earning twenty thousand pounds for the year up to her death, and forty-eight thousand pounds the year before, how she might have earned a flat million in cash is unclear."

"I wasn't trying to mislead you," Parth muttered, in a bitter tone that was apparently his version of an apology. "Valeria was beautiful and witty. She lit up every room she entered. I suppose she must've had an admirer. But just because she had an admirer," he continued, voice rising, "doesn't mean there was a quid pro quo. Gulls said it outright, Valeria must have been some man's mistress, and the flat was their love nest. I almost spit in her face. Valeria was pure. She was a virgin. You know how I know this?"

Tony shook his head.

"Because she wasn't married," Parth said triumphantly. "That's how I know. There are still pure, perfect, true women in this world. Valeria was one of them."

As he spoke, Parth's hands moved, catching Tony's attention. They were hugely oversized, just like his nose, mouth, and ears. It was easy to imagine those hands wrapping a cord around a woman's neck and ending her life. The way Parth bristled as he recounted DC Gulls's reasonable—indeed, obvious—inference about Valeria Chakrabarti's mystery benefactor made him seem slightly unhinged. Was he a man who would kill, not for some specific end, but merely to relieve his feelings?

Yes, Tony thought, disliking Parth all the more. *But not the way Gulls was killed. He'd either do it here, the moment she enraged him, and make up a story to cover it, or he'd let her go and do what his sort always do—try and ruin her professionally, by getting her demoted or sacked. I suppose he might hire someone to kill her, like many a rich man before him, but that would require a cooling-off period. Parth's at the mercy of his emotions. More of a hair-trigger than a slow burn.*

"When the investigation began, several of Valeria's friends told the police that she had a boyfriend. Regarding this supposed romantic partner," Tony began.

"Mickey Post-Hewitt," Ken said from the corner of his mouth.

Tony looked at him.

"Oh. Forgive me, Lord Hetheridge, I didn't mean to intrude. Only I thought you might appreciate a nudge."

"I know the names of all the principals," Tony said. Paul, who'd controlled himself rather admirably until that moment, looked as though he might choke on suppressed laughter.

"But as I was saying, about Mr. Post-Hewitt," Tony resumed, "He flatly denied that Valeria had any romantic partner, much less him. He claimed she's always been single —not uninterested in a partner generally, just unattached. Still looking. She was frequently photographed on Mr. Post-Hewitt's arm, but of course he doesn't date women. Do you have any suspicions about Mickey?"

"Suspicions of murder? No. Mickey wouldn't have harmed her. He wept as hard as I did. He was gutted, poor sod."

"Yet he lied to you for two years. He let you believe Valeria lived with him in Notting Hill, rather than at the secret flat in Shepherd's Bush."

"He was afraid I would disapprove of the admirer."

"He told you that?"

"In so many words. He said men loved Valeria from afar.

That she was a good girl, but if one wanted to make a gesture and give her a flat in Shepherd's Bush, why not?"

"So we've established that Mr. Post-Hewitt would lie to you," Tony said. "Imagine for a moment that Valeria was in love with a man you wouldn't approve of. Married, perhaps. Or someone you'd met and intensely disliked. How would you have responded?"

"I would have told her to get rid of him. And she would've done it. She obeyed me in all things."

"As far as you know."

Parth glared at him again.

"Yet she lied to you, too."

"Now you listen to me, Lord So-and-So—"

"Forgive me, Mr. Chakrabarti, but according to your own sworn statement, she did. You stated you knew nothing about the flat in Shepherd's Bush. You had no idea who might have given Valeria the money in cash to rent it. You told the police she was frequently out of the country because she was a full-time model, and the rest of the time she lived with Mr. Post-Hewitt in Notting Hill. These may be lies by omission, but they're still lies."

"No. If I didn't know what was going on, it's because I was too busy. Not paying proper attention," Parth flared. "Who cares what I said the day she died? I was a madman. Do you know what she looked like after hitting the pavement? Can you imagine what it did to me, seeing her that way?

"There I was, feeling as if God had deserted me, as if the world had ended, and the police were under my nose asking all sorts of questions. They should've been going door to door, searching for the man who killed her, rounding up witnesses. Instead, they asked me a hundred inane things. So I got it wrong. She never lied. I was too busy—in those days GTFO was all that mattered to me. I'm being punished for it now, of course. But Valeria never told a single lie and I resent the implication that she did."

Tony, who'd read about Parth's pressure group GTFO, had no desire to pursue the topic. Having spent this much time with Parth, it was clear the group's rather startling acronym was chosen purely for shock value. Parth liked to keep people afraid, off balance, inwardly cringing as they awaited the next eruption. Poor Ken Hussy was practically hugging himself with anxiety as he waited be of use. Anything to make Parth happy and then to bask in that accomplishment for a single golden moment.

Tony said, "Mr. Chakrabarti, when it comes to the dead, I understand the desire to remember only the best. And please believe me when I say Valeria was clearly an exceptional daughter. You formed a special bond with her—"

"I had to. You know what her mother did. Mandy and the pool boy. All of London can hum that tune," Parth said. He didn't sound particularly angry about it; rather, his eyes flashed with the satisfaction of trotting out his favorite grievance. "The pool is right here, did you know that? You're sitting on it. I filled it in two days after she scarpered off to Greece. I could never swim in it again without thinking of her and Tassos. Besides, with her gone, I had work to do. The hard work of raising three children alone. Antonio isn't worth mentioning, and Octavia—well, she's an embarrassment, isn't she? I paid to have her ears bobbed and her nose shaved down and she's still a gargoyle. But Valeria was my beautiful little helper. My angel."

"Of course." Tony tried again. "My point is this. If you will accept that Valeria might have had a lover, and will search your memory accordingly to provide us with names, it will open a new avenue of investigation. Forensics have proved inconclusive. Witnesses weren't able to supply anything about the killer, except that he was tall and possibly large."

"She had no lovers. She was a virgin," Parth growled.

"Then let's revisit her closest friend, Mr. Post-Hewitt. I understand he's receiving financial assistance from you—"

"Why not?" Parth cut in. "He's a good person. No head for business. Plays in a band but never earns much. His parents are out of the picture and he can't keep a man to save his life. I'm a charitable man. Why only give to stink holes across the globe when I can give here, to someone my daughter loved?"

"When last I spoke to Mickey Post-Hewitt," Paul put in, surprising Tony, who thought his psychic admonition to keep mum had been received and obeyed, "he expressed considerable gratitude to you, Mr. Chakrabarti. I think he wouldn't hurt you for the world. And his friend Valeria is dead. If she had a secret that Mickey thought might or might not help the police, but would definitely wound you, I reckon he'd stay quiet rather than take the risk."

"No, he would want her killer exposed. Caught. Put away forever," Parth declared.

"But suppose it's only an inkling? Nothing but a name," Paul continued. Tony was pleased to see that despite Parth's blatant hostility and AC Deaver's manifest lack of faith, Paul's confidence was undaunted. He'd evolved a great deal since the days when a black look from Lady Margaret could send him into a tailspin.

Paul continued, "I could pop round Mr. Post-Hewitt's place to see him as soon as we leave and ask again, for the hundredth time. But I doubt he'd open up without your express permission, sir."

Parth seemed to consider it. Then he stood up, abruptly signaling the interview was over. "Ken. Get in touch with Mickey. Tell him to come by for a late lunch." To Paul he said, "I will talk to Mickey and decide for myself. I'm promising nothing." Then he asked Ken, "Is Antonio still in the house?"

"Yes, unless he left in the last half-hour, Mr. Chakrabarti."

"If you find him inside, tell him to get out. I can't bear the sight of him. Talking to police always stirs me up. Then I see his face and wonder how God could be so cruel, to take Valeria and leave me him."

Retrieving a silk robe draped over an unused chair, Parth slipped it on and belted it, covering his munificence at last. The sunglasses went back into place, too. "Lord Hetheridge, as I said, I'll indulge DI Bhar by questioning Mickey Post-Hewitt again. But I warn you, if this turns out to be another blind alley, it will only strengthen my conviction of a cover-up."

"You've levied that accusation more than once," Tony said. Parth loomed over him, forcing him to look up, so he spoke harshly to emphasize his lack of intimidation. "Have you any evidence of it, or only pure emotion?"

Parth grunted. "I'm pleased to be asked. Here's how I see it. Valeria is killed. At least two people witness her murder, yet neither of them can describe anything useful about the man who threw her from that window. One claims he was looking at his electronic fare meter. The other says he saw a tall shadow—then recants almost immediately to say he's sure of nothing.

"The first police arrive on the scene within seven minutes. Yet the killer is gone from the area without a trace. Nothing on CCTV cameras—of which there are many—and no witnesses who saw the killer flee.

"A forensic team that has worked with the Met for many years is dispatched to Valeria's flat within the hour. This flat that means so much to you, that supposedly proves she had a sugar daddy"—his lip curled—"and was leading a sinful life. What does the team find? Nothing. Nothing except Valeria's DNA, and her cleaner's, and Mickey's, of course.

"How does that happen, Lord Hetheridge? How can a supposed love nest yield no hairs, no fingerprints, no DNA profile of a lover? Thank God Mickey was performing on stage in front of a hundred people the night Valeria died, or I'd be forced to conclude it was him. How can there be nothing else? It's unbelievable. You can't expect me to accept it."

"The UK has an extensive DNA database," Tony said. "But if the killer had never been in trouble with the law before—"

"Yes, yes, of course, that's the standard reply. Then there's Scotland Yard. What sort of detectives do they assign? DI Bhar with his jokes and his foolishness, and DC Gulls, who I didn't wish dead but I damn sure wished off my daughter's case. Now she is, and they've dug you out of the MPS crypt to come tell me in the poshest of accents that all is well. It isn't! It's a cover-up! I know it is."

"And why would the Metropolitan Police wish to protect Valeria's killer?"

"You tell me." Parth jabbed a finger at Tony's face. "You. Tell. Me."

* * *

"Your Mercedes is parked just on the other side of that hill," Ken Hussy announced unnecessarily, scurrying in an undignified fashion to get in front of Tony and Paul so as to lead them away from Parth. "Follow me."

Tony glanced back. Parth lingered under the big umbrella, peeking beneath his shades to read something on his smartphone. Maybe the act of rising had only been a power play, an excuse for him to end the interview by literally looking down on his guests. As if to confirm Tony's suspicion, Parth dropped back into his chair, belted robe straining across his midsection, and began swiping on his mobile.

"Lord Hetheridge, DI Bhar, it's been a pleasure," Ken said

as they crested the hill. Away from his boss's bad temper, he was upbeat and friendly, putting out positive vibes the way Chernobyl put out ionizing radiation. "I do hope if you have occasion to return to Highgate House, it will be—" He broke off. "Antonio? Is everything all right?"

Parth Chakrabarti's twenty-seven-year-old son was ambling from the house to the multi-story garage, dragging a wheeled suitcase behind him. "Fine, Ken. Just fine."

"That's good. May I ask, erm—where are you going?"

"Didn't my father tell you to get rid of me?"

"Well, as a matter of fact, he said something about needing time alone. But that was two minutes ago. How did you...?"

Tony and Paul swapped glances. The greenest detectives on earth wouldn't get into their car and drive away from this. When Antonio regarded them with some interest, Tony nodded pleasantly at the young man.

"His rages are cyclical, Ken. It's time for another one. I can feel it, and I'm getting out before the storm hits." Antonio resembled Parth in many ways—height, broad shoulders, the kind of heavy musculature that can easily run to fat. But while his facial features were bold, they weren't exaggerated to the point of ugliness. He possessed that gently jaded aura belonging to children of the very rich: he'd been there, done that, got the t-shirt, donated the t-shirt to charity, and now found the memory faintly embarrassing.

"No offense," Antonio went on, smiling at Tony and Paul, "but the presence of you lot speeds up his natural rage timetable. I won't say you triggered him—he's raged all my life. But Scotland Yard is definitely an accelerant."

"Yes, well, the detectives are just leaving." Ken turned and seemed dismayed to find Tony merely standing there, with the SUV still dormant and no keys in hand. "You *are* on your way to another appointment, are you not?"

"We are," Tony said equitably. "Mr. Chakrabarti, it's good to meet you. I'm Tony Hetheridge. Retired chief superintendent, now consulting with the Yard on your sister's case. Would you have a moment to chat with us?"

"I don't think—" Ken began.

"You work for the other Mr. Chakrabarti, mate, not me," Antonio said.

"Yes, but while you're on the premises, it behooves me to—"

Antonio giggled. It was very high-pitched, incongruous with his solid physique. "Behooves? Ken, love, you're embarrassing yourself. Daddy can't hear you, he's down at the scene of the crime, doing what he does best. Making money. Or what he does second best—bullying women on Twitter from his GTFO account. He's the biggest troll in the UK, figuratively and literally."

"Scene of the crime?" Paul asked in a light tone, as if hoping to get in on a joke.

"The burial ground. The swimming pool where dear old Mummy fell in love with another bloke and decided to chuck it all for a new life. Daddy filled it in and paved it over, but in his head, she's still floating inside it, making eyes at Tassos the pool boy." Antonio studied Paul with some interest. "You second or third generation?"

"Second."

"We're from Mumbai."

"My mum and dad were from around Raipur," Paul said. "Me, I'm straight outta Clerkenwell."

"How's cop life?"

"Living the dream." Smoothly, Paul produced his card, passing it to Antonio. "I see you're trying to get on, but once you settle, give me a ring. I know your father has his doubts about me, but I'm not messing about. I promise, I'm committed to catching Valeria's murderer."

Antonio's eyes narrowed as if reevaluating Paul for any hint of insincerity. Then he shrugged. "First I have to talk my little sister, Octavia, into letting me crash at her place. Then we'll see."

"Octavia is more than welcome to join us," Paul said. "I realize DC Gulls already interviewed you both, but sometimes a second interview helps."

"Yeah. I wasn't feeling it when the lady detective talked to me," Antonio said, as if he couldn't be expected to make a special effort for anything, even his sister's murder investigation, if the fancy didn't strike him. "And Octavia has a thing against cops. She hates you lot, full stop. But I might be able to talk her round. Then we could talk to you together."

Ken said, "I realize you may find this intrusive, Antonio, but in light of what you've just said, I'll have no choice but to inform your father. Mr. Chakrabarti has been very clear that—"

"Ken, Ken, Ken." Antonio bestowed a mild smile on the former estate agent. "I'm an open book. Tell him anything you like. By the way, gentlemen, Ken here had a thing with Valeria for a couple of hot months, did you know that? Back when he was new to Highgate House and she was feeling the itch. Tell them all about it, Ken. I'm off to get my car and make my getaway before Daddy changes his mind and tells the gatehouse not to let me out."

CHAPTER 13

*K*ate was almost finished with "Children of the Moon," a werewolf episode from the 1980s *Hammer House of Horror* TV series, when Tony entered the bedroom. His tie was off, he was limping slightly, and he didn't exude that quiet satisfaction that denoted a successful day in the field. Still, he lit up when he saw her, propped against the pillows with a bevy of baby shower gifts arranged on the bed.

"They did it," he murmured. "They dared to actually do it."

"Indeed they did. I was completely in the dark until an hour before it all kicked off."

"For the record, I told Margaret it was madness. I urged her and Vivian to talk Emmeline out of it. But Emmeline insisted. Judging from how very pleased you look—and beautiful, I might add—I must conclude the ladies got it right and I got it wrong."

"Yeah. Oh, Tony, it was *such* fun. And the food! To die for, every morsel. Plus there was a chocolate fountain. Whenever I got up for the loo, I had another go at it."

"Were Henry and Ritchie allowed to participate?"

"Of course. Mrs. Snell supervised Ritchie. I let Henry go wild." Kate shrugged. "He told me he's taking up fencing again, and he promises to ride more at Briarshaw this summer. He deserved a treat. Besides, I just don't have the heart to ride him all the time about his weight. My mum did that with me, and I still have her voice in my head, poking at me nonstop. I don't want Henry to feel the same way twenty years from now—that inside his skull, Kate's harping on the size of his trousers."

"Yes, well, I think it's natural to want to keep him nearer a healthy weight," Tony said, sitting down near the bed. "But not everyone's meant to be slim. And since Henry's way of coping with criticism seems to be eating more, it's a vicious circle."

As he spoke, the voices on the telly surged, making them both glance over to see what was going on. The program's so-called hero, whom Kate considered an idiot, was arguing with a heavily bearded, flannel-clad woodsman. Behind the woodsman's shaggy head, the dark was rising.

"That bloke's a werewolf," Tony remarked.

"Well-spotted. Never mind him, look at my loot. How about this? What do you think?"

"Haven't the faintest. Is it for food preparation?"

"No. It's a multi-stage bath," Kate barked. She passed over the plastic tub, shaped to resemble a blue whale, for his inspection.

"See the mesh sling? It adjusts to the baby's current size for the proper support. Very ingenious." She took it back and handed him another present.

He said, "But this is a white noise machine. Surely babies sleep well enough on their own?"

"We'll see. It came from your cousin Lucinda Perkins-Jones, and she was very proud of it. According to her, the

Hetheridges and the Perkinses are poor sleepers from early childhood and need all the help they can get."

"Ah, Lucinda. The old battle-axe. How is she?"

"Perfectly lovely, thank you very much. I happen to like her, and she's not a battle-axe, whatever that means. Besides, she's younger than you are."

"Impossible."

"Of course she is! She was the first of your relatives to turn up, and my favorite, but you know what? I have to admit, the rest weren't bad. And they were all on their best behavior under Lady Margaret's eye," Kate added, smiling at the memory of how their acid-tongued friend rode herd on the partygoers. "As an introduction to all the family members you've spent years hiding from, I think the shower went brilliantly."

"I haven't been hiding from them. I've simply kept occupied in a variety of ways. Ways that made it impossible for them to locate me." Tony sounded amused. "As for Lucinda, you're quite right. I was confusing her with my aunt Lucille. Lucille is my father's youngest sibling, which makes her at least eighty-five, assuming she's still living."

"Of course she's living. She turned up, briefly. Just long enough to say the fire destroyed everything good and worthwhile about the house, and the restoration was a total botch. Also to wonder aloud where all the family portraits had gone. She *was* a battle-axe."

"Whatever that means."

"In her case, it means if you picked her up and flung her into a gang of armed men, she'd knock their blocks off." Kate giggled. "The Honorable Lucille Hetheridge. Completely terrifying. And there was a strong family resemblance. After she left, Lady Margaret said she looked like you in a frock and pin curls."

Tony shuddered.

"Then there's your cousin Daphne Abguillerm, who isn't a blood relation of yours, but married into the Breton part of the family. Oh, yes, ancestry came up a great deal," Kate said, pleased at his look of astonishment. "Daphne is my age with two kiddies. We're already following each other on Instagram. I think we might really become friends. And she brought my favorite prezzie by far." Kate passed over a gift she'd chosen to keep in its box. "Have a look."

Tony removed the lid. On top of the tissue-wrapped bundle was an old photo. It was a color print, faded by time. In it, a small boy with dark hair grinned at the camera, a newborn in his arms. Kate had first assumed the infant to be female, as it was dressed in a long lace gown, but Daphne had explained that for traditional christenings, the garment was appropriate for either sex.

"Good God, it's Lee," Tony said. "My elder brother. Called Leonard after my father. Lee for short. Doesn't he look marvelous? Must have been about seven years old. I suppose the unprepossessing runt he's holding is me."

"Yes, and I'll treasure it forever." Kate took back the photo rather jealously. "Go on, dig a little deeper."

Groaning, Tony withdrew a vintage christening gown, yellow with age, from within the tissue paper. With it were various tiny accessories, including lace booties and a lace bonnet.

"It's Victorian," Kate said triumphantly.

"It's ghastly." Tony looked appalled. "I've heard stories about this set being passed around every time a baby's due, and I must say, it looks even worse than I imagined."

"But it's so old. It's an heirloom. Do you know what passed for an heirloom in the Wakefield family? My mum's old Rolling Stones concert t-shirt. Steel Wheels was the tour, I think, but I can't swear to it. This set is a true Hetheridge family tradition."

"It's moth-eaten. I mean that literally. See?" He pointed at a tattered edge.

"You look as if you're on the verge of saying no child of yours will wear it."

"Do I have to?"

"You wore it."

"I beg your pardon, I did not. Look again at the photo. That ridiculous costume someone wrestled me into is mostly satin. It's also white, not a decrepit sick yellow."

"Where's the satin gown now?"

"In the attic at Briarshaw, I expect. Or shipped off to some other unlucky recipient when my mother was still alive."

"Tony. I want one photo of Nipper wearing that christening set. I mean it. Say you'll let me or I'll take your baby photo and—and show it to Paul. He'd love to see the old guv in a pretty dress."

"Go ahead. Paul deserves a treat after the beating he took from Parth Chakrabarti. Total Teflon. Let it all bounce off him and went away with a smile on his face."

"I did notice you limping a bit."

"Oh, that's nothing."

For a few hours, Kate had almost put DC Gulls's murder out of her mind, but reference to the Valeria Chakrabarti case brought it back. It came in waves—grief, disbelief, anger. There was nothing to do but let it wash over her. "Anything about Amelia?"

"Not yet. But she was in the habit of writing an end-of-day report before leaving each night. All that will soon be recovered from the Met's cloud servers and turned over to Vic's team. He's personally handling the matter. I wouldn't bet against him in his present mood."

"Is Sean in the clear?"

"Far from it, I'm afraid."

141

"Oh, no. Gut feeling?"

"I find it impossible to imagine him killing her for any reason. But something is off about his alibi. It remains to be seen exactly what."

"What about his demeanor?"

Tony shrugged. "To me, he seemed guilty of something. But that's the trouble with a case that hits so close to home. You can never rely on your objectivity."

"What about Valeria's murder? Anything good?"

"Nothing until the very end, and it was all down to Paul. He seems to have hit it off with Parth's son, Antonio."

"Lady Margaret said he was named after *Much Ado About Nothing* and the name fits."

"Perhaps. I'm reserving judgment. Maybe he's only squashed by his father. Hiding his light under a bushel, as it were, out of self-preservation."

"Well, Lady Margaret and Lady Vivian gave me the short course on Parth's runaway wife, Mandy Haystack. He came off like an old-school woman-hater."

"You could make the case he's more misanthrope than misogynist."

"You could, if you could get your tongue around it."

"I mean, Parth's an abusive personality, full stop. Can't go a moment without beating his chest and bellowing that he's king of the world. But I'll concede he may generally despise women more than men," Tony said. "Except for his perfect Valeria, of course."

"I think if you find her boyfriend, you find her killer."

"No argument there. But Parth is obstructive. He claims she was a virgin."

Kate giggled. "No—really?"

"Yes. A twenty-nine year old, model-beautiful, worldly, jet-setting woman, completely untouched by male hands." Tony shrugged. "But getting back to Antonio—this afternoon he was provoked into uncovering the bushel somewhat. He didn't reveal the identity of the boyfriend Valeria clearly had, at least I don't think so, but he named a past romantic partner of Valeria's. That's a break in the case."

"Who is it?"

"Ken Hussy is his name. He's Parth's dogsbody, whipping boy, and mood ring. He changes color according to how Parth feels at any given moment. Apparently Ken and Valeria had what I would characterize as a serial fling six months ago."

"What's a serial fling? Oh—you mean they hooked up sometimes but never really dated."

"That's it. As a matter of fact, Antonio described it rather colorfully as 'bog hookups.' Parth throws a lot of parties at Highgate House. When Ken and Valeria got a chance, they sometimes slipped away to an upstairs bathroom."

"Classy," Kate laughed. "Six months ago, eh? So unless Ken Hussy was her Shepherd's Bush benefactor, she was cheating on the man who provided that all-expenses-paid flat."

"Assuming they had a relationship meant to preclude others, yes."

"Oh, they did," Kate said. "Men don't lay out that sort of dosh for a love nest without expecting to be the only rooster in the hen house." She paused. "I bungled that, didn't I?"

"It's a mixed metaphor, I think, but the sentiment is valid."

"That could make the dogsbody the other man, as far as Mr. Love Nest was concerned. Maybe the reason Valeria was tossed out a window—a jealous rage."

"Yes. I'm not sure if Mr. Hussy followed the logic that far —he certainly claimed to believe that a confession on his part would do nothing to aid the investigation. We were out on the drive near my car when we met Antonio. He'd packed a bag and was more or less running away from home for the umpteenth time. Mr. Hussy tried to throw his weight around and Antonio grassed.

"After his confession, Mr. Hussy all but got down on his knees and begged us never to tell to Parth. I think the only thing that preserved that last shred of dignity was the fear his boss might glance out a window and see him pleading on the ground."

"What's your sense of him?"

"Born toady. Masochistic streak plus an addiction to being within sniffing distance of the finer things."

"Killer?"

"I don't know. I would've appreciated your take on him."

"Yes, well, I can't wait to get back out in the field. I really mean it," Kate added. "I was surprised by the number of women who insisted to me today that once I held Nipper in my arms, I'd never, ever want to go back."

"I suspect after a reasonable interval, you'll want nothing more. You're a workaholic, as you well know. Nipper might change that overnight, but I'd be surprised. We're luckier than most, in that there's no financial angle."

"Yeah. To be honest, Tony, if I wasn't on bedrest, I'd be out there right now, demanding my share of the Gulls investigation."

"Yes, of course. Not sure you'd get it. Michael is—I don't know what. Uncharacteristically volatile about the whole thing. But this is the first time in fifteen years or more that he's lost someone working for one of his direct reports."

"What part of the Gulls case did he give you?"

"Nothing. He told me to keep my nose out of it. I—" Tony paused to look at his mobile, which was emitting a *whirr* from his inside pocket. "Oh, what a surprise. He's at the gate this very moment, requesting the code."

"Did he really say keep your nose out of it?" Kate was incensed. Michael Deaver had never been her favorite person

—in the early days of her service at the Yard, he'd been on record as skeptical that women could effectively serve—but over the years he'd stood by Tony, especially after other members of the Met's top brass decided to force his retirement. Deaver had also done a great deal to assist the Hetheridges during the crisis with Sir Duncan, and that meant more to Kate than all the rest.

Tony said, "He was an arse, if I'm being honest. I expect that's why he's out front, to mend fences. I'm tempted to pretend I'm not at home. But I want in on the Gulls investigation as much as you do. So I'll bring him into the library, offer him a drink, and see what I can winkle out of him."

"Winkle away. The next episode on my disk is 'Carpathian Eagle.' That sounds like a cracker, doesn't it?"

"It does," Tony said, rising with a wince. "Bloody knee. Whenever I forget, it reminds me."

"Wear that brace I bought you."

"I don't need it."

"Knee replacement surgery," Kate hummed, lifting her face for a kiss. "I'll set it to music if I must. Suppose you fall over again?"

"If I do, I'll get up. Watch your horror movie." Instead of kissing her cheek, as she expected, he kissed her lips. Not just a peck, either, but a longer kiss.

"Lord Hetheridge. What on earth do you want of me?"

"Only that. I'll be back up in time for dinner. Possibly with some real news to report."

CHAPTER 14

*M*ichael Deaver was fifty-nine years old, but seemed older. A tall man with a long, saturnine face, white hair, and perpetually compressed lips, he often looked as if he'd just absorbed some unfathomable body blow. At the Yard, Tony had been his subordinate for many years, and while he found Deaver's glass-half-full-of-hemlock outlook occasionally bleak, he'd always assumed the difference in their temperaments had to do with their divergent career paths.

Both had made chief superintendent around the same time, but while Michael set his sights much higher, Tony had settled in for the long haul, convinced he could rise no higher without unbearable levels of aggravation. Michael was willing to play politics, participate in ceremonial meetings that did nothing but stroke egos, promote a weak officer if his superiors insisted, and show a good officer the door if the Powers That Be told him to. That had been Tony's fate not long ago, when his unusual marriage to Kate, his subordinate and nominal protege, gave his enemies the firepower they'd long yearned for.

In his comfortable perch as perpetual chief superintendent, Tony had been able to work murder cases, rescue
promising young detectives, and arrange his career to his
liking. Because he worked harder than men half his age and
had the record to prove it, he'd felt no qualms about playing
by his own rules. Michael Deaver was a company man, as the
Americans said, with all the rights and privileges thereto.
Tony was his own man, which was why at almost sixty-two
he looked younger and seemed happier than his old friend.
There was a spring in his step—apart from the intermittent
limp.

Deaver had turned up in his own car, a rather nice old
Jaguar S-type that was spoiled by its dreary green color.
Hemlock, Tony thought for the hundredth time upon seeing
his ex-boss emerge from it. *Even the vehicle carries an aura of
gloom.*

"Good of you to let me in," Deaver said, stretching his
mouth in a semi-smile as they passed through the foyer. "I
half expected you to pretend you weren't at home."

"Not at all. This Gulls situation has everyone on edge,"
Tony said. "Follow me to my office. You haven't seen it, have
you?"

"No. You don't consult with clients here, do you?"

"That wouldn't do at the moment. Not while the Fan
Club," he said, meaning Sir Duncan's most passionate devo-
tees, "is still issuing death threats and whatnot. I use the
office to tackle the work I bring home, or to escape from
Henry and Ritchie—"

"We heard that," Henry shouted from the living room.

"Just testing you. Top marks," Tony shouted back. "As you
see, voices carry in the old pile rather more than I should
like, but during the renovation, I had my office sound-
proofed. I'd offer you refreshments, but the temporary cook
is rather at a loss. How about a drink?"

"Please God. How's Kate?"

"Radiant. She promised to slap me if I said it once more in her hearing, but it's true. Upstairs hating every minute of bedrest and watching old horror movies."

Deaver must've cottoned on to Tony's hint about Henry and Ritchie being in earshot, because he refrained from mentioning Gulls's murder until they were safely inside the office. Taking a seat on the red leather sofa, he said, "About this afternoon. Sorry I snapped at you, old boy. That was beneath me. All I can say in my defense is, my nerves are worn down to nothing."

"It's forgotten," Tony lied. He would forget, eventually, but the downside of having an excellent memory was retaining thoughts and feelings long past their sell-by date. "Still take scotch and water?"

"Yes. Large one, if you don't mind. I promise to metabolize it before I get back behind the wheel."

"You're welcome to stay for dinner. We're having beef fillet and asparagus. If you don't help me eat it, most of it may go to waste. Kate, Henry, and Ritchie gorged on a catered lunch during Kate's baby shower this afternoon." Tony set out two glasses, opened the crystal decanter, and poured a generous quantity of Glenlivet in each. Splashing in a bit of water, he asked, "How's Monique and Stuart these days?"

"Ah, you know Monique. She's like a fine quartz mechanism. Runs silently and flawlessly without winding," Deaver said of his wife. "As for Stuart—well. He'll return to Oxford next semester to become a Master of Philosophy in Celtic Studies." He sighed. "I suppose I should be glad he's wasting his life in a genteel, socially acceptable way, instead of shooting up under a tree like Gregory Marquand. But it rankles to watch him flutter about, searching for the most meaningless thing possible to peck at."

"He seemed quite happy, last time I spoke to him," Tony said, handing Deaver his drink, then settling into the wing-back near the cold fireplace. "To quote Paul Bhar, that's not nothing."

"Wait till little Evvy pierces her nose and runs off with a guitar player. Then his views on childrearing will take a quantum leap." Deaver tasted his drink, but if it pleased him, he gave no sign. "What about you? How's the PI life treating you?"

"Rather well. Satisfying in its own way, but no big cases lately. Which is probably why I treasure my consulting work with the Yard."

"Yes, well, if you can do anything with the Chakrabarti case, you'll be working a miracle. Which you're quite capable of doing," Deaver added, squinting at him over his glass. "You realize Parth has spent the last six weeks torturing the MPS, from the Commissioner of Police right down to the custodial staff, don't you? He's determined to find fault with us. Not long ago I had a meeting with the risk management team—twelve whey-faced lawyers and ten political liaisons—and they don't think any suit he can bring will have the slightest merit. Still, he has the time, money, and malice to drag the Met through the mud from now till the end of time. Are you aware of his social media escapades?"

"His son said something about it. Called him the biggest Twitter troll in the UK."

Deaver snorted. "Yeah. Half the time I used to agree with him. 'Gone too far' is an apt description for plenty of things happening in this country. Happening *to* it." He took another drink. "Oh, I know you probably don't agree. You can play the maverick all you like, you're rich and titled and a living incarnation of privilege, in the latest sense of the word."

"That's why I stay off Twitter."

Deaver actually laughed, which was so rare Tony found it startling.

"It's a wonder we get on at all," Deaver continued, shaking his head. "I married to get ahead. You held out for passion. I had a child because that's what one does. You scoffed at the idea until you were sixty and then went wild. I played the game, got the promotions, got the power—such as it is—and you thumbed your nose at all of it. The one thing we have in common is the job."

"For most of my life, the job was *the* thing," Tony said honestly. "And I still want every single murderer caught and punished, never to kill again. I want justice blindfolded with her sword sharp. We've always been of one mind about that."

Deaver sighed.

A prickle went up Tony's spine. He put down his glass. "What?"

"I'm worried about Kincaid. I have reason to believe he might have killed Gulls."

"Why?"

"His alibi's shaky. Vic and I agree about that. And the way he and Gulls behaved—in so underhanded a fashion, seeing each other without disclosing their relationship to their superior officers—speaks ill of his character. I—"

"Amelia Gulls was never underhanded," Tony broke in, surprised by his own vehemence. "What they did was technically wrong, a bit of rule-breaking, but morally neutral as far as I'm concerned. She and Kincaid had an affair. So what. Add them to legions of coppers from the beginning of time."

"Of course you'd consider it morally neutral. You blurred all the lines between work, romance, and friendship," Deaver said. His fingers tightened on his glass. "Anyway, if it offends you, I withdraw the remark. My point is, I have a bad feeling about Kincaid, and he was one of your junior proteges back at the Yard. As you said, we've always been of one mind. I want to be sure we're on the same page as to how to handle the crisis, should he be proven guilty."

"What do you mean?"

"Just what I said. If Kincaid killed Gulls, how will we handle it? The public isn't over the Everard case. Everywhere I go, someone's bleating about the breach of trust. Everard's killer was one bad apple, and probably a right bastard, but he was one man," Deaver said firmly. "Most officers will give their lives, their health, their very sanity for complete strangers, and the almighty public shrugs that off. But let one psychopath commit the sort of crime regular citizens commit every day, and suddenly all policeman are assumed monsters until proven safe."

"I agree with all that. But Michael, there's no handling this. If Kincaid killed her, God forbid, ours is not to reason why. We make the arrest and turn the evidence over to CPS. If there are extenuating circumstances of any kind—and I can't imagine what those would be—it will be up to his counsel to mount a defense. The commissioner of police will do what she does, and the legal and PR departments will do what they do. It'll be a black eye and a sodding humiliation, but that can't be helped." He leaned forward on the edge of his seat, resisting the urge to grasp Deaver by the shoulders and shake him. "Do you *know* he's guilty? By God, if he is, don't let me near him. If I ever lay hands on him, I'll be the next one arrested, and with cause. I saw Amelia Gulls lying dead on the floor. It's a sight I'll never forget."

"No, Tony. I don't know that he's guilty," Deaver said sharply, shaking himself as if waking from a trance. "I have only my instincts, which maybe aren't as keen as yours. And I have my fears for the institution and for policing as a whole, which as I said before, you can afford to wave away. You glory in being a maverick. I'm an institutionalist, first and foremost, and the idea of Scotland Yard being dragged into a national scandal makes me physically sick."

Tony realized he was breathing too fast, and made a concerted effort to calm down. Staring at his glass, he bit the inside of his cheek, one of the few indulgences he permitted himself when his emotions spiked this way. If Deaver had still been his superior, he would've kept silent. But he was a free agent now, and the temptation to speak won out.

"If you're so worried about a potential crisis, there's a simple solution to your problem. A way to protect the institution," Tony said in a cold, clear voice. "Stop investigating Gulls's murder. Not so the public can tell. Just forget to read the reports. Find excuses to reassign the investigators. In private meetings, repeat what you said about Gulls being underhanded. That should poison the well—"

"Tony."

"And then take Kincaid under your wing. Reassure yourself it was a one-off, just boys behaving badly, and not likely to occur again. That way the public is spared the scandal and—"

"Tony! Enough. You're dead set on thinking the worst of me, aren't you?"

"I'm giving you a variation of what Parth Chakrabarti thinks of the MPS as a whole. That Scotland Yard gave up investigating his daughter's murder early on, for reasons of their own. That Forensics came back with nothing useful, and the witnesses were weak, and our knocking on doors and wearing out shoe leather amounted to exactly zero for a very good reason—it was all a sham."

Deaver sank back against the sofa cushions and closed his eyes. "He'll parrot that line for the rest of his life. I don't suppose he warmed up to you at any point?"

"Far from it."

"Well, don't blame yourself for not getting anywhere. The

case has been ice cold for ages." Deaver's brief flash of anger was gone; he was back to sounding mildly suicidal, which for him was normal.

Tony said, "I never said I didn't get anywhere."

Deaver opened his eyes.

"Actually, it was Paul who wedged a foot in the door," he continued. "He's arranged tomorrow to re-interview Antonio Chakrabarti, who is on the outs with his father at present. Antonio said his sister Octavia, who belongs to various pressure groups and has what might be called an adversarial relationship with the police, will join the discussion."

"The son doesn't know anything," Deaver said. "He's admitted he was never close to Valeria. The other daughter, Octavia, knows even less, but she might pretend to have secret information. She's been arrested three times in violent anti-government protests, you know. Held in contempt for courtroom outbursts. Paul's aware of all this, of course, and I hope he won't let his eagerness for a break in the case blind his good sense. Will you be there for the interview?"

"No. I should think if the personification of privilege turns up, as I believe you called me, it would push Octavia into active hostility." Tony picked up his glass again, shifting it from hand to hand as he pretended to examine the whiskey's color. He knew Deaver wasn't at his best; the loss of Gulls, the fear that Kincaid might be implicated, and the strain of Parth's sustained attack all weighed on him. They rarely discussed home life—for their friendship, it really was the job, first and foremost—but Deaver's remarks about his wife and son had been startlingly bleak, even for him. Tonight, the man's doom-and-gloom aura didn't seem like a defense mechanism; more like a cry for help.

"Antonio did tell me and Paul one salient fact that's new," he said at last.

"What?" Deaver snapped.

"Valeria had a fling with Parth's confidential assistant."

"No. That toothy fellow? The one with all the hair?"

"The very same. Ken Hussy."

"Well. Look into it. But it was ancient history, I suppose."

"No. Six months ago. Antonio referred to the affair as a series of bog hookups. Ken begged us not to tell Parth. He said it was meaningless, and it would destroy Parth's rosy-eyed view of his daughter for nothing." Tony paused. Deaver's intensity was startling. "You think we've hit upon something?"

"I hope so. Is anyone checking on Hussy's alibi?"

"Yes, Paul assigned someone from his team. According to Hussy's diary, on the night Valeria was killed, he was at Highgate House, debasing himself to Parth. He doesn't always sleep at his place of employment, but that night he did, because Parth was preparing for a GTFO conference and wanted all hands on deck. We'll see if Hussy's account can be verified. If not, we'll get his prints and DNA to compare to a couple of unknowns recovered from Valeria's apartment."

"So if Paul is handling the Chakrabarti children, what's on the program for you tomorrow?"

"I'd like to talk to Sean Kincaid. Man to man, off the record. Then I'd like to retrace all the steps of his alibi, on the record of course, and see what comes up. I agree there's a wobbliness to his story. While I very much hope that will turn out to be grief and anger distorting his ability to explain himself, it still must be investigated."

"No. Vic Jackson has charge of the Gulls case. He's a new man since he quit drinking, Tony. Gone are the days that I can snatch a case out from under his nose just because you show an interest." Deaver knocked back the rest of his drink. "Sorry. There I go again, addressing you as an inferior in the chain of command. When in truth, of course, you're a consultant beholden to no one. And my superior in every way that matters, as our surroundings so aptly reveal." He set the glass down with a *thud*.

"Michael. What's wrong?"

Deaver let out a short, unpleasant laugh. "Everything. And I require an answer. How else do you plan to consult with Paul Bhar?"

Tony sidestepped that again, saying stubbornly, "I understand Vic is SIO of the Gulls case, but I can't believe he'd object to some help. He's been short-handed ever since Kate took leave, and now he's lost Gulls and been forced to sideline Kincaid. I'm not sure what, if anything, I can pry loose from the Lin Wu Chen case, but there's always Leland Marquand at the Peel Center. I can prod him about his son's suspicious death. Which might suit you, since I have reason to believe the case was reopened at your request."

"Damn you. You put your finger on it," Deaver said softly. "I'm afraid I can't divulge the nature or source of the new information I received. But it's quite suggestive, Tony. I expect Gulls muffed it somehow—she was too young for that investigation, too green. I know she was one of your favorites, but to be honest, I always found your confidence in her misplaced."

"What about Leland? Do you have confidence in him?"

"I did. Now I'm not sure. You probably heard he came back to the Yard for a confrontation with Vic and made a bloody spectacle of himself. Not behavior to inspire confidence in a man's innocence."

"So you think Leland might have killed his son?"

"I don't want to, if that's what you mean. But I can imagine it. He was a hands-on copper before he made detective. Remember that televised rescue a few years back? Two children taken by a pedophile? One of the rescuers fractured his knuckles on the perp's face during the arrest. That was Leland."

"I do remember. I was all for giving him a medal," Tony said. "But I will admit, the sort of man who'll lunge for the bad guy's throat may just as easily attack an innocent young woman, if he truly believes he has no other way out. If Gulls uncovered something..." He paused, considering. "Do you know if IT has given Gulls's recovered reports and evidence logs over to Vic yet?"

"In part," Deaver said. "You know IT. There's always a reason why the task takes longer than it should, or why what ought to be possible just can't be done. It might be another week, or never."

"True. So I'd rather not wait. With your permission, I'd like to drop in on Leland Marquand at the Peel Center tomorrow."

"Granted." Deaver stood up and stuck out a hand. "Are we good?"

"Of course." Tony shook it. "Home now?"

The other man pulled a face. "Please. I'm heading back to the Yard. Give Kate my best." He exited Tony's office, head up but shoulders drooping.

CHAPTER 15

With Kate on bedrest and Harvey sunning himself in Saint-Tropez, bedtime at Welle-grave House was a trying affair. On that particular night, dinner went off poorly because Tony had little appetite—his mind was still replaying and relitigating his conversation with AC Deaver. Meanwhile, Ritchie and Henry, still full from baby shower treats, refused to do more than play with their food. When Kate also sent her plate back largely untouched, that was the final straw for the temporary cook; she gave notice, saying she knew when she wasn't wanted. Mrs. Snell paid the woman in full, wished her all the best, and gave her the keys to the street.

"I say good riddance. As for breakfast tomorrow, I'll handle it myself," she informed Tony. "The agency will send a replacement by teatime, they promise."

"I'm not worried about that in the least," he said honestly. "But I'm sorry to tell you this is Ritchie's bath night. I know the form of it," he said, wincing at her blank look of horror. "But he's rather elusive in act one, and exuberant in act two.

That is to say, the first part involves chasing him and the second part involves being splashed in the face. I don't think I can manage him alone. Henry might be able to lend a hand, except I just sent him upstairs to finish his history essay. It's due tomorrow and he'll need an hour to get it done."

For a moment, the woman who'd seen him through countless murder investigations and intra-office political upheavals seemed to wilt. Then her chin lifted, her magnified eyes gleamed behind her specs, and she quoted Elizabeth I.

"'I know I have the body of a weak and feeble woman, but I have the heart and stomach of a king, and of a king of England, too.'"

"That's the spirit. You start the bath and I'll begin negotiations to get him undressed."

It took every minute of an hour to do the job, but Tony had assisted Kate in the operation enough to understand that direct appeals to Ritchie never worked. He didn't care if he smelled bad. Nor would he concede that his itchiness would be solved by bathing. When Tony entered Ritchie's bedroom, his brother-in-law was listening to an episode of *The Mandalorian* on the Disney streaming channel while working on a LEGO creation. It was abstract, nothing but yellow and red bricks, and unfathomably fascinating, as with all Ritchie's LEGO art.

"I found this in the bathtub," Tony announced, holding something up.

Ritchie, who declined to look, kept right on fitting plastic bricks to plastic bricks. "No baby."

"But it is a baby. A child. Grogu," Tony said, naming a *Mandalorian* character.

"Grogu." Ritchie stopped with the bricks and looked up. He gestured possessively; that was his shorthand for *give it to me.*

Tony regarded the bath toy as if he wasn't quite sure. "He tells me he lives in the tub."

Ritchie got to his feet. He no longer sprang up, nimble as a child, when he rose from the floor, and tonight he grunted a little, annoyed by his own stiffness.

"Oh, yes. Middle-age comes for us all," Tony said. "Those of us who are lucky, anyway. Let's see about Grogu's claim that he lives in the tub."

Once Ritchie was successfully lured into the lavatory, and when he saw that Mrs. Snell was armed with soap and towels and that a warm bath already awaited him, he bowled them a spin ball. Undressing rapidly, he decided to join Grogu, Boba Fett, and various other *Star Wars* characters in the water without delay.

"Don't look at my thing," he told Mrs. Snell as he stripped.

Tony bit his lip. Ritchie, who had no notion of privacy and often wandered out of his bedroom clad only in underpants, had accidentally or on purpose shown that particular bit of flesh to every member of the household multiple times. Poor Mrs. Snell had probably glimpsed it on more occasions than she could count, and was still coming to work each day.

Weak and feeble woman, my arse, Tony thought as they cracked on with getting Ritchie scrubbed, rinsed, and shampooed.

After his bath, Ritchie went back to his room in clean pajamas, Mrs. Snell retreated downstairs for a well-deserved sherry, and Tony went to Henry's room to make sure the homework was finished. Henry, like many bright kids, would do nothing but coast if permitted. If Kate and Tony didn't keep after him, he'd mostly fritter his time away, counting on his own native cleverness to let him put off school assignments until the last minute—a bet that didn't always pay off. Therefore, Tony made it his business to know exactly what

Henry was meant to produce in any given week, and wasn't above confiscating beloved devices if those tasks went undone.

"And what can you tell me about warfare in the ancient world?" he asked by way of greeting.

Henry, already in his pajamas but playing an Xbox game, paused the action to say solemnly, "Genghis Khan and his armies wiped out ten percent of the world's population."

"Did he? How?"

"Riders on horseback shooting the composite bow, for one thing."

"What's a composite bow?"

"It's a specialized weapon," Henry declared, warming to his subject, "that took great skill and anywhere from five to ten years to create..."

In the master bedroom, the telly was blaring as usual, but Kate had fallen asleep sitting up. Tony paused for a moment to see what Peter Cushing and Christopher Lee were up to—they seemed to be fighting to the death, as usual—and then cut it off. As was his habit, he took a shower before bed, trying to luxuriate in the hot water but mostly failing. Gulls been working on three cases: Lin Wu Chen, Gregory Marquand, and Valeria Chakrabarti, and she'd been dating Sean Kincaid on the sly. Did the answer lie there, in those circumstances? Or was there something else?

When he emerged from the bathroom, hair toweled dry and sticking up, terrycloth robe belted loosely around him, Kate was awake. She hadn't turned the TV back on. Instead, she was fooling with her laptop, going at it from the side, since she no longer had a lap.

"Not working, I hope," he said mildly.

"Just a little. I started with Xiuying Chen—Deputy Director Chen, if you want to be precise. Just the run-of-the-mill stuff any detective would do. She's led a nice, successful, boring life. Very much the anonymous civil servant until her son died."

"I wonder if Gulls dug up anything more."

"She didn't. IT gave Vic all her notes on the Lin Wu Chen case. When I rang, he said he'd found nothing but a lot of due diligence and emailed me the file. He also warned me not to tell you, since I'm not supposed to be working."

Tony wanted to scold her, but he also wanted a quick look at Gulls's notes. He compromised by asking, "You're all right? I don't want you overexcited. First the baby shower, now this."

She flashed him that smile, the one that was utterly without artifice and always made his heart turn over. "No Braxton Hicks. No sharp pains or agonizing pressure. Not even any reflux, which is amazing, considering how I ate today. It feels good to sneak a little work in."

"Fair play. Let me see."

Getting into bed still in his robe, he positioned himself to see the laptop's screen without making Kate shift. "Yes," he said after a quick perusal of Gulls's final notes on the Lin Wu Chen case. "The mother has pushed hard, which is understandable, but there's a dearth of physical evidence. She suspects Mr. Parker, the boyfriend, who has an airtight alibi. What does he do for a living?"

"Hospital porter. There's documentation of his presence on-shift at St. Thomas's Hospital during the time Mr. Chen went missing. Not only the time card, but sworn statements from eight coworkers."

"Did Gulls re-interview Mr. Parker?"

"Yes. I will say, I can see why Deputy Director Chen dislikes him so much. First, he was the beneficiary of Lin

Wu Chen's will. Mr. Chen had some cash and property inherited from his grandmother, and it all went to Parker. Second, it wasn't too long after the burial that Parker moved in with another man. A sixty-five-year-old retired flutist in Putney."

"May-December romances are all the rage."

"You'll never hear me say otherwise. Anyway, they were married," Kate continued, "and divorced in record time. The retired flutist's family brought suit against Parker for undue influence. They claimed the old fellow was in the early stages of dementia and Parker was using him for material gain. Trying to get himself into the flutist's will."

"By the pricking of my thumbs," Tony murmured.

"What?"

"Mrs. Snell quoted Queen Elizabeth I earlier tonight, and I'm quoting Shakespeare. 'By the pricking of my thumbs, something wicked this way comes.'"

"On that, Shakespeare and I agree. I wonder...do you think Parker hired someone to kill Chen?"

"Anything's possible. Amateur killers aren't known for keeping mum, though," Tony said. "They tend to turn around and blackmail the person who hired them."

"Amelia seemed to zero in on Parker for a while. She even checked with the hospital staff to see if he might have slipped out of work during the crucial period. The answer is no. He could've left campus for a very short time, but there's no scenario that gives him enough of a window to kill Chen, dump his body, and get back on the job before anyone missed him."

"Then he's innocent. Or there's a doppelgänger."

"Oh! I just watched an episode from the *Hammer House of Horror* that was about doppelgängers. 'Two Faces of Evil.'"

"Was it good?"

"No, it was one of the worst things I've ever seen. Definitely since Dr. Laidslaw confined me to bed. Still—what did you call it? The itching of your thumbs?"

"Pricking."

"Yes, well, when it comes to Orrin Parker, I have the infuriating sensation he got away with murder. I don't know what else about him I can look into, but I'll sleep on it. Maybe tomorrow something will occur to me." She shut the laptop, shifting it to the bedside table. "How was AC Deaver?"

"Somewhere between miserable and despondent."

"So normal?"

"No. Rather worse," Tony admitted. "As a consultant to Scotland Yard, I would never be so unprofessional as to repeat key details of a sensitive conversation..."

"Right."

"...but as your husband, I'm sorry to tell you he suspects Sean Kincaid. Full stop. If not Sean, then possibly Leland Marquand. As for Gulls, Michael wasn't terribly complimentary about her abilities..."

"Of course not. If he had his way, there would still be an A4 division and we'd all be branded with pink Ws."

"He's Cressida Dick's subordinate and has been for some time."

"Did you ask him if he likes it?"

Tony chuckled. "No. Anyway, Michael thinks it's possible that Gulls touched a nerve with Marquand. That perhaps he felt cornered and decided to shut her down."

"That's absurd."

He looked at her, surprised.

"Think about it. The risk of hunting a detective constable, stalking her in her home, killing her, and then getting away without leaving a trace—I can't imagine how desperate Marquand would have to be to attempt such a thing. At least with Sean, awful as the idea is, it makes sense, in a twisted way. So many love affairs end in violence, we hardly need an explanation any more. But Gregory Marquand died under muddy circumstances, after a long battle with drug addiction...any good defense counsel could probably get his father off, unless someone dug up a videotaped confession."

"Michael wouldn't disclose why he wanted the case reopened. Not even to me. As I said, his mood was—bleak. That's not the right word."

"Suicidal is the word you usually use."

"Yes, but—given his demeanor, that hits a little too close to home. He's worried for the institution. Bad enough that Gulls was murdered. Bad enough that a wealthy, powerful, and extraordinarily loud individual like Parth Chakrabarti is accusing the Met of a cover-up. But if an officer, active or retired, killed Gulls..."

"I imagine he's bricking it, wondering how to sweep the evidence under the rug so the public never finds out."

For the second time, Tony looked at his wife, genuinely amazed. "You believe that of him?"

"Of course I do. Oh, I know he's your friend, and he shielded you for years, or so you say." Kate sounded dubious. "All I know is what I've seen. He'd sell his own mum cheap if it meant good press for the police. The Everard thing is his worst nightmare, but not for the same reason it's my worst nightmare. Because it was splashed all over the country—all over the world—and there's no way of blurring it, no fig leaf to hide behind. It's the same with Gulls—if a policeman did it, he'll want to mitigate the facts somehow."

"I've always thought Michael would do anything to protect his people. I've said so, more than once."

"Do you still believe it?"

For some reason, he couldn't bring himself to tell Kate she'd been right about Deaver's fervent wish to "handle" the Gulls situation, as opposed to following the evidence where it led without fear or favor. Belatedly he realized that he'd considered it such a blatant transgression, it had left him shocked. Generally Tony believed himself too old, sophisticated, and worldly to be shocked by much of anything. But hearing Assistant Commissioner Michael Deaver express such a view had shaken him to the core.

Instead of answering Kate, he sidestepped, telling her of his plan to surprise Leland Marquand between classes at the Peel Center.

"Congratulations, you've stopped calling it Hendon."

"Yes, well, must move with the times or be run over, I suppose. Ready for lights out?"

"Yeah. Tony, I hate to bring this up, but a little while ago I checked the calendar and realized tonight was supposed to be Ritchie's bath. You know how hard I've worked to get him on a schedule that's set in stone. Everything completely predictable. I don't think we should try and wait until we can get a fully vetted assistant," she said, meaning a paid carer. "But with me on bedrest and Harvey away, that means—"

"It's done," he said nonchalantly, watching her face.

"What's done?"

"Ritchie's bath. He had it this evening. Mrs. Snell and I officiated, but Ritchie, Grogu, and Boba Fett were the main players."

"You remembered. And you just did it?" She gazed at him, hazel eyes wide.

"Naturally."

"That may be the sexiest thing you've ever said to me."

"Well, in that case..." He took her hand, drawing it under the loose confines of his robe.

She laughed. "Hope really does spring eternal with you. Tell you what. I'll give you a cuddle. Maybe a kiss, since you're going to let me take a picture of Nipper in his heirloom christening gown. You are, aren't you?"

"His?" Tony asked.

"His. Hers. Who knows. I never thought I'd hear you say the words Boba Fett. My mind is reeling."

"Then this is an opportunity not to be missed. Extinguish all lights," he ordered the room, which had no choice but to obey.

CHAPTER 16

hen Paul Bhar woke up, he suffered a dizzying moment of incomprehension. He wasn't home—meaning his mum's place—and he wasn't asleep on a couch at the Yard, which had happened a lot during two years of staffing shortages and rising crime, including terrorist attacks. No, he was in his own bed, the one he shared with Emmeline, and the thing on his face that had teased him awake was morning sunshine.

"Em!" he bellowed, alarmed. He hadn't slept through the night since the week before Evvy's birth, and had never expected to again.

"Coming," his wife sang from the kitchen. Entering the bedroom with Evvy nestled in her arms, she gave him a smile. "Morning, glory."

"I don't remember Evvy crying out. Did she sleep through the night?"

"Lord, no. She demanded her feedings right on schedule. This girl knows what she wants, when she wants," Emmeline said, shifting the infant, who made a fussy noise. It was a sweet little sound, and Paul responded to it like Pavlov's dogs to *ring-a-ding-ding*.

"Give over," he said, opening his arms.

Emmeline did. Evvy, who'd come into the world with lots of wispy dark hair, was wearing a pink all-in-one. His mum, Sharada, was mad for pink baby clothes, and had loaded Paul and Emmeline up. Of course, Emmeline might have enjoyed choosing a few pieces herself, but she thought lasting peace with Sharada was worth a few compromises.

"Evvy," he crooned, staring into her huge dark eyes. She also had his coloring, but her dainty nose and mouth were pure Emmeline.

She made the gurgling sound he interpreted as wanting to be held against his chest and obliged her. To Emmeline he said, "You let me sleep in. What's the occasion?"

"I felt sorry for you. You're already burning it at both ends. So I did the nightshift alone. Don't get used to it," she added. "Kate's baby shower was a triumph, as I knew it would be, but I need a recharge. Today's going to be nothing but tea, telly, and naps with baby."

Paul cocked his head to Evvy, who was dozing, and pretended to listen to some whispered directive. Then he told Emmeline, "Come here. Evvy wants me to tell you something."

"Oh, really?" She leaned in.

"Closer."

She leaned in closer.

"We love you." Paul kissed her lips.

"You great soft melty tub of goop."

"I'll take that as a minimal show of affection."

"Minimal? I can prove how much I love you. I let you sleep." Grinning, Emmeline took Evvy back. "But if you want to show your face at the Yard by nine o'clock, you'd best be up and in the shower before too much longer. And Paulie?"

"Yeah?"

"See to your hair, love. It's shaggy."

Surprised, he touched the nape of his neck and realized she was right. "I—I must've forgot to get it trimmed. I can't believe it. That's never happened before."

Laughing, Emmeline told the sleeping baby, "Daddy forgot his vanity for you, Evvy, m'dear. It'll probably never happen again. But it's still a miracle."

* * *

PAUL DID MAKE it into Jackson's office by 9:15 a.m., which wasn't bad considering he stopped at a barber shop on the way. Before his marriage, he'd booked regular appointments at a pricey establishment that sold hair and skin products for the discerning gentleman. In those days, he considered two things—the fee and the post code—as barometers of a shop's suitability. Now he just wanted his hair de-shagged, sharpish. The shop he picked, one of those manly places that kept poncy side services to a minimum, did a fine job for a fair price. He put a recurring alert on his personal mobile to go there every two weeks. Falling down in the grooming department was a slippery slope; he didn't want to end up like Vic Jackson, with dandruff and powdered doughnut sugar decorating the shoulders of a badly-fitting, off-the-rack coat.

Joy was still a bit under the weather, demeanor-wise, which for her meant only a cheerful "Good morning" without any small talk. There was an aura of fatalistic expectation settling over Homicide. The Toff Squad, often the punching bag of other departments for the perceived cushiness of its investigations, was down by three: Kate on maternity leave, Kincaid filling in with another unit, Gulls dead. Usually when the going got rough, policemen cranked up the trash talk and the swagger; overconfidence had propelled most of the officers through other hard times, and would surely do so again. But today Paul caught a hint of something else—disbelief as well as fear. It was as if subconsciously, everyone on the job knew something was very wrong, but no one had yet put their finger on what.

Good thing Mum is too wrapped up in Evvy, not to mention writing her latest novel, to interrogate me about work. She'd be convinced my life's in danger. Which it always is, technically.

Jackson was at his desk, reading specs perched on the end of his nose, studying a sheaf of documents. His eyes flicked up when Paul entered. "Close the door behind you, Bhar."

Paul did so. "How's tricks, guv?"

"Bloody awful, as you very well know. Pollack at Queen's Scientific rang me this morning," Jackson said, referring to one of the independent labs the Met turned to when the FSS and other large companies were too busy for a quick turnaround. Hugh Pollack, a former MPS medical examiner-turned-lab founder, had worked with the Toff Squad since the early days, when Tony Hetheridge and Michael Deaver were DCIs who investigated cases together. Pollack was always willing to lend a hand if AC Deaver asked, and would assist in the lab himself to expedite forensic testing on the case of a copper killed in the line of duty.

"What did he find at Amelia's flat?" Paul asked eagerly, taking a seat.

"Hairs from fourteen unique individuals, not counting Gulls and Kincaid. All colors—black, brown, blond, red, and gray. You're in there, and so is Kate."

"That's twelve to play with. How many of the others are from her colleagues?"

"We're working on it. Prints came back from twenty-two unique individuals, not counting Gulls and Kincaid. Those were easy—you, Kate, and seventeen Met employees. That leaves three sets of unknowns. First pass through HOLMES 2 gave us nothing, but I put a man on it."

"Other types of DNA?"

Jackson shrugged. "The usual piddling bits of this and that. As for IT, they procured Gulls's work product regarding that uni student who drowned in the Thames, Lin Wu Chen. I found nothing in them. Kate's antsy on bedrest, so I sent them to her. For all the good it will do."

"What's that you've printed off the computer?" Paul asked, teasing gently. Jackson disliked computers and screens of all kinds. He preferred to waste pots of ink and reams of paper printing out digital files so he could hold them in his hand, crumple them melodramatically, and occasionally wave them under someone's nose.

"What IT has recovered of Gulls's early work on Gregory Marquand and Valeria Chakrabarti. Some of it wasn't backed-up properly, or so they say," Jackson added with a scowl. He distrusted IT technicians even more than the devices they serviced. "What they've given me is just more of the same, ad infinitum. That manky bloke with the mole above his lip promised me yesterday on his old mum's life that he'd have the data in my hand by noon. That gives him three hours, and I'm holding him to it, by God. The idea that Gulls didn't back up her work properly? Please. I should give him a slap just for suggesting it."

"What about Sean Kincaid? Has someone visited Kentish Town Police Station, or that pub he claimed as an alibi?"

"Deaver rang me about that this morning. He's putting outside men on it. Box 500 blokes," he said, meaning officers attached to MI5, the UK's domestic counter-intelligence and security service. "He said he doesn't want you or Tony gumming up the works. Tony in particular was a mentor to both Gulls and Kincaid; anything dispositive he found would be immediately challenged on those grounds. If he exonerated Kincaid, he would be accused of helping a promising young man; if he destroyed Kincaid's alibi, they'd say he was hellbent on vengeance for Amelia Gulls."

Paul blew out a sigh. "I didn't think of it like that. I doubt Tony did, either. I suppose that's why Deaver's the man in charge. He understands the political angles. I hope there's no subtle, four-dimensional chess sort of reason why Tony can't go and talk to Leland Marquand?"

"No. Deaver's all for it. I don't know who the AC likes for Gulls's killer, if anyone. For all I know, it's Marquand. He always likes to point his best mate Tony in the most promising direction." Jackson sounded more than a little peevish, but that was typical of him. Paul thought his guv's real issue wasn't jealousy of Tony's relationship with the assistant commissioner, but rather that Gulls was dead and no clear leads had yet emerged.

"Now what about you, Paulie my lad?" Jackson asked, making an effort to sound hale and hearty and almost succeeding. "How do you plan on making queen and country proud?"

"I have an afternoon appointment with the younger Chakrabartis. Octavia has a place in Croydon. A flat above a Ladbrokes on George Street."

Jackson scowled. "That's no place for a multimillionaire's daughter."

"Apparently she prefers to live differently. I checked into her background a bit. She's been on the outs with her father since she was fourteen years old. Went off to live with an aunt on the Haystack side of the family. Sort of unofficially emancipated."

Putting down the wad of printouts he'd been studying, Jackson began rummaging in the papers on his desk, a task akin to combing the sands of the Sahara with his bare hands. Paul watched politely for a minute or two, looked out the window for as long as he could stand it, then broke down and checked his personal mobile. Emmeline had sent a picture of Evvy looking grumpy. Her bottom lip was pushed out and her hands were balled into tiny fists. The text below read, *Those who displease me will pay!*

"What are you smirking at?" Jackson asked.

"Hmh? Oh, sorry. Baby pics. Never fear, I'll spare you," Paul said, hoping Jackson would show a little interest, but he never did. Unless you had a picture of a dog, preferably a hound, Jackson wouldn't bite.

"Look at this." He handed Paul a printed email dated five days before. "Gulls sent it to Kincaid—from her personal account to his. He voluntarily turned over his computer yesterday. IT's pulling it apart, but they got this right away."

Paul studied the email. It read,

Babe, the mayor was no help. Neither was the embassy. Am trying ICMP but don't know where to start. Know anyone?

"ICMP," Paul said. "Is it related to Parth and his men's rights group? Let's see. We know what GTFO means in the common parlance. ICMP—is it Idiots Claiming Male Privilege?"

"International Committee on Missing Persons," Jackson said drily.

"Huh." Paul thought about it. "First she tried a mayor and an embassy—you don't reckon it was Greece, do you? Was she trying to track down Valeria's mum who ran off with the pool boy?"

"Seems so."

He whistled. "Talk about grasping at straws. Still—we've tried everything else, except a deep dive into Ken Hussy, exestate agent and ex-hookup. And I have some good people on that already."

"Since you have idle time between now and your visit to the Chakrabarti spawn," Jackson said, returning the printed email to his desktop information hoard, "why don't you call the Greek embassy, and the mayor of Athens or wherever Mandy Haystack ended up, and see for yourself what line Gulls was pursuing. Even if you dig up nothing, it still might give you a conversation starter with Antonio and Octavia."

"Maybe," Paul said doubtfully. "I think Antonio won't need much grease to be candid. But he already warned me that Octavia might not say anything at all. Her official statements to the police are virtually all yes and no answers. No explication unless it's dragged out of her."

"She despises our kind," Jackson said, not sounding terribly broken up over it. "Mind you, if she's ever attacked on the street by some druggie with a knife, I reckon she'll scream for a cop like everyone else, and be glad at the sight of one. Even the people who hate us the most expect us to always be there."

Paul couldn't argue with that. "Right. Whatever happened to Mandy Haystack is the name of the game. Maybe the pool boy returned to London under cover of darkness to chuck his stepdaughter out a window. Mind you, he must be pushing forty by now. That makes him a pool man, doesn't it?"

"Get out, Bhar," Jackson said. He was glaring down at a fresh handful of printouts.

"Yessir," Paul said, and did.

CHAPTER 17

he Peel Center on Aerodrome Road in North London was a facility Tony could take pride in. After an informal tour of the police academy, he realized he should've come for a visit long ago, and wondered why he'd left it so late. On campus there was ample space for didactics, equipment training, and operational drills of almost every description. Kate and Paul had both come through the Peel Center, and while the MPS was currently experimenting with an alternate career track—one that essentially plucked recruits right off the street—Tony felt that officers who received formal training would always have a leg up. In another life, he could see himself teaching classes there, making his own small contribution to the next generation of constables, detectives, and specialists. But given his responsibilities at home, the flexibility of a PI's schedule suited him better. Besides, he wasn't ready to close the door on active murder investigations just yet.

Leland Marquand was teaching a module on interrogation techniques when Tony slipped into the back of the small auditorium. The recruits were clustered down on the first three rows, listening intently and taking notes. At uni, kids cultivated an aura of boredom, and would torment any schoolmate who seemed conspicuously intent on learning; there was no greater sin than being too earnest. Here, that wasn't the case.

At Hendon—make that the Peel Center—the pupils understand, for the most part, that what they learn may save their lives. And enable them to save many other lives in the bargain.

Slipping into an aisle seat, he listened as Marquand, who chose to lecture from a chair with only a glass of water and a laptop at hand, came to the end of his lecture.

"...because the essence of a good interview isn't asking the right questions. Not in the first, most crucial phase. It's listening. If you revisit that video I presented on Monday morning—and I suggest you watch it multiple times, if you haven't already—the first twenty-two minutes, which might have seemed unbearable in its long pauses and interminable backtracking, is the key to the confession that comes almost three hours later. During those first twenty-two minutes, the detective conducting the interview makes no effort to intimidate the subject. Why is that, do you think?"

A hand went up.

"Ms. Drummond."

"Because the circumstances and surroundings are already intimidating. Beyond a certain point, too much pressure is counterproductive."

"Yes, precisely. I will also mention that while the detective doesn't take a stab at intimidation, he also refrains from trying to befriend the subject at that point. Which is markedly different than the sympathetic turn he takes at the end whilst eliciting the full confession. Why do you think he waits? Mr. Neeley."

"Because to come on too strong would seem insincere."

"True. I had another answer in mind. Anyone?" Looking

around the room, he caught sight of Tony, blinked in surprise, and managed a weak smile. "We have a distinguished visitor. Chief Superintendent Hetheridge, would you care to weigh in? I realize you haven't viewed the video in question, but from the context you may already have an opinion. Why would an interviewer who intends to show sympathy toward the end of session, particularly if he can draw out a confession, refrain from any such overtures in the interview's first twenty-two minutes?"

"Because in the beginning you speak as little as possible. You do nothing to direct the witness. You listen, and let what you hear direct you."

Marquand rose. "Well. There you have it. I understand half of you are about to take a driving course at our sister facility up the street, and the other half have signed up for a cybercrimes seminar, so I shan't burden you with more reading. I do suggest that you view the interrogation video at least once more, in its entirety, and try to guess when the interviewer decides to go for a full confession. We'll discuss it at the top of the class on Monday. That's all."

The students gathered their things and filed out. A few gazed curiously at Tony, as if trying to decide whether or not they ought to be impressed. He nodded pleasantly, glad that Marquand hadn't called him up to the stage to address the group. His knee was still troubling him, and if he had to show himself to raw recruits, he wanted to stride confidently, not hobble like a old warhorse on its last go-round.

"Hetheridge. How are you?" Marquand asked warily. "I can't say I'm happy to see you."

"No, I expect not. But I come in peace. The declaration itself is proof, isn't it?" Tony waited where he stood, as Marquand climbed the steps to meet him near the auditorium's exit. "If I begin by coming on this strongly, it's proof I'm not in search of a confession, isn't it?"

The other man forced out a humorless chuckle. He was about Tony's age, with sparse gray hair on the fringes of a bald spot and a pugnacious look that didn't match his rich and cultured speaking voice. Despite the loafers, tweed suit, and rimless specs, the shadow of the fighter was still visible, clinging to the teacher like English ivy to red brick. Tony could easily imagine Leland Marquand throwing a punch, and thought he might actually see it, if this meeting went anything like the man's last visit to Scotland Yard.

While he was sizing up his ex-colleague, his counterpart returned the favor. "How long has it been?" Marquand asked. "Three years?"

"Something like that."

"I heard the top brass tossed you out on your arse."

"They did."

"And that you finished Sir Duncan Godington on a rooftop. With your bare hands."

"I did."

"Didn't think you had it in you."

"I had strong motivations. And no other weapons in sight."

"You know what they say about your wife, don't you?"

Such provocative phrasing ordinarily put Tony on his guard, but something in Marquand's tone indicated the man was softening. "What?"

"She's too young for you, too pretty for you, and since you married her, you seem ten years younger."

He shrugged, smiling.

"It's all true, isn't it? Lucky bastard." Marquand actually cuffed Tony on the shoulder, a little harder than was really necessary. "If we must talk, let's do it in my office."

The office in question was a hole in the wall, but sufficient for Marquand's needs. There was a desk with a straight-backed chair in front of it, a bookcase, and a wall calendar hanging where the window should have been. Glancing around the room, Tony noted the two framed photographs on Marquand's desk. One was an old picture of him and his wife; another was a more recent one of her in front of a tree. She sat in a wheelchair with a knitted throw over her legs.

"How is your wife these days?"

"Fine. Well, not fine at all, of course. The loss of Gregory triggered a progression of her MS. She uses the wheelchair all the time now, when before she only used it occasionally." Marquand dropped heavily into his swivel chair behind the desk. "And yes, I have no picture of my son in the office, because I prefer not to see his face. You can chalk that up to a guilty conscience if you wish."

"I understand you had words with Vic Jackson over the reopening of the investigation."

Marquand rolled his eyes. He moved the swivel chair from side to side, as if he might erupt with nervous energy at any moment.

"I spoke with Vic, day before yesterday," Tony continued in the placid tone he used for hostile interrogations. "You know him. No hard feelings. He's had to ask forgiveness himself too many times."

"I shouldn't have taken it out on him. I know damn well the order came from up the food chain." Suddenly he met Tony's gaze with blazing acuity. "They cast you out after a distinguished career—no, I'll say it, a brilliant career—and yet here you are, playing consultant for them. Still doing the bidding of politicians, whether they call themselves that or not, who've long since forgotten what it means to uphold the law. Why?"

"It's good to keep an oar in," Tony said vaguely. "To be honest, I'd rather be working the Amelia Gulls case. One of our own, cut down in her prime. Did you know her?"

"Of course I did. She was here last week, a day after my row with Jackson."

"What did you talk about?"

Marquand gritted his teeth. "Have any of your interviewees taken a swing at you?"

"Many, I'm afraid. Why? Does that question touch a nerve?"

"Because you must know the answer. I'm sure she would've put it in her notes." He sighed. "Rather acute questioner. Put me off with her style. Friendly chatter, encouraging smiles, the demeanor of a preschool teacher. I imagine she would've been a force to be reckoned with, had she been permitted the time."

"Indeed. Unfortunately, her computer and mobile devices were stolen, presumably by her killer. Doubtless IT will recover the documents soon, but I didn't want to wait. So I decided to come here and chat with you, to see what Gulls might have concluded."

"Chat," Marquand repeated. "You know, I'm glad you began by asking after my wife's health. Poor Cathy suffered so much during the initial investigation. If I'm being honest, Gregory put us both through hell from age fourteen on. I have it on good authority that when a child goes wrong, the parents are to blame, full stop. Very well. For myself, I can only assume I spent too much time working and not enough time providing a strong role model. Or perhaps a caring role model. But Cathy gave that boy everything. And all he gave her was grief."

"I assume he began using at fourteen?"

"Yeah. MDMA. Marijuana. Then heroin. It's as if he died sometime in his mid-teens, but the body kept going. The addict kept going. But when I looked in his eyes, there was no one there. No one I recognized."

Tony would've preferred to keep Marquand talking, but

the man was once again gazing at him acutely, as if expecting an answer. Not wishing to sound glib, Tony said carefully, "I understand in such cases, the addicted person must want to recover. No one can want it for him."

"I think so. Heaven knows Cathy and I tried hard to want it for him. We did interventions. Rehab programs. Intensive aftercare. Family therapy. Gregory always told us what he thought we wanted to hear, but it was all lies. Every time I turned my back, he was using again. Even keeping him at home—a grown man on lockdown, like a child—didn't keep him from getting more gear. He'd meet people online and they'd come round the back door with a hit for him. Strangers helping strangers get their hands on one of the most dangerous and addictive substances on earth." He shook his head. "Brotherhood of man."

"Surely Gregory knew injecting himself in the carotid could be fatal," Tony said.

"He knew. He brought it up to Cathy and me a year before it happened. Said sometimes when he thought of dying, that seemed like the best way. One last blissful trip as he ascended to heaven."

"Then you're satisfied he died by suicide?"

"As much as anyone can be."

"His body was found in Epping Forest. Did that place have specific meaning for him?"

"I couldn't say. Not to the Gregory I knew—the son that died long ago. To the addict Gregory, it might've meant something." As Marquand spoke, color crept up his cheeks. "Why don't you ask me if I threatened his life? If I behaved like the monster he described on social media?"

"Did you?"

"Yes, many times, when he drove me past my limit. I screamed things at him, horrible things. I told colleagues at the Yard he would've been better off dead. I thought I was venting, sharing something awful to men who'd seen every terrible thing under the sun and might understand. They didn't. They trotted to the SIO and said I'd planned to kill my son right out in the open."

"Marquand," Tony said sharply. "You may have convinced yourself that's the objective truth, but it isn't. Three of your colleagues were questioned and they answered honestly, albeit regretfully. I reviewed the transcripts this morning. Each one went on record as saying you were a good detective, incapable of murder, and your angry statements about Gregory were not meant in earnest."

"Yet the investigation continued..."

"Because Gregory used Facebook and Twitter to complain about his family life, and he made some very florid accusations. I reviewed that data, too. May I give you my personal opinion of those posts?"

Marquand nodded.

"Gregory's relationship with you may have been irretrievably broken, and his personality might have been warped by his addiction. But when he wrote those posts, he was still a prodigiously verbal, clever young man, more than capable of getting his meaning across. I won't say he was framing you, but those remarks were calculated to humiliate you. And clearly, they succeeded."

Marquand, who'd looked ready to lunge across the desk at Tony, seemed to deflate. "That young woman, DC Gulls. She said the same. I'm sorry she's dead. The media made it sound as if she was ambushed and executed in her own home."

"Yes."

"And according to the grapevine, either her boyfriend did it, or a person connected to her Met caseload. That poking around in cold cases triggered her murder. But not my son's case, surely."

"Did you open up to her? Give her anything new?"

"Perhaps in a way. Maybe because she genuinely asked after Cathy's health. I'd been holding in something for a long time, and on impulse, I told DC Gulls."

Tony nodded.

"It was hard. It cost me a lot. But in the end, I felt better. She said she wouldn't write it down. I wonder if that's true."

"Tell me."

Marquand sighed. "First you have to try and imagine how it was for Cathy and me. See what we saw." Appearing to select an empty spot on his desk, he stared fixedly at it, either remembering or trying not to remember too much.

"It all came to a head just after Christmas. The worst Christmas ever. I was in and out of Kentish Town Station at the time, helping the borough chief, and if you look back at the logs, you'll see I was there for twelve hours the day Gregory died. It's a false entry. I had the day off and I was home, helping Cathy get the house in order. Christmas had been so painful, we wanted to pack away every trace of it.

"Gregory had finally admitted he didn't want to get clean. In his view, everyone was addicted to something—drugs, caffeine, drink, telly, etc. We had it out in the living room, the three of us. As we argued, Cathy and I dismantled the tree. Gregory just drifted about, contributing nothing, only rambling about himself and his philosophy of life.

"I said if he was so far gone as to tell himself intravenous heroin is the moral equivalent of too much telly, there was no hope of him ever recovering, and he might as well leave. That perhaps his so-called friends, the ones who seemed to enjoy his social media rants so much, would put him up, or go and squat with him under a bridge. I was vicious. So angry I threw a glass ornament at his head. He ducked. It shattered." Marquand paused to glance up at Tony, as if to gauge his reaction. Then he continued,

185

"Gregory said that was my problem—to me, everything was a moral question, and objectively 'moral' is a meaningless word. The hobgoblin of my little mind. I was on point of ordering him out of the house. Chucking his clothes into the street and all that. But you can't legally evict a person that way. And anyway, I thought Cathy would object.

"I used to accuse her of coddling him. But something in her broke that day. When I remember her face, how it looked when Gregory said the word 'moral' didn't mean anything, I hear that glass ornament smash against the floor. Not a loud sound at all, but final.

"She said, 'Gregory, if you want to die, for God's sake, do it. Put the needle in your neck and go for broke. At this point I think I would find it a relief.' It was the cruelest thing I ever heard her say, yet I tell you, Hetheridge, I wanted to cheer. I almost did cheer. Poor Cathy, long-suffering Cathy, was finally driven to hit back." Marquand met Tony's eyes again, and this time he expected an answer.

"I understand," Tony said truthfully.

Marquand's gaze returned to the fixed spot. "Gregory laughed at her. His high-pitched laugh. He laughed like a maniac. I thought, well, of course he doesn't care. He hasn't given a fig for either of us in ages. Afterwards, he wandered back upstairs and we carried on packing up Christmas for another year. Forever, as a matter of fact, but we didn't know it then.

"At dinnertime he didn't come down, but that was typical, too. By then Cathy was doing what she always does, blaming herself and exonerating him. I decided to have a shower before bed, and she went up to his room to apologize for what she said. Her scream got me out of the bathroom. Gregory was in bed, the needle still in his neck, already cold. I reckon he must've taken the fatal dose immediately after she told him to.

"What I did next, I did for her. She fell apart, you know. Completely and utterly. I thought she might lose her mind then and there. Spend the rest of her life in a secure facility.

"I tried to make her understand." Marquand's voice trembled. "She didn't kill him. She didn't force him to do it. She made a remark under pressure, a cruel remark, perhaps, but only a remark. For years Gregory taunted us by threatening to kill himself—to take one last glorious trip and leave us to pick up the pieces. Cathy threw it back in his face, yes, but he asked for it. Perhaps he didn't even mean to die. Who can say?"

"Did she listen to you?" Tony asked.

"No. She was unreachable. It was as complete a break with reality as I've ever seen from someone who wasn't under the influence. I thought about what the next few hours had in store—the questions, routine questions, that would cut her like knives. I had to help her. And I did.

"I carried her back to our bedroom, confiscated her phone, and pulled the landline out of the wall. I found an old sedative prescription—one I kept hidden under a loose floorboard because otherwise Gregory would've nicked it—and made her swallow the pills. Then I said she must get in bed and try to sleep while I took care of everything.

"I was very careful, Hetheridge. I rolled the body up, first in a sheet, then in a rug from our spare room. When I was sure the street was clear with no one about, I carried the rug with Gregory inside to my car and put it in the backseat. I didn't take my mobile or Cathy's—I left them in the kitchen pantry, so it would seem like we spent the entire night at home. As for Gregory's phone, I extracted it from his hip pocket, broke the ruddy thing, and left it in his room. I wanted to provide the police with a reason he might go off to get high without taking his mobile.

"With Gregory in the back of the car, I started driving,

trying to think of places around London that meant nothing to our family. Spots without a connection to us, even an obscure one. Finally, I hit on Epping Forest. By then it was about three in the morning and I realized if I kept driving about, that in itself would be suspicious. I pulled over in a secluded spot and waited in the car, alone with Gregory's body, until sunrise. It didn't feel strange. It didn't feel like anything. I was used to him being there in a sense, but not there. All I thought about was Cathy.

"Around six in the morning, I found the park rangers' access road and used it to get Gregory into position under a tree. I rolled him around a bit in the grass first, to try and muddy the forensics if any hairs or fibers from home were attached to his body. Then I cleared out. The sheet and rug went into a wheelie-bin along the way.

"As you know, it worked. By the time Gregory was officially discovered, I was on the job and Cathy had somewhat regained her footing. Even between the two of us, I pretended for a time that Gregory didn't die at home—that what I told the police was true, he left the premises to get high and never came back. Cathy pretended, too, during the investigation. I truly believe that pretense saved her sanity. If she'd had to tell detectives, over and over, what she said to Gregory before he took his life, it would've destroyed her."

"I take it she's dealt with the reality now?"

"Yes, and you see the result." Marquand's gaze shifted to the portrait of his wife in her wheelchair. "I can't bear to think of what it would do to her if I'm brought up on a charge of obstruction of justice. Or indeed any of the lesser charges that go along with what I did. The lies I told to cover it up. Even so..." He sighed. "There's a cost to hiding the truth. There's a cost to being suspected and knowing you deserve that distrust. Which is probably why I ranted and raved at Vic Jackson when I heard the case was reopened. And perhaps why I broke down and confessed it all, at long last, to DC Gulls."

"As I mentioned, I don't yet have her notes," Tony said. "But obviously she didn't escalate this new information up the chain of command, and no one has notified CPS. I think she believed, as I believe, that nothing is to be gained by making an example out of you."

"You mean that?"

"Yes. You violated various statutes, of course. If I suspected you or your wife of murdering your son, it would be different. In that case, it would be in the interest of society to pursue what justice we could, even if it only amounted to a charge of abusing a corpse or giving false evidence to authorities. But I don't suspect you or your wife murdered Gregory. I think it happened just as you described. In which case, especially in light of your distinguished record, it's best to let things stand."

"Gulls said the same." Marquand's eyes shone; he blinked them clear. "The other one was all right, too. At pains to assure me he considered Gregory's case closed and this wasn't harassment. He only wanted—"

"The other one?" Tony broke in.

"Yes. Young blond man. Kincaid. He visited me at home Sunday night. When I opened the door to find CID on my front step, it gave me a bit of a turn, I don't mind telling you. But he wasn't after me. He was after something else."

CHAPTER 18

For a moment, Tony forgot to view Marquand as an interviewee; he started to address him as a colleague. Then he remembered himself, clamped down on his excitement, and modulated his breathing. When it came slow and steady, he knew his bland policeman's mask was back in place.

"I'd like to hear about DC Kincaid's visit."

Marquand emitted another humorless laugh. "I imagine you would. I haven't gone witless just now. I know what I say may provide his alibi if he's suspected of killing Gulls. I'm only surprised it took you two days to ask me about it."

"Kincaid didn't mention you when he described his movements."

"No?"

Tony shook his head.

"Well. That surprises me. I mean..." He sighed. "I wish it surprised me. Something's wrong inside the Met. It's upside down. It's obvious—like looking at the skyline and seeing Elizabeth Tower on her head. You sense it, don't you?"

Tony shrugged. "My personal life is complex just at

present. I mean that in the positive sense, of course, but not so long ago it was different. Kate and I were in recovery mode at my farm in Devon. So I'm afraid the time when I experienced the Yard as a sort of phantom limb, not really attached but still transmitting, is long past."

Marquand studied Tony as if weighing his truthfulness. Then he began to report as if on duty, speaking briskly and without the emotion that had colored his description of Gregory's death.

"Cathy and I were having a quiet Sunday night in, as usual, when Kincaid turned up on my doorstep. Cathy was already in bed, reading, and I was downstairs watching telly when he knocked. The time was just after eleven o'clock. I'm certain of that for two reasons—first, because I was up past my usual hour, and second, because I was watching a BT Sport program that airs at eleven.

"I didn't know Kincaid, though I may have dealt with him glancingly in the past, but as I said, the sight of him gave me a turn. He looked like CID. Practically smelled like it, so clean-cut and serious, with waves of responsibility radiating off him. Accompanied by a partner, of course. A tall bloke in the street, hanging back near the corner.

"For a second, I thought Gulls had turned on me. That this was the vanguard of a new nightmare that would destroy my teaching career and do untold damage to my poor wife. I'd like to believe I kept a shred of dignity—that my terror wasn't plain as day as I stood there, gaping at him—but naturally it must have been, because the first thing he did was go out of his way to reassure me. He introduced himself as a close friend of Gulls. From the way he said it, and the little smile he gave, I surmised the connection wasn't just professional.

"Anyway, I wanted to believe him, but I was still rather shaken. I asked about the tall man lurking near the corner.

Kincaid looked a bit sheepish. He said it wasn't a man, or a Met partner, but a woman he'd allowed to tag along. Someone involved in a separate investigation. Apparently he was trying to build trust with her, and she'd called him a liar on certain points, so he let her follow him to prove he was on the level. He promised me she wouldn't be privy to anything we spoke about, unless it happened to somehow touch on her own concerns, which was unlikely. She was just waiting to see if he actually entered my house, or if his presence at my doorstep was a ruse.

"I did let him in, but I was still nervous, so I decided to take control of the conversation and steer it onto steady ground. Rather than let him ask about Gregory, I pretended to expect something else. I said, 'I reckon you want to ask about the Mandy Haystack case. Since I was SIO of the investigation that followed her alleged disappearance.'"

Tony was stunned. Only with effort did he keep his jaw where it belonged, as opposed to the floor. "Remind me how long ago that was?"

"Twenty-one years ago. And two months and some odd days, if you want to be exact," Marquand said. "It was a Toff Squad case before there was one, officially. Back then, when a crime intersected with the rich, titled, or influential, each investigatory team was handpicked on a case-by-case basis. At the time, you were dealing with a stolen da Vinci, weren't you? The *Rothesian Madonna?*"

"That's right."

"And you got it back, didn't you?"

"Yes. Took a couple of months."

"Well, while you did that in the full glare of TV lights and print reporters, I snooped around Parth Chakrabarti's life for about six days, trying to decide if his wife Mandy really left of her own accord. He used to keep her isolated at their mansion, Highgate House, taking care of the children—apart from the maid, the pool boy, the cook, and Parth's personal assistant, Mandy hardly knew anyone. But after she stopped coming to her regular salon to get her hair done, her stylist rang the MPS tip line and said she thought Parth had done his wife in.

"I interviewed the stylist at length. Very *Educating Rita*, if you remember that one—a working class girl who'd bettered herself, got a place in a posh salon, and was always reading to improve her mind. According to the stylist, Mandy was desperately unhappy with Parth, but thought leaving him was out of the question. He'd told her if she divorced him, he'd fix it so she'd never see the children again. The eldest daughter, the one who went out that window not long ago, was under ten at the time. The other two were much younger. According to the hairdresser, Mandy always teared up at the idea of a custody battle. She was convinced that Parth could manipulate the whole thing to his satisfaction.

"I asked the stylist about Tassos Vlachos, the infamous pool boy. Apparently he was quite handsome, popular with the cook and the maid, and not the brightest man who ever lived. That was the only thing the stylist remembered Mandy ever saying about Tassos—that she thought he was stupid. Apparently he tried to overcharge Parth on chlorine tablets, and Parth had words with him. According to Mandy, Parth was so paranoid, he examined every invoice with a fine-tooth comb. To try and blatantly cheat him was the mark of an idiot.

"At any rate, that was all the stylist could tell me about Mandy and Tassos. I asked if Mandy had flirtations or extra-marital love affairs, and the hairdresser said that would be about as smart as tripling the price of chlorine and thinking Parth would pay up. *He* had other women sometimes, especially when traveling out of the country, and made no secret of it. Yet he was always checking up on Mandy, accusing her of adultery, and so on."

"Having met Parth, it's hard for me to imagine him being truly satisfied with any person or situation."

Marquand gave a wry smile. "Then he hasn't changed since I dealt with him all those years ago. Before I ventured into the lion's den, I practically begged the stylist to give me a weapon to take with me. Had she ever seen Mandy with a black eye or her arm in a sling? No, nothing like that. Had she ever witnessed Parth being verbally abusive? No, it was all hearsay—what Mandy confided to her while her high-lights developed. So I asked, when she heard about Mandy running off with Tassos, what made her disbelieve the story? What convinced her to stick her neck out and involve the police?

"She said, 'Two things. First, there was no affair. Second, her kids. If Mandy didn't take her kids, she didn't go.'"

Tony digested that. In missing persons cases, he'd often heard people make similar statements about mums who'd disappeared. Frequently it was true—the seemingly heartless mother who ran away from her kids was eventually found decomposing in a ditch.

"Yet your investigation turned up nothing?"

"No. Not that I had a free hand, or anything like it," Marquand said. "Parth was very much the wronged man, pushed into single fatherhood by a harlot and her toy boy. Mandy's parents were dead and her sister wasn't much of an advocate. Not after Parth paid her a quarter million to be his live-in nanny for the next several months, while he found his footing as a dad. As for Tassos, he'd burned his bridges in Greece and Wales before coming to the UK. He was present illegally, which no one had bothered to notice, and made several enemies since his arrival. Bad debts, broken hearts, that sort of thing.

"I couldn't trace Mandy and Tassos by air to Greece, though Parth insisted that as she packed her bags, she said they were going to Karpathos to live with his mum. These days, not being able to easily trace an air traveler would be a huge red flag. In those..." He shrugged. "It was a different world. People traveled under assumed names for a lark and got away with it. No one took airline security as seriously as we do now. Nor did we have so many high-tech tools at our disposal.

"Anyway, after five or six days, I felt the all-seeing eye upon me, if you get my drift. Michael Deaver called me in—he'd just been made a commander—and broke the news that unless I had persuasive new evidence that CPS would rally behind, the investigation was over. He understood how upset I was—how much it galled me that Parth might have got away with murder. Double murder, no less. After that, I counted Deaver as a friend, and still do." Marquand sighed. "When Gregory's investigation was reopened, I should've gone to him instead of reading Vic the riot act. But Assistant Commissioner Deaver is even busier than Commander Deaver, and I didn't want to add to his woes. You know what a sad old sod he is, or pretends to be."

"I never thought of his general gloom as a put-on," Tony said with a smile. "May I share something with you, off the record?"

Marquand blinked. "Of course."

"I have reason to believe Michael Deaver is the person who triggered the new investigation into your son's death."

"No. Not possible."

"Would you care to hear my reason for saying so?"

"Not until you hear mine for why it couldn't be. Michael already knows the truth."

Tony stared at him. "What?"

"Yes. I confessed to him ages ago, about three days after

the fact. I was so full of guilt and confusion, I was desperate to come clean. I didn't go into nearly as much detail with him as I did with Gulls, or with you just now. He wouldn't allow it. I said Gregory killed himself at home, in his room, and in a sort of dazed panic I moved the body somewhere else. That was as far as I got before he silenced me."

"What did he say?"

"I'll never forget it. He put both hands on my shoulders, looked me straight in the eye, and said, 'You're a damn fine detective. Memory-hole this. Never speak of it to me or anyone else again.' Which is what I did, until the burden became too great."

Tony absorbed that, genuinely at a loss. First, the bombshell that Kincaid had visited Marquand during the time of Amelia Gulls's death. Second, the long-forgotten connection between Marquand and Parth Chakrabarti. Third, negative investigatory findings that suggested Parth might had killed his wife and her purported lover. And fourth, the news that Deaver not only knew the truth about how Gregory Marquand's body ended up in Epping Forest, but that he'd already absolved Leland Marquand of criminal wrongdoing.

What was all that in my office, then? The sighing and head shaking about whether Marquand could be capable of murder?

He could ask Deaver directly, of course. But first he needed Marquand to talk him through the encounter more fully, and see if it carried the ring of truth.

"You told Deaver. Three days, you say, after Gregory was discovered in the forest?"

Marquand nodded.

"How was Cathy at that point?"

"Still in bed. Taking sedatives from her GP and being looked after by her best friend. I still feared for her sanity at that point. But I had to unburden myself to someone in authority, or I thought I'd go mental, too."

"Where did this meeting take place? At the Yard?"

"God, no. I wouldn't have dared. I remember the day quite well. Seventh of June, four years back. A Monday night, still bright outside, so before eight o'clock in the evening. The reason I'm so certain is because of Gregory, of course. Gregory died on a Thursday night, was found on a Friday morning, and by Monday evening I rang Michael's home number. Said I had to see him, because I was going off my head."

"How did he respond?"

"Kindly, of course. With genuine sympathy. He has a difficult relationship with his own boy, you know. Nothing like Gregory's problems, but still—there's a certain grim fellowship between men with problem sons. May you never join us," he added with a mirthless smile. "Said if I came by his home in St. John's Wood, he could give me a quarter hour's moral support."

"How did you get there? To his home in St. John's Wood?"

"I drove our car. I assure you, it really happened. Even if it didn't, and it did, you aren't going to trip me up by getting me to mention a car in one version of the story and the tube in another."

"Old habits." Tony followed it up with another seemingly innocuous question: "Who answered the door?" As a frequent guest at the Deavers' home, he knew that during that particular time period, Monique had employed a slender Yugoslavian maid named Petra. For the last two years, however, Monique's maid was a plump Yorkshire woman called Beth. To name the wrong woman would be an easy mistake to make, and a significant one.

"Michael let me in," Marquand said. "He said it was the staff's night off. No maid, no cook, and his son off at school. Just him and Monique having a sort of date night."

Tony raised his eyebrows. He'd never heard Deaver employ such a phrase in his life.

"I know, it seems out of character for the old cadaver, doesn't it? I can't help but smile now, looking back, though at the time I was so miserable, the happy aura in the Deaver house set my teeth on edge. All the upstairs lights were burning and music was playing—dance music, very upbeat. I could hear Monique laughing in the next room. Michael said she was watching a funny program on telly."

The happy aura, Tony thought. It was ingrained in him not to argue with the interviewee if he could help it, but the story seemed to have veered into fantasyland.

"Where did you have this talk you described? The memory-hole discussion?"

"In the foyer. With the inner doors closed, so Monique could watch her program in the living room without being disturbed. I reckon she never knew I was there."

"Right." Tony struggled to maintain his poker face. "Anything I've neglected? Other details that would render the picture more complete?"

"You sound just like Kincaid. Or rather, he sounds just like you, since he obviously idolizes you. A good egg, Kincaid. Can't imagine him hurting any woman, much less a wee thing like Gulls."

Tony felt it then—not exactly the pricking of his thumbs, but an inner tingle that meant he'd drawn very close to the heart of the case without realizing it.

"You've given me some unexpected information," he admitted. "One detail that stands out is the tall woman lurking on the street when you found Kincaid at your door. You said he was trying to gain her trust, and she had nothing to do with your son's case, but with something else he was working on. Did Kincaid say anything else about her? Anything at all?"

"I don't recall. I was so shaken, I didn't absorb the facts as I usually do. I realize Sunday night wasn't long ago, but I'm struggling to remember precisely what he said. Possibly that she was a government type? Or did he say anti-government type? Someone traumatized by an unsolved murder. She needed extensive courting before she could accept he was acting in good faith."

Could it be Lin Wu Chen's mum? Deputy Director Chen, working secretly—and reluctantly—with Gulls and Kincaid?

"So, allow me to restate what I've heard," he said slowly, gaze never leaving Marquand's face. "You learned the investigation into Gregory was reopened. For four years you've been trying to memory-hole your part in obscuring the full truth about his death, but the news the case was reopened almost sent you over the edge. You went to the Yard and verbally attacked Jackson. He responded by sending someone who was arguably his most personable detective, Amelia Gulls, to see you.

"You were hostile at first, but she won you over. You decided to make a full confession, as you'd intended some years ago. And so you began with your trip to St. John's Wood? The meeting with AC Deaver?"

"No, I started with the day Gregory died, just as I did with you. I didn't want to wantonly bandy Michael's name about, and perhaps force him to deny something. But when she seemed to waver a bit, as if not quite sure she could absorb what I told her without consulting a superior, I told her the whole thing."

"And she told Kincaid."

"Evidently. Maybe it was just pillow talk. A strong argument for why coppers who sleep together should work in different departments," he said, sounding very much like a teacher imparting best practices. "And when he turned up on my doorstep, I tried to distract him with the Chakrabarti angle, since Gulls had found that interesting, too. But no. Kincaid only seemed to care about that meeting between me and Michael. I told him about it twice. Then he thanked me, apologized for the disturbance, went back out into the night. Next morning, I woke up to the news Gulls had been killed." Marquand paused, then asked, "Did he really never mention this as part of his alibi?"

"No."

"Shouldn't you give him a ring and ask?"

"I've been warned off."

"By whom?"

"AC Deaver."

"Oh. Well. In that case, I'm sure there's a reason," Marquand said. "At least now you see it couldn't have been Michael who sent down the order to reopen the investigation."

Except he told me himself that he did. So either this man is lying, or my friend is.

CHAPTER 19

"Wotcha, Katie-Kate?" came the voice over speakerphone.

"Wotcha yourself, Big Daddy." After Evvy's birth, Kate had started calling Paul that, and she enjoyed the sound of it too much to stop. "Done with the Chakrabarti kids?"

"Haven't even started. I turned up in the neighborhood at three o'clock, texted Antonio, and was told under no circumstances to knock on Octavia's door before half-three. On the dot. According to him, she goes to pieces if cops change the rules while the ball's in play."

"Ah, the unforgivable sin of turning up early. She'll go down a treat, I can just feel it. Tony told me how Parth behaved. Are you working yourself into a lather over round two?"

"No, it's raining again, but I don't care. I'm window shopping." He sounded nonchalant. "They may be Parth's spawn, but there's no way even two little ones can equal the original. And even if it does turn out to be another bloodbath, worrying in advance won't help."

"My goodness. Pearls of wisdom." Kate was genuinely

impressed. Many of Paul's longstanding anxieties seemed to be on pause since his daughter's arrival, possibly because he was too knackered to notice them. She hoped he wouldn't begin projecting those fears onto Evvy the way his mum, Sharada, projected hers onto him—or, indeed, how Kate had recently caught herself projecting her own body image woes onto Henry. Maybe it was an inevitable byproduct of parenthood? If so, Kate thought they ought to make a pact; she'd monitor his projections if he monitored hers.

Paul asked, "So how are you feeling?"

"All right. Massive indigestion. It didn't get me yesterday, so it's twice as bad today. Also bored and impatient. I went through all my presents a second time this morning. One of the Hetheridge relatives didn't get the memo and bought me a gorgeous Stokke carry cot. Heather gray with a black and white interior. Very stylish."

"You'll use it."

"Probably not," she sighed. "The special carry cot arrived in the post last week. Etsy is a marvelous place. It's exactly, and I do mean exactly, what I asked for."

"Then why are you whinging?"

"Because I didn't expect anyone to give me a carry cot, and now that I've held the Stokke, I like it better. Oh, well. If I don't use it, I'm sure to get invited to someone's baby shower before long, and I'll regift it."

"Have you heard from Tony? I tried to ring him to see how his talk with Leland Marquand went, but I got the 'Sorry, I'm driving' message."

Kate made a contemptuous noise. "You really think he phones me in the middle of the day to rev me up with juicy details about his murder investigation? I should be so lucky. At most, he'll ring to say he loves me and then quiz me—not very subtly—on whether I'm observing the rules of bedrest.

But I did get a cryptic text from him. He must be onto something, because he reverted to guv mode."

"Saying what?"

"I shall read it aloud for maximum effect." Kate picked up her mobile, cleared her throat, and said in a passable imitation of her husband at his most imperious: "'I trust you are not working, but if you are, drop the Lin Wu Chen matter entirely.'"

"That romantic son of a gun."

"I know. Fortunately, I have my spy working the ground floor, and he provided a bit more information."

"I assume you meaning Henry?"

"Who else? He's always listening. I mean it—the kid doesn't miss a thing. He told me that around two o'clock, Tony rang Mrs. Snell on her mobile. She took the call in the kitchen, so Henry, being Henry, slipped in to eavesdrop. He heard her say she'd consult Mr. Briggs at Blevins-McNeil for an estimate of depth limitations and cost per hour."

She waited for *ooh*s and *ahh*s. They didn't come.

"I see. So who's Blevins-McNeil when it's at home?"

"Come on, Big Daddy! You know." Kate gave him an extra five seconds, then said, "Mobile Underground Surveyors. The GPR people."

"What? Like genetically modified livestock? Frankenfood?"

"That would be GMOs. This is GPR—ground penetrating radar."

"Oh. Well. That's sort of—" He seemed on the verge of saying "boring" when he stopped. "Wait. Are those the people who check for buried power lines or cracked foundations but sometimes turn up King Richard III under a car park?"

"Yes! I'm so excited. You know something's up when Tony has Mrs. Snell doing that kind of legwork."

"It *is* exciting. However, I regret to inform you, you're not supposed to get excited."

"That ship sailed when someone killed Amelia. But I'm sublimating it into the Lin Wu Chen case. Or more accurately, I'm channeling it into an amateur review of Orrin Parker's social media activities."

"Didn't Tony literally just forbid it?"

"He's not the boss of me. Not anymore. And I did say this is purely amateur. No probable cause, no sneaky police tools in use," Kate said, scrolling through Orrin's Twitter feed as she spoke. "Just me, a good citizen, reading the public posts of a potentially not-so-good citizen. I saw something in *Hammer House of Horror* that made me wonder."

"About what?"

"Doppelgängers."

He laughed appreciatively.

"No, I'm serious. Well, kind of. I have to do something, Paul, even if I just make it up. If you had any idea how frustrating it is for me to be—"

"We've been through that," Paul cut across her. "No offense, Kate, but we've been *all* through that. Just wait until bouncing baby Hetheridge arrives. You'll have cause to look back on your days of leisure and lament."

"You're barmy. There's no leisure, even in bed. Just more and more things piling up, undone. Anyway, I reckon if Tony doesn't want me messing about the Chen case, it's because he's checked into the victim's mum and decided she has enough power to cause trouble for us. Either that, or he's planning on paying her a visit, and doesn't want my fingers in the pot."

"And the ground penetrating radar?"

"I haven't the foggiest. I keep trying to relate it to Gulls's building—a way to nail the person who ambushed her in her flat—but it doesn't add up. What do you think?"

"I think I have fifteen minutes of window shopping left, and then it's time to confront the Parth-spawn. I—hang on. Just how, precisely, do you comb through someone's social media looking for a doppelgänger?"

"Oh, I don't know. Really, I'm just snooping," Kate admitted. "From what I've seen so far, Orrin Parker likes porn, *Bright Star* celebrity news, and trolling TV presenters who never dignify his comments with an answer. He doesn't makes any reference to his past relationship with Lin Wu Chen, or the quickie marriage and divorce that came after. And he rarely interacts with anyone he seems likely to know in real life. I found one tweet, to a bloke who goes by @BorntobeMild and has a picture of a koala as his avatar. It says, 'Happy birthday to you is happy birthday to me.' And yes, they do have the same birth date. Could it be a twin?"

"Could it be his other Twitter account? Plenty of people have more than one. What personal details does @BorntobeMild offer?"

"None. But he seems to like porn, *Bright Star* celebrity news, and trolling Paul Hollywood and Jeremy Clarkson."

"It's a boondoggle."

"What's that mean?"

"A snafu."

"As in higgledy-piggledy?"

"Close enough."

"Go back to work," she said, and rang off.

CHAPTER 20

*J*n Paul's experience, when it came to London homes for twenty-somethings to let on their own, completely without family help or any sort of financial assistance, those homes were typically dumps. And of those dumps, there were three varieties.

Variety One: the genuine menace to health and safety. Such places, shoddily insulated, were sweltering in summer and bone chilling in winter. Poor plumbing meant bogs that didn't flush and sinks that were perpetually backed-up; uncontrolled rising damp led to spongy floorboards and black mold. Usually owned by an unscrupulous landlord who lived far away, with rents collected by an unpleasant, if not downright dangerous, enforcer, Variety One dumps were the province of the desperate. As a young copper, Paul had been in and out of them constantly; now, as a member of the Toff Squad, he rarely came near them.

Variety Two: the bearable hovel. These were sometimes examples of genteel poverty. They might be once-gracious buildings, not quite historic, not universally recognized as worthy of preservation, parceled out in flats that squeezed several people into what had been designed as a single-family home. In other cases, the bearable hovel was a slap-dash new-build, already sagging after only a few years, with cheap carpet, peeling paint, and a baked-in sense of ennui. Variety Two dumps differed from Variety One in that the former had functioning locks, adequate heating, barely adequate cooling, and no black mold or unflushable toilets. Their landlords probably still lived elsewhere, and might or might not be unscrupulous; it was an unscrupulous world.

Variety Three: the vortex of neglect. Unlike the dumps that came before, vortices of neglect were mostly down to the inhabitants, who either didn't care how they lived or were too poor, busy, or overwhelmed to make a good showing. Octavia Chakrabarti's small flat above the Ladbrokes, which turned out to be boarded up, belonged to Variety Three.

"Hiya, Scotland Yard," Antonio said cheerfully, opening the door to wave Paul in. "Come through. No sole sanitizers here! Alas, the maid hasn't been in. Sit anywhere you're not afraid to put your bottom. You might have to shift some stuff."

People often made self-conscious cracks about the maid not being in to excuse dirty dishes in the sink, or a string of clean laundry waiting to be pulled off the indoor line. The flat Antonio currently shared with his sister looked as if it hadn't been cleaned or tidied in a year, if ever.

On the windowsill were three scraggly potted plants, each one terminal. A flatscreen TV hung lopsided on the wall, its black cord snaking inelegantly over the chair rail and across the carpet for anyone to trip over. Various posters were pinned up, giving the flat the look of a basement that hosted political meetings:

MAKE ART NOT WAR

RISE RESIST REVOLT: THE GREENS
FEAR IS THE CURRENCY OF CONTROL
WHAT IF I TOLD YOU THEY'RE ALL LYING?

The kitchen stank of sour milk and rubbish that was probably evolving into some new life form. Used crockery, mostly bowls and spoons, had been discarded all along the bar top that divided cooking space from living space. Antonio had answered the door with a bowl and spoon in his hands; following Paul's gaze, he grinned and said, "We're big on muesli, me and my sis. Quick to prepare, quick to eat, minimal cleanup. Well—assuming we ever do." Taking a final bite, he turned up the bowl, drank the milk, and added the dirty crockery to the pile.

"Don't be shy, come through, come through. I'm not my dad. Don't tell me the old man broke you. He loves to get into people's heads. Make then scared of their own shadows."

Paul didn't think it would be wise to tell Antonio that general disgust, as opposed to lingering intimidation, was the reason he hadn't sat down. The living room had a futon, a recliner, and a bean bag, and not one of them looked fit for human occupation. The futon, covered in a stained and ragged blanket, was piled with books, open boxes of snacks, Blu-ray cases, and a laundry basket full of knickers. The fact those knickers were in a basket implied cleanliness, but he didn't want to chance it by coming too close. The recliner seemed to have been rescued from a landfill—its worn brown upholstery had a greasy shine—and the bean bag was clearly a repository for soiled garments. On top of the pile, someone's Calvin Klein cotton stretch trunks occupied pride of place.

"Oh. Sorry. At Dad's place it's all about presentation. Here, we're maybe a little too informal." Antonio crossed to the futon, transferred everything onto the coffee table or floor, then pulled off the blanket and put it back on inside-out. The result was far more inviting.

"Cheers, mate," Paul said, taking a seat.

"There he is. I don't know why I agreed to this," said a harsh female voice. It was Octavia Chakrabarti, entering from the bedroom with a scowl on her face. "If you came here for advice on how to appease my almighty father, you can stand up and walk out. There's no appeasing him, ever. Not unless you can resurrect my sister."

Paul, who'd seen many photos of Valeria Chakrabarti, marveled in the lack of resemblance. In Valeria's face, there'd been a great deal of Mandy Haystack; her bold stare, pursed lips, and high cheekbones. Like her younger sister Octavia, Valeria had been tall, but her figure had been typical clotheshorse: flat chest, narrow hips, long legs. Octavia was bigger than most men both in height and girth; like a man, she carried almost all her extra poundage in her stomach. As for her face, she was pure Parth; anyone who'd met the father would instantly recognize the daughter.

"I'm not here to talk about Mr. Chakrabarti," Paul said, giving her what he hoped was a respectful smile. He didn't dare go for winning; he doubted he had the stuff to win over Octavia. Not unless he tattooed an anarchy symbol on his forehead and joined Feminists Against Censorship.

"I'd like to ask you and your brother some questions. Many will seem familiar. A few may seem beside the point. But if you'll just bear with—"

"Why should we answer anything? Antonio has talked to you at least once, to that miniature girlboss at least twice, and maybe someone else for all I know. As for me I—" She cut that off. "You're not going to do anything about my sister. MPS is just putting on a show, that's obvious. You people excel at profiling and harassing the underclass. At exacerbating violent situations. But not at solving crimes after the fact. Not unless you've already decided who's destined to take the fall. Why haven't you done that yet? Picked someone who lives near Valeria's building to be the killer, I mean. Wasn't there any ex-con or political malcontent in a ten mile radius you could stitch up?"

Paul sighed. In years past, he would've argued with her, or poked fun at her relentless animosity. But despite a night of uninterrupted sleep, it was mid-afternoon and he was already yearning for a nap. A coffee would've been nice, too. But even if Octavia had offered refreshments, he wouldn't have dared to consume them.

"Look, Ms. Chakrabarti. I get how you feel about the police—"

"No, you don't." She was still on her feet, glaring down at him from her impressive height. Antonio put a hand on her forearm.

"Why don't we sit down?"

"How can I? The recliner's cover is in the wash and your dirty underpants are on the bean bag."

"True. I didn't realize you had such high standards. Hang on." Antonio gathered up his discarded clothes, disappeared with them into the bedroom, and returned with a black satin sheet. "Brought it from home. Still smells like lavender." He took a big whiff of the sheet to prove its freshness, then shook it out like a tablecloth and draped it over the recliner. "Take your pick, sis!"

Octavia lowered herself into the bean bag. Given her stature, she looked incongruous in it, like a parent wedged into a preschool-sized chair. Antonio made himself comfortable in the black satin-bedecked recliner.

"All right, let me start over," Paul said, hanging onto his patience with both hands. "I don't know how you feel in your heart about the police, but I know about your pressure groups, some of the protests you've attended, and your arrest record. I—"

"I'm proud of all that."

"I'm sure you are. The thing is, you seem to have certain ideas about me personally that just aren't true. First, I don't care how Darth—sorry, Parth Chakrabarti feels about me. It's—"

Antonio hooted. "Darth Chakrabarti! Haven't heard that since Year 6. It's still true. Though didn't you think he was more like Jabba the Hutt out on the patio?" Putting on a deep alien voice, he boomed, "Bring me Solo and the Wookiee!"

Octavia broke up. Just like that, her hostility crumbled into helpless laughter. "You are so bad," she told her brother, clearly delighted.

Paul chuckled, too. "Yeah. Freudian slip there. I don't like your father, and to be honest, I don't trust him. Early on, I had the wacky theory he killed your sister. I know, I know, he loved her more than life itself. Seems like that was actually true. Still, all I have from the eyewitness who watched Valeria go out the window was a big, tall person. A man who—"

"It's not just men who are big and tall," Octavia put in.

"True." Paul was still have trouble finishing complete sentences without being interrupted, but at least the mood had lightened. "Anyway, my personal feelings about Mr. Chakrabarti aside, I do want to find Valeria's killer. If you doubt that for some reason, let me put it in more personal terms. A friend of mine was ambushed and strangled to death on Sunday night. Maybe you saw it in on telly?"

"Not really a fan of TV news," Antonio said.

"The papers?"

"I'm off mainstream print news at present," Octavia said airily. "Right now it's all about citizen journalism for me."

"Then you don't know DC Amelia Gulls was found dead Monday morning?"

"Oh. Lost one of your own, eh?" Antonio's gaze sharpened. "So that's why you were at Dad's house yesterday."

"Gulls? You don't mean that wee little doll of a detective? The girlboss?" Octavia sounded shocked.

Paul nodded.

"She's dead? Strangled? Oh, for the love of—oh." Octavia pressed a hand to her chest. "Oh, no, how awful."

"Did you become friendly with her?" Paul was surprised by the strength of her reaction.

"What? No. Only—never mind, it's personal." Octavia's mouth twisted like she was fighting back tears. "Poor thing. Nobody deserves that."

"I met with Gulls, too. She was nice enough. How old was she?" Antonio asked.

"Oh—thirty, maybe," Paul said. "Thirty-one at the most."

"Same age as Mum," Antonio said to Octavia.

"Yeah. A sweet nature, too, for all that she chose to be a cop," Octavia agreed. "It's always the ones who don't deserve it that go too young."

Paul paused to be sure he'd heard that right, then asked, "Your mum, Mandy Haystack. I thought she was in Greece. Are you saying she's dead?"

"What do you think, mate?" Antonio gave him a wry smile.

"Of course she's dead," Octavia snapped. "You've been down to the patio right? The place we call the scene of the crime. Couldn't you feel it?" She shook her head. "I swear, sometimes what I take as malevolence is just pure stupidity. A mum supposedly runs off. Days later her husband's ruddy swimming pool is *filled in*..."

She was still talking, but Paul's personal mobile, although

silenced, was ringing. It was currently set to ring through only for two people: Emmeline and Tony.

"One second," he muttered to Octavia, and put the phone to his ear. "Kind of busy, Chief."

"Are you interviewing the Chakrabarti children?"

"Yeah."

"I'm sorry to interrupt, but I have a couple of questions I'd like you to relay."

"All right. Are you still at the Peel Center?"

"No, I finished up there some time ago. Since then I've been checking into various things. Lightning research—the kind that requires calling in old debts. Moreover, I disobeyed AC Deaver and rang Kincaid to ask him some questions."

"You did."

"Yes. He did lie to us yesterday, but perhaps not without cause. What he said was quite illuminating, but unsubstantiated. I'd very much like to know if he's being honest or still lying. You can help me decide."

"How?"

"By asking the Chakrabarti children two questions."

Paul listened as Tony framed his queries. One was for Antonio and Octavia. The other was for Octavia alone.

"Sorry about that," Paul said, slipping the mobile back into his pocket. He took a deep breath. "That was my colleague, Tony Hetheridge. He was there with me and your father, on top of the white cement patio, at Highgate House yesterday. Since then he's been poking into another case Gulls was working on when she died. It's possible she uncovered a crucial bit of evidence and was killed for it."

Octavia opened her mouth to speak, but Paul held up a hand. "This is important. Tony has two questions. The first is for both of you. In your opinion, is ground penetrating radar likely to uncover the bodies of Mandy Haystack and Tassos Vlachos inside the filled-in pool?"

"Yes," Octavia cried as if she'd been waiting all her life for someone to ask.

Antonio popped the recliner's lever, a move which instantly rendered him sitting upright. "Take care. He'll never let you do it, mate. He'll have your job. He'll have your bosses' jobs. He'll ring Boris and Rishi and Gordon and they'll make your life a living hell because their big, bad donor tells them to. If we thought anyone could get away with jackhammering that patio, we'd have done it already. But Dad always wins. He does. And fighting a losing battle won't bring Mum back."

"It's true," Octavia said miserably. "I wish it wasn't, but it's true."

"We'll work that out later," Paul said. "I can't promise you anything except this—if Tony thinks there's probable cause, he'll find a way. If he doesn't, at least we entertained the idea, and didn't let Parth scare us into not even daring to say it out loud. Here's my second question. It's for you, Octavia." He paused again, not fully understanding what he was about to ask, but hoping her answer, should she choose to give one, would shed some light at last.

"Why did you insist on accompanying DC Kincaid to the house of Leland Marquand last Sunday night?"

CHAPTER 21

Octavia smiled a little, dropping her gaze self-consciously. Though she wasn't anywhere close to Paul's notion of an attractive woman, the gesture softened her features. It was almost endearing.

"That's easy. Lack of trust."

"You didn't trust him?"

"I didn't trust myself. My reaction to him," Octavia said. "At first, I wasn't very helpful with Gulls. If I'd known what was going to happen to her, I would've been nicer. But the police rub me the wrong way. I've always thought they exist to serve people like my father. My mum, Tassos, all the powerless people...they don't matter."

She paused, then continued, "I wasn't only being provocative, you know. When I said I was surprised Scotland Yard didn't just put names in a hat, pull one out, and announce, 'Person X killed Valeria Chakrabarti.' Because my father matters and he must be served. I'm sure no one cares about Valeria. She was just another woman. A kept woman. Living by the rules of the patriarchy—marching in step with it.

Selling pictures of her pretty face and body. Selling the rest of her, too."

"We all do things we're not proud of," Antonio said.

"True. Maybe if I'd been the beautiful one, I'd be doing the same." Octavia shrugged. "Anyway, Gulls kept coming round, and I warmed up a little, but still I kept my guard up. I could've told her that we know Mum's under the patio, that we can feel her there, but what would she do about it? Like Antonio said, it's hard to even imagine going against Dad."

"I understand he sends you both an allowance," Paul said neutrally.

"In my case, to stay away when I'm not wanted," Antonio said, and laughed.

"I don't know why he sends me money. I give it away," Octavia said. "Parth Chakrabarti has been supporting all the fiercest social justice groups in the UK for years and has no idea, because it's all done in my name."

"So you, at least, would be willing to risk being cut off financially," Paul said.

"Sure. But if I really angered him, he'd destroy me. At the least, he'd ruin my life. Get me evicted, have the police run me out of London, all that stuff. At worst, he'd actually kill me, like he killed Mum. I think after you take one woman out of the world, removing the next one comes easier.

"Anyway, in the course of talking to Gulls about Valeria, we made what she thought was progress, and she wanted more from me, and I got cold feet. Ghosted her. So she sent Sean—DC Kincaid—to talk to me. The moment I saw him, I thought she'd reached right into my heart and pulled out my type." Octavia winced. "I don't mean to say I fancied him—"

"You totally fancied him," her brother put in.

"Maybe I would've, only he told me he was dating Gulls. Helping her with a tricky situation."

Paul asked, "Tricky? How so?"

"Tricky enough not to give me real specifics," she said with a laugh. "All I know about it is, Gulls interviewed an ex-copper, Marquand he was called, and that geezer told her something that absolutely couldn't be true. She checked and rechecked and proved it was impossible. It started her down a different road—Sean called it a "funny road." But I knew he didn't mean funny. He meant dangerous.

"Anyway, Sean met me late for a coffee Sunday night. He'd just been to Kentish Town Station on a fool's errand and said he was trying to decide whether or not to bother Marquand at home."

"Was he dreamy?" Antonio asked.

"Shut it. And yes, he was very charming. I felt like a teenager. I had to keep reminding myself he was the enemy. He wanted Valeria's entire history again: how many boyfriends she'd had, what sort of men she dated. He knew Dad was mental to call her a virgin. She wasn't. She liked men—older, powerful men."

"Counterpoint: Ken Hussy. Not much older and about as powerful as a jock strap," Antonio said.

"Oh, that was just Valeria acting out. She and Mr. Top Secret were on the outs at the time. She punished him with secret hookups. Said he was the jealous type, so whenever she and Ken locked themselves in a bathroom to do the deed, she could hardly keep from laughing. She loved picturing how angry Mr. Top Secret would be if he ever found out."

"I take it Mr. Top Secret is the man who paid for Valeria's flat?"

"Her flat. Her upkeep. Her entire life."

"A married man?"

"Of course. They're always the most possessive. The most crazy-jealous."

"Did you know his real name? Or was he just Mr. Top Secret to you?"

"She wouldn't ever say his name," Octavia said. "In the beginning they were looser. Then it turned serious, and before you knew it, she wasn't even living with Mickey Post-Hewitt anymore, just pretending he was her flatmate. It was all very hush-hush. She forgot that I'd seen him once. In the early days, at Maxim's."

"Maxim's? Is that a person? No—you mean Maxim's Casino, don't you?" Paul asked, naming a posh gaming house in South Kensington.

Octavia nodded. "This was a few years ago. Dad's a member, and he can do whatever he likes, so when I was fifteen, he took me there to see a magician who was doing a command performance in one of the private rooms. That may be the one and only time in my life I wore a party dress and tights," she added with a grin. "During intermission, I went in search of the loo. I passed through the main gaming room and saw Valeria sitting at a table. She was the only woman in a sea of men. They were all sort of interchangeable in evening dress. She stood out. She looked so perfect and beautiful in her red dress, with her hair falling over her shoulder." Her smile was sad. "I was always jealous of my sister's looks, but I was proud of them, too. I took her picture."

"With your phone?"

"No, this was so long ago, I took it with a camera. One of those retro instant things—point, shoot, shake, and *voilà*. A photograph."

"If you hadn't been a little girl in a party dress, they would've booted you for disrupting the tables," Antonio said. "Maxim's has standards, you know."

"No one cared. Valeria just laughed. Later that night she pointed at one of the men in the picture and said he was her boyfriend, and his name was top secret."

Paul sat up straight. "I'd like to see that photo, please."

"That's what Gulls said. So I showed her. But she couldn't be sure of recognizing any of the men. She wanted to take the picture, or at least take a scan of it with her phone, but I got cold feet. That's when I started ghosting her."

"But why?" Paul asked.

"Because I don't help cops," she shot back, astonished that he would even ask. "I'd already told her a load of family secrets. I more than met her halfway. I dragged out a picture of Valeria at her most beautiful. And Gulls was like, I don't know, I'm not sure, I'll need a copy and a sworn statement, and I pumped the brakes."

"I guess that makes sense."

"Sean said the same thing over coffee Sunday night. Charmingly. That's when I started distrusting myself again," Octavia said. "I thought, what do I even know about this man, except that he chose to work for one of the most corrupt, abusive, tainted organizations on the face of the earth—"

"No offense," Antonio put in cheerfully.

"Plus I thought of what my friends would say. They'd think I'd lost my mind. That's my motto." She pointed to something behind Paul's head.

He turned. The slogan on the poster read,

NEVER NEVER NEVER TALK TO THE POLICE

"So I decided to put Sean on the spot," Octavia said. "I asked how he knew that Gulls was really on to something. He said she'd fact-checked part of the interview and confirmed it wasn't true. I said, what if she misunderstood? What if it was all a mix-up and they both got into trouble for getting it really, really wrong?

"*That* hit a nerve," Octavia said with some satisfaction. "He said yes, he was treading on rotten ice, but he'd taken the precaution of quote-unquote forgetting his mobiles so no one could trace his movements. That probably should've been proof enough for me, but I'm stubborn and pushed for more. Finally Sean said that even though it was getting late, he could go by Marquand's house and revisit the story Marquand told Gulls to make sure there was no misunderstanding. I tagged along. Stood in the street and watched him go in. It all seemed legit, so when he came out, I said he could come round the next night and collect the photo. But he didn't."

"Yeah. He's been temporarily transferred to a different unit while we investigate Gulls's murder. Why didn't you just give him the photo that night?"

"Because I didn't have it on me. And it's not here," she added, puncturing his hopes with a cruelly sharp needle. "It's in a safe deposit box with a few of my treasures. When you get banged up and harassed as much as I do, you don't take chances. My old flat was raided twice. This one could be, too."

"Not if you stop bringing home fugitives," Antonio said.

"'Fugitive' is an overly broad term." Octavia looked at Paul. "That's it. Did you expect more? I'd think my poor mum with a swimming pool for a grave would be enough for anybody."

"Did Valeria agree with you about that? That your father killed your mother?" Paul asked.

Octavia and Antonio exchanged a glance.

"When you're the favorite..." Antonio began.

"It's hard to see the truth," Octavia finished. "If she'd been on our side, we might have been able to go to the police together and *make* them jackhammer that patio. But she wasn't on our side. She was off playing lady-love to Mr. Top Secret. And he's probably the bastard that killed her. Especially if he found out about her little hookup habit."

"Do you think Ken Hussy was Valeria's only, erm, outlet?" Paul asked.

Antonio laughed.

"Not even close," Octavia said.

Paul's silenced phone rang again. He jumped a little—the thought always shot through his brain that it was Emmeline calling to say something terrible had happened to Evvy—but the screen bore Tony's name. Relaxing, he put the phone to his ear and said, "Question one: yes. Question two: because she was assessing his trustworthiness. Octavia happens to be in possession of a photograph that may answer an important question about Valeria."

"Paul." Tony sounded grave.

"What? It's a total success. Aren't you..." He tailed off, slightly unnerved. "Aren't you calling to hear the answers?"

"No. Something terrible has happened."

"What? It's not Kate, is it?"

"Nothing like that," Tony said quickly. He took an audible breath. "Paul, I need you to prepare yourself. I'm sorry to be the one to tell you. We've lost someone else."

His heart leapt into his throat, and for a frozen second he was aware of absolutely everything around him: Antonio's curious half-smile, Octavia's suspicious gaze, the sour milk smell, rain pattering against the window.

"Tony. Please don't say it's Kincaid."

"No." Another pause. "Vic Jackson left the Yard around noon and told Joy he'd be back in the afternoon. Not long ago he was found lying dead on the pavement by St. Edmund's Street."

"What? Vic?"

"Yes."

"Dead?"

"Yes."

Paul said the first thing that came into his head, though it was a stupid question, and one he knew the answer to, at least when in his right mind. "Where's St. Edmund's Street?"

"Near Primrose Hill."

"Did he have a heart attack?"

"No. He was shot in the back of the head. Execution style."

Paul heard himself make a kind of exclamation, not a shout, but definitely a loud noise from his diaphragm. Antonio and Octavia were becoming visibly alarmed, so he forced himself to tell them, "Another dead cop." Then he rose and exited the flat, taking his mobile onto the stairs so he could hear the rest in relative privacy.

"Someone killed Vic Jackson in the street?"

"Not on the street. There was no blood at the scene. He was killed elsewhere, taken to St. Edmund's Street and dumped. It's a quiet stretch, no shops, not much foot traffic during the workday."

"What's the AC doing about it? Who does he have on the scene?"

"DAC Pelham's in charge. And he's called in Box 500. Things are upside down, Paul. There's a forensics team in Jackson's office and another one in his house. The Yard itself is practically in lockdown. I don't have the credentials to find out the things I need to know. I'll need your help with that."

"Of course," Paul muttered numbly. "So—you're saying he left the Yard around noon, told Joy to expect him back, but he never returned and some citizen found him dead on St. Edmund's Street?"

"Yes. It happened around three o'clock, but identification took time because Vic's wallet, watch, and mobiles were missing. The medical examiner thought he looked familiar and queried some colleagues. One of them recognized Vic's face."

"I feel like I'm dreaming."

"Then wake up," Tony said brutally. "Your life is in danger. Even Emmeline may be in danger, insane as it sounds. I have a hunch what's going on, but whether I'm right or wrong, precautions must be taken. You mentioned a photo that might answer questions. You mean the one Kincaid was after?"

"Yes."

"I need it. Get your hands on it however you can and text me the image at once. But first, ring Emmeline. Tell her to lock the door and admit no one but me or you."

"For God's sake, if you have a hunch, tell me," Paul demanded, and Tony did.

*a*s Tony entered the master bedroom, Kate said, "Well. I don't believe it. You're home right on time for once."

"Yes, well, only to check in and see that you're obeying doctor's orders." He smiled at her, willing himself perfectly calm, unassailably normal. As he'd sat in his parked SUV outside the tall iron gates, waiting for Henry to send him that day's randomly generated passcode, a text had arrived from Paul. It showed a lovely young woman, Valeria Chakrabarti, seated at a gaming table with four smartly dressed older men. Three were strangers to Tony. The fourth was not.

"Which movie is this?" he asked, making a point of glancing toward the screen as if he cared, or could spare the lurid images even a thought.

"*The Creeping Flesh*. When they put the word creeping in the title, it was a hint," Kate said.

Entering the deep walk-in closet and eyeing a row of boxes on the top shelf, he asked, "How was lunch?"

"Not great. I woke up with reflux. Brekkie didn't settle. I

forced myself to eat half a sandwich and some soup, but it's weighing on me like a ball of lead."

He removed the lid from the first box, checked the contents, replaced the box and tried the next. Pleased at his still-reliable memory—years ago he'd packed away the item he sought, yet recalled its location almost precisely—he called, "I'm glad you're not skipping meals. How was Henry's day at school?"

"Don't shout," Kate said from behind him, and he jumped.

"What are you doing up?"

"I'm allowed to get up for the loo, thank God. What are you rummaging around up there for?"

"Oh. My, erm, knee is a bit wobbly. You mentioned that brace. I thought perhaps I might give it a go."

"Well, I suppose you could wrap your shoulder holster around your leg in a pinch, but I doubt it would be very comfortable." She smiled at the black leather contraption. "I didn't know you had one."

"Doesn't every copper?" He placed it carelessly on a shelf, as if intending to put it back in the box.

"I'd rather fancy seeing you wear it." She gave him a wicked smile. "After Nipper comes, of course. I'm not feeling very seductive just at the moment. Can you believe it—I had a bit of an accident earlier. Wet the bed. Don't tell anyone. I almost cried, I was so mortified." As she spoke, she waddled toward the bathroom. Tony watched her go, wondering if he should take the opportunity to slip out of the room with the shoulder holster in hand. But he couldn't leave without a proper goodbye.

"Kate." Following her into the bathroom, he took her by the shoulders and turned her around. Cupping her face in his hands, he kissed her on the mouth, long and hard. Kate was the first to break away—pleased, astonished, and more than a little pained.

"Tony, I've got to *go!*"

"Sorry, love. I'm off to meet Paul and chew over the case. Not sure when I'll be back. If someone comes looking for me, tell them to bugger off. I mean it, no guests tonight. Keep the locks in place and the alarms on."

"Fine by me. The last thing I want tonight is company."

"Good. I love you," he said, a touch more emphatically than intended. Then he left her to relieve herself, picking up the shoulder holster on his way downstairs to get his gun.

CHAPTER 23

*B*y a quarter to seven it was raining steadily. Tony, who'd left his SUV parked two streets away from his target, was thoroughly wet when he reached the house in St. John's Wood. Passing through the little gate on the property's east side, he could've gone directly to the elegant terrace, which he knew well from Monique's summer garden parties. Instead, he cut through the raised herb beds, leaving deep prints in the soil with every step. The grand French doors that opened onto the terrace weren't the house's only rear entrance; there was also a back door, used by the staff, that opened onto a boot room.

He tried the door, found it locked as expected, and withdrew a small leather pouch from his coat. It contained three tools: a trip wire, a specially ground hex key, and a bump key. The latter item was all he needed to get him out of the rain and into the Deavers' house.

The boot room had that cheerful shabbiness common to the informal spaces of stylish homes. Macs, cardigans, and towels hung from pegs; beneath them was an unpretentious assortment of battered family footwear. After wiping his mud-caked shoes on the boot scraper, Tony tested the soles of his wingtips on the tile floor, assuring himself they wouldn't slide. Inside the brace, his left knee felt steady as a rock, despite the ripple of nerves in his belly. He hadn't lied to Kate about giving it a go. He might die in the next few minutes, but he damn sure wouldn't fall down in front of an enemy because a joint failed him.

As he rubbed his hair dry with one of the towels, his mobile vibrated. Pulling it from his pocket, he checked the message, sent a one-word reply, and tucked the phone away again. Removing his Glock 26 from the shoulder holster for another once-over was tempting, but he resisted. He'd checked it in the SUV before setting off. Another check now would only be stalling.

The boot room opened onto the kitchen, which as he had surmised turned out to be empty. No plump Beth from Yorkshire at the cooker tonight, and doubtless no Monique watching telly downstairs. If Deaver had asked Vic Jackson to drop by at noon for an impromptu meeting, he'd surely done so with deadly intent. That meant getting his wife off the premises and sending the maid home early so he could shoot Jackson, clean up the mess, cram the body into a vehicle, and drive it away to be dumped.

At the door which led to a hall connecting the kitchen to the rest of the ground floor, Tony paused to listen carefully. No voices or sounds of movement. Satisfied, he eased open the door with his shoulder and risked a look. The hall, brightly-lit by wall sconces, was empty from end to end. On the wall hung a large, gilt-edged mirror over a credenza with a vase of dried flowers. The mirror reflected part of the living room, but not all of it. No one was visible in the glass. Nor did Tony see anything out of the ordinary. Just a plush sofa, part of the coffee table, and a bit of the room's centerpiece, a grand piano.

Reminding himself to take slow breaths, Tony edged closer to the opening between hall and living room. One step. Two steps. He was poised for a third when a note sounded on the piano. Middle C.

Biting the inside of his cheek, he eased the Glock from his shoulder holster and held it in the high compressed ready position.

Another C note, followed by a two-octave arpeggio. Not really music—finger warm-ups.

At least I know where his hands are.

Music was one of the things he'd once had in common with Michael Deaver. They'd both had lessons in their youth, and both played rather better than average, though Tony had abandoned the practice for lack of time. He'd always assumed it was the same for Deaver; that he kept the big black piano chiefly because Monique liked the way it looked.

How many other wrong assumptions have I made?

With the gun still in position but pointing slightly down, Tony stepped into the living room as the arpeggio gave way to scales. Shielded by the grand piano's raised lid, he made it to the instrument and was approaching the bench from the left when Deaver's head jerked up.

"Oh! Gave me a turn." He blinked at Tony as if trying to decide if he was an apparition. "This house is a morgue when it's just me. Keep seeing things out of the corner of my eye. Are you really there?"

"Yes," Tony said.

Lifting both hands from the keyboard—he had long fingers and an enormous reach—Deaver said, "You don't have to point that thing at me, you know. I got rid of my gun. Took it apart after I did Jackson. Chucked the parts in various bins. And a sewer."

"That was wise." Tony lowered the gun only a fraction. His arms and shoulders already ached with the tension of holding a ready position, but he didn't think his body would've allowed him to put the weapon away, even if he wanted to. "But ringing Vic and luring him here? Not wise. Sheer desperation. Was it because he'd read Gulls's reports and knew what she knew? Or because you commanded IT to hold back the data and Vic was demanding to know why?"

"The latter. I was within the scope of my authority, you know." A hint of a slur, as well as the glass of whiskey sitting atop the piano, suggested that Deaver had had quite a lot to drink. "Vic's authority as SIO came from me. I could choose to withdraw it at any time, and I did. I told him I'd hand-picked a man from MI5, highly regarded, and the rest of the investigation would be done under his direction."

"I don't imagine Vic liked that."

"No. He wouldn't be quiet about it. See, Tony—I'm putting my left hand on my thigh," Deaver announced in the same slurring voice. "And now I'm gently, *gently* using my right hand to pick up my drink. See? Don't pull the trigger, old man, there's a good fellow." He had a sip, then set the cut crystal glass down again. "Be terrible if you shot me full of holes because I went for my drink," he added with a smile.

"Haven't seen you smile like that in some time," Tony said. Now that they were face to face, his nerves had evaporated and a glacial calm had settled over him. If he felt anything, he couldn't name it. He was empty of everything but purpose. "Except in that photo of you at the gaming table with Valeria Chakrabarti. You looked so much younger and happier, you were almost unrecognizable."

Deaver seemed to ignore that. "I know what people say about me. Mr. Gloom. Captain Kill Yourself. Even at school, the other boys used to tease me about it. But pessimism was my shield, and Monique's never seen any other side to me. Only she did. Valeria." He studied Tony with something like admiration—the exhausted admiration of a man who knows he's beaten and can't help but grudgingly cheer for his adversary. "How did you unravel it?"

"First, the way Gulls was murdered. It suggested a killer well-versed in criminal investigations. Kincaid was the perfect suspect, naturally, but I simply couldn't believe it of him. We started looking into Gulls's final caseload. As I told you last night, when we talked to Antonio, we found out about Ken Hussy. How despite her long-standing secret relationship with you, she liked to meet Ken in bathrooms for a bit on the side."

Deaver's eyes flashed. "Slut."

"Ken, or Valeria?"

"Both. But he owed me nothing, so I don't care about him. Valeria—I bought and paid for her a hundred times over. Every part of her was mine by right."

"If you felt that strongly, why all the creeping about? Why not divorce Monique and marry her?"

Deaver again went through the exaggeratedly slow process of retrieving his drink. This time he finished off the whiskey, though he held onto the glass, gripping it tight.

"Tony. My God, Tony, you're such a fool. Why would I destroy a marriage that's done so much for my standing? I told you, Monique is like a fine quartz timepiece—no noise, no winding required. Of course, she'd castrate me if I humiliated her. But a private love affair?" He chuckled. "Not everyone lives by your code of conduct. You would've destroyed Marquand for moving his son's corpse to Epping Forest and then lying about it, isn't that right? You would ruin a man and his wife without a second thought, just to satisfy yourself that the great Lord Hetheridge enforces the law without fear or favor. You should've heard yourself the other night. So pompous. So unbearably self-righteous."

"Perhaps. You might as well know, after hearing Marquand's story, I believed him. If he'd come to my home a few days into the investigation, determined to take his punishment, and if I'd been in your role, I, too, would've given him absolution. But in my case, if he'd heard an unseen woman laughing merrily in the next room, it would have been my wife. Not Valeria Chakrabarti enjoying the run of the place because the real mistress of the house was away."

Deaver stared at him. "No. Not that. It couldn't be. That's the thread you pulled? Since the night I killed Valeria—since I threw that slut out a window for betraying me—I thought I'd swept up every crumb. Put out every fire."

"Handled things, you mean," Tony said pointedly, with rising disgust.

"Yes. I got Pollack from Queen's Scientific to process the scene. Every fingerprint, every hair, every bit of DNA from me was destroyed by him personally. The lab listed it as a contamination accident. For a while I was afraid Parth would find out somehow and raise Cain, but he never did."

"What about how you disappeared from the scene?"

"It wasn't hard. A friend requisitioned the CCTV camera films. Only one neighbor saw someone of my description leave the building, but I sent the same friend to talk with the witness and he recanted."

"Did he come cheap?"

"Five hundred pounds. I call it a bargain. It was all going well, despite Parth's constant agitation, until Gulls put her nose in. The next thing I knew, she'd written a memo to herself marked private that said something like, 'I have reason to believe a senior, decorated officer was involved in the murder of Valeria Chakrabarti and I shall proceed appropriately.'"

"Did you access that from the MPS servers?"

"Of course. Phil Gimble in IT always provides whatever I need. I pulled his fat from the fire once. And damn it, Tony, overseeing her work product was completely within my purview," he slurred, trying to take the high ground. "Documents created on Met-issued devices aren't private, whether you mark them confidential or not. And nothing stored on an MPS server is beyond leadership's reach."

Tony again bit the inside of his cheek. The idea he was emotionless, entirely possessed by his task, had gone, replaced by a blackening rage. Hearing the man he'd once called a friend justify his actions on a technicality, yet show no remorse for three coldblooded murders, was almost more than he could bear.

"But really, you're telling me it was Marquand's story that tipped Gulls off? How?" Deaver demanded.

"Because she was a damn good detective." Tony's voice echoed within the expansive living room. As if in response, the rain outside came down harder, battering the tall French doors. Beyond the terrace, the backyard was sunk in darkness. Tony knew the sun hadn't set long ago, but outside it looked like midnight.

He continued, "Gulls didn't blindly accept what Marquand told her. She fact-checked the details. And as it turns out, Monique was on a week-long health retreat in East Sussex. Which meant either he lied about confessing to you, or you lied to him about the identity of the woman in the next room."

"Why didn't she come to me about it? Ask me, instead of writing that blasted memo?"

"Because around the same time, she was working on Octavia Chakrabarti, who had an old photograph of you and Valeria together—"

"Impossible. I don't believe it."

"—taken at a gaming table when Valeria was twenty and you were about fifty. Your hair was still dark then, and you looked rather carefree, so Gulls couldn't be certain it was you. Because she was careful, and understood that to accuse a man in your position without hard evidence would end her career, she turned to Sean Kincaid for help."

"But don't you see how provoking that was? She'd written that strange memo to herself, leaving out everything except the unnamed suspect and the fact Kincaid was helping..." Deaver looked at him imploringly. "Is it possible you have no sympathy for me? None?"

"Why did you arrange to have the Marquand case reopened? Simply to wean Vic's team off Valeria's case?"

"Yes. A shiny object with some actual guilt, no matter how minor, for them to discover."

"And the tip about Kentish Town Police station. The call that kept Sean busy and away from Amelia's flat during the crucial time. That was you, I presume?"

"Of course it was. I didn't dare hire a professional, or even another cop who'd break the rules to help me out. Not for a young woman like Gulls—photogenic, small in stature, sure to trigger all the usual media sob stories. No matter how much I trusted the man who did it, he might later decide to blackmail me. I'd be at his mercy for the rest of my life. To safely handle her, I had to get rid of her myself."

Handle her, Tony thought bitterly, drawing on depths of self-control he never knew he had. The gun wasn't just in his hand, it was a part of him, ready to fire.

"And you sent your friend Pollack's team to handle forensics for Gulls, just like Valeria. He won't have cause to thank you for the patronage when I'm through with him. Accessory after the fact times two. Two that I know about. Heaven knows how many other cases he compromised with made-to-order lab data. Did he work on the Kimberly Urquhart case? If he did, we'll soon find out."

"Self-righteousness again. You ought to get on your knees and thank God for Pollack," Deaver shot back with sudden savagery. "Sometimes we need a little magic from the lab.

The courts are stacked against us. Juries have been trained to expect airtight DNA evidence every time, or they acquit. There's nothing worse than watching someone you nailed get off. All because a jury held out for absolute scientific evidence, when a perfectly good circumstantial case was laid at their feet."

"That sounds like the man I once knew," Tony said coolly. "When Marquand told me about his son's overdose, he said something that rang true. He said his child died years before, during his struggle with addiction, and only his body went on. When did you die, Michael?"

Deaver stared at him silently for so long, Tony thought he wouldn't answer. Then he said: "When I killed her. Valeria."

Tony waited.

"I'd toyed with the notion for weeks," Deaver said after another lingering pause. "Even when things were good, I'd look at those casement windows and fantasize about chucking her out. I was always suspicious of her. Jealous when she flirted too much, or wore provocative clothes out on the town. To put my mind at rest, I hired a private detective. I thought he'd come back empty-handed. But he brought pictures. Terrible pictures.

"The night I confronted her, she laughed at me. Said if I wanted to truly possess her, I should ante up. Put a diamond ring on her finger and be done with it. Instead I picked her up and threw her out the window. And died," he added almost as an afterthought.

"You're going to wish you had. You must realize I didn't come here alone," Tony said. "Paul Bhar texted me not long ago, from inside your garage. After he discovered the blood-stained tarp in your Jaguar's boot, he called in MO19. I imagine they have us surrounded, though with all these interior lights burning, they can't be seen. You'll be going with them. Marching out of this house and into infamy."

The blood drained from Deaver's face. He still sat just as he'd been when Tony surprised him: on the piano bench with his legs forward and his torso swiveled, the sheet music propped on the rack in an untidy pile. He still held his empty whiskey glass, his big hands tightening around it as he absorbed his situation. Imagining those long fingers wrapping a cord around Amelia Gulls's throat, it was all Tony could do not to aim the gun and pull the trigger.

"It will be an ugly spectacle," he said. "The ugliest in the Met's history. Just think—had you allowed Gulls's investigation to play out, you would've had your day in court, and maybe got off. Most people would've given you the benefit of the doubt, and as you mentioned, Pollack eliminated all the forensic evidence. Now you're a confessed triple murderer, and two of them were cops. Maybe you won't destroy the institution, Michael, but God knows you did your level best."

Deaver's lip curled. "That pleases you, does it? And for what? For what will I be sacrificed? Valeria was a tart. Gulls was a nothing, a nobody, in over her head. And Jackson—come on, Tony, he was an embarrassment. No one will miss him. Put them all together and I'm still worth ten of them. And the Met, everything it stands for, is worth ten of me."

"Stand up, Michael. We've talked enough. It's time to walk to the front door."

Deaver didn't move. His hands still clutched the glass. "You and Paul, eh? You think your word alone can convict me? I'll say you two conspired against me. Came here together, planted evidence in my garage, then called in the lads with guns. A bloody tarp. That's all you have? Please!"

"Jackson's watch, wallet, and mobiles were wrapped in that tarp. Why didn't you get rid of them? Like you got rid of your gun?"

"Because I didn't. I didn't get rid of it!" Exploding up from the bench, Deaver hurled the cut crystal glass in Tony's direction. When it shattered against the marble tiles, shards flew up, but without sound. All Tony heard was a series of booms, loud as the unmaking of the world. Three all-encompassing sounds that bled into each other, *boom-boom-boom.* Then sheet music was fluttering around the grand piano, the pistol once hidden beneath the music was on the floor, and Assistant Commissioner Michael Deaver was on his face at Tony's feet.

* * *

"I DIDN'T ATTEMPT to render aid," Tony muttered. He was sitting on the piano bench, and had been for what seemed like forever. His neck and shoulders ached and his head pounded. The first specialist inside the house had apologized when confiscating his gun, but Tony had felt only relief when the young man gently pried it from his grip. Once it was gone, he never wanted to touch that particular weapon again.

"Sorry, say again?" Paul's face loomed over him, sympathetic. Unable to sit still, he'd been pacing near the piano, making a little circuit to the French doors and back. Outside, it was raining even harder, drops rattling against the glass, and the firearm specialists had tracked mud and rainwater into the house. Monique Deaver and Beth from Yorkshire would have their hands full with the clean-up.

"My ears are still ringing," Tony told Paul. "I'm trying not to shout. I said I didn't attempt to render aid."

"It's all right, I did. He was dead. Three shots, all center mass."

"Who's in charge?"

"Everybody. An entire clown car of coppers just unloaded out front. Plus MI5 and maybe almighty MI6, assuming they exist. My vote's for existence. Movies don't lie." Paul hesitated, then said more gently, "Can I step away from you for just a minute? Only I need to ring Em. It's been three hours since I gave her the lockdown warning, and she was scared out of her socks."

"Sorry about that. She was probably in no danger. I over-reacted to the threat. When I realized Michael killed Vic, he seemed no better than a mad dog to me. I thought he might do anything, anything at all, just to give himself a bit more time."

"You didn't overreact. Good God, Tony. He tried to kill you." Biting his lip, Paul seemed to argue silently with himself. Then he reached for something on the coffee table and offered it shyly.

"A tissue?"

"Yeah. Take it. You're crying."

"Oh." Tony blotted his eyes. Apparently the salt he'd been tasting was tears. "So I am. I keeping thinking about her. DC Gulls. Amelia. Such a good detective doing brilliant work. And being strangled for it." There was more to say, but his voice failed. Paul, looking as if he might weep himself, leaned down to awkwardly pat him on the shoulder.

"Right. I'm dashing away, just for half a sec, to ring Em. Five minutes tops, then I'll be back. Hang in there."

Tony was barely aware of Paul leaving. As for how long he was gone, he had no inkling. The passage of time seemed as distorted as his post-gunshot hearing. It seemed that one minute Paul was gone, and the next he was there again, grin-ning incongruously and bouncing on the balls of his feet.

"So." Dark eyes bulging, Paul stared hard at him as if expecting a reply.

Tony rubbed his left ear, which seemed to have borne the brunt of the report. Digging deep inside himself for any remaining patience, he said, "I take it Emmeline is pleased you're unhurt."

"Oh, sure. She's texted me a hundred times. I had to

explain the specialist took our mobiles and haven't given them back yet. The scene manager laughed in my face when I asked. But she let me ring Em using Deaver's landline. You should've heard Em at first. Hell of a reception I got for being alive. Nothing but shouting. Then she switched directions, said she loved me and she was going straight to my mum's to drop off Evvy. Then on to St. Thomas's Hospital. Even if she missed the main event, she wanted to give moral support." Another flashing grin, another bounce on the balls of his feet.

"The hospital? Why? We're not going there," Tony said dully. "I imagine they'll keep us here for another hour or two, then escort us to the Yard to wrap up."

"I know. Em isn't going to the hospital to meet us. She's going to meet your son. He was born an hour ago."

"Sorry, say again?"

"Your son," Paul said firmly. "He's here. Kate's fine. He's fine. Thirty-seven weeks is preterm, but it's late preterm, and Em said the neonatal unit didn't whisk him away. That means he's breathing well and can probably come home in a day or so."

Tony found himself eye to eye with Paul. The other man hadn't leaned down; Tony had surged up from his chair in one move. Something was in his hand—the crumpled tissue. He blotted his face again, cast it aside, and cleared his throat.

"Kate's all right?"

"Yes."

"The baby's all right?"

"A healthy boy. Maybe he'll need a little TLC since he came early. But he's good, Chief."

"But how did this happen? I read up on first time labor and delivery. It can take days."

"Not if you're brass-knuckled Katie," Paul said, seizing Tony's hands with pure delight. "This is secondhand from

Em, but apparently Kate thought she had a bad tum? That her stomach had bothered her since early morning? And when her water broke, she thought she'd wet the bed. So labor was seriously underway before sunset."

"And then what? Did Mrs. Snell drive her to hospital?"

"Henry rang for a Black cab," Paul said, squeezing his hands again. "He took charge, told Kate she was having a baby whether she believed it or not, and rode with her to hospital. If not for Henry, she probably would've given birth at home—still swearing it was just indigestion."

"That's my boy," Tony murmured. "My clever boy. And now another boy..." Suddenly he was aware that he was still clutching Paul's hands. Letting go of both at once, he grinned at the other man. Then he threw his arms around his friend and embraced him as heartily as he'd ever embraced anyone in his life.

CHAPTER 24

*O*nce for an English assignment, Henry Hetheridge had written a seven hundred word essay called, "What People Might Be Surprised to Learn About Me." The first bullet point was, "I can rough it." When called to the head of the class to read it aloud, that claim had drawn some snickers from the usual suspects, but it was true. In the days before he'd come to permanently live with Kate, he and Maura had dwelt in unheated flats, eaten catsup sandwiches for dinner, and nicked the odd item. (Maura had generally performed the operation, but once Henry himself had walked out of Poundland with a package of boys' underpants stuffed under his jumper.) To Henry's way of thinking, his experience during Nipper's birth proved that while he might look a bit soft, where it counted, he had steel.

It started when he'd gone up to the master bedroom after dinner. He always wandered in around that time, partly to check (on Tony's orders) that Kate was eating enough, and partly to see which Hammer horror movie was on. Kate hadn't touched her dinner and was in a thoroughly cranky mood, even by her standards. Every ten minutes she got up to stretch, or press her hands to the small of her back, or walk around the bed. Then it was every eight minutes. Then every five. Henry, who knew nothing about contractions except what he'd seen on telly, had picked up his mobile and consulted Google. What he saw caused him to announce, "You're in active labor!"

"Rubbish. Labor pains hurt. Like, screaming and crying hurt," Kate had said. "Like when Sir Duncan broke my knee, or when I was in rehab leaning to walk again."

Henry, who understood experientially that grownups could be dafter than the doziest donkey, had sent a text to Tony but received no reply. Looking back, he now knew that Tony must've been heading to St. John's Wood to confront Deaver, but at the time such silence was mystifying. So he'd gone downstairs to tell Mrs. Snell, who'd informed him he knew nothing about labor and not to be hysterical. Harvey was still in Saint-Tropez, of course, and the newest temporary cook had gone home. Returning to the bedroom, he found Kate still pacing with a scowl on her face. Deciding someone had better to take control, he'd rang for the Black cab.

When the car arrived, Kate put a coat on over her pajamas and let Henry lead her downstairs without complaint. Apparently by then, things down in lady-part land had progressed so much, even the most bloody-minded adult could no longer deny the truth. Mrs. Snell, who had the grace to look mortified as Henry was proven right, promised to stay behind and look after Ritchie, who wasn't alarmed in the least. He even gave Henry and Kate a cheerful, "No baby," as they left.

The first hour at the hospital had been exciting. Henry hadn't planned to stay for the birth, but since it was already in progress, he remained with Kate and held her hand. When a young nurse fretted over Kate's chart—the birth plan included an epidural, completely impossible at such a late stage—an older nurse had laughed and said, "When they're too tough to know what's happening, you can save the pain meds for after the fact."

Henry was rather proud that Kate didn't give a full-throated scream, not even once, although she did grunt a few times while squeezing his hand. After all the horror-flick screams he'd heard coming from her television over the last few weeks, he'd expected something really dramatic from a woman truly in pain, but no. Kate could rough it, too.

Nipper didn't seem happy about being born. He was small, only two and a half kilograms, and bald and red all over. Henry secretly wouldn't have blamed Kate for being disappointed, or for discreetly quizzing the doctors as to whether Nipper was likely to improve in the looks depart-ment, but she seemed almost overcome with pride. Seeing her, exhausted but radiant, beaming down at the baby on her chest, Henry was surprised to realize he wasn't jealous. He felt proud of himself, like he'd helped accomplish something vital—almost as if he'd temporarily stepped into Tony's shoes.

"What do you think of him?" Kate had asked.

"He's little."

"He is at that. And shouty. That's good. You need strong lungs to cry so loud. Come here, kiddo."

When Henry drew close, Kate planted a kiss on his fore-head. "You're my hero, did you know that?"

The declaration pleased him so much, he immediately tried to think of something reassuring to say. "Dad still hasn't texted, and neither has Paul, but I got hold of Emmeline. She said they're busy with a case and it might be hours. So I told her everything, and she said she'll come when she can, but it could be tomorrow. So I reckon I'll stay with you and

Nipper. That chair is pretty soft, and I'll bet Sister will give me a blanket."

"Thanks, love. I wouldn't want to send you home alone in a cab, anyway. And I'm not sure nurses are called 'sister' anymore."

"They are if they supervise the ward. I googled it."

She'd grinned at him, returned to her wordless happy contemplation of Nipper, and gradually fallen asleep. Henry was in the guest chair, a blanket up to his chin as he played Minecraft on his phone, when Emmeline turned up, *sans* Evvy for once.

She tried covertly inspecting Nipper without waking Kate, but that was a no-go—Kate joked that she slept with one eye open and sometimes Henry thought she really did. Rather than be annoyed by a visitor, Kate was overjoyed to see her. When their excited talk devolved into ultra-technical, down and dirty, not-fit-for-children's-tender-ears stuff, Henry decided it was time for an expedition. He wandered around that wing of the hospital's public spaces, was informed of the rules, found the vending machines, found the lavatories, was told off for snooping in a janitor's closet, and was given a packet of crisps by a pretty nurse who said he was cute. Roughing it was like going on a quest—a few surprises, a bit of danger, and the occasional treasure.

The moment Henry returned to the ward, he noticed a change in energy. Emmeline, sitting at the foot of Kate's bed, stopped talking when she saw him. Kate no longer looked uninhibitedly happy and radiant. She looked like a copper on bedrest. Nipper wasn't there.

"Where's the baby?" Henry asked, alarmed.

"Getting his Vitamin K shot and some tests. It's all right," Kate said. "He really is strong for thirty-seven weeks. They'll bring him back any minute now."

"Then why do you look like that?"

"Like what?"

"Like something's happened."

"Things *did* happen, but not to us. Tony's fine. Paul's fine. They cracked a murder case and you know how long it takes to process a scene."

Henry had stared at Kate. "No. There's something else. I know it."

"Well. My boss. Vic Jackson. Remember him? I used to call him the plonker. Then he had a change of heart, so to speak, and after that we got on all right. He even came to Wellegrave House once." She sighed. "He's dead. Someone shot him."

"Oh. Are you...okay?" he'd asked awkwardly. All he could think was, *It's not Dad. It's not Paul. We're all right.*

"I'm okay," Kate said, voice breaking. "I'm just... you know...emotional. Poor Vic. He deserved better. Just like Amelia deserved better."

"Yeah, but Dad caught the bad guy, right? He'll go to prison?"

"He's gone to the morgue," Kate had said with no particular satisfaction. "But the damage he's done will go on for years to come."

* * *

AROUND FIVE O'CLOCK THE next morning, Henry was startled awake. The ward was gloomy rather than truly dark, and a blurred figure he instantly recognized as Tony was next to Kate's bed. Putting on his specs, he saw she was asleep, and Nipper was, too, snug in his moveable cot parked nearby.

Smiling, Tony put a finger to his lips, then beckoned for Henry to follow him out to the nurses' station, where they could talk softly without causing a disturbance.

"I'm proud of you," Tony said.

"Kate did all the work. You know her. Always game."

"Yes, well. Quite. Shall I take you home?"

"No. I don't mind sleeping in the chair. I'm really very good at roughing it." Eyes roving over Tony, he added, "You look a bit tired, though."

"I am."

"You weren't in danger, were you?"

"What? No, of course not, not at all. You know, last night you demonstrated great initiative as well as great responsibility. When Paul told me how you handled things, I felt as though I left Kate in good hands." Tony smiled. "Are you ready for more responsibility? Helping smooth the way with Ritchie?"

Henry nodded. He'd momentarily forgotten about his uncle, who famously resisted any and all changes to his surroundings and routine.

"He'll be up in a couple of hours. I wonder if you might take the day off from school—I'll ring the headmaster to explain—and tell Ritchie it's a *Star Wars* day. Get him to watch *The Mandalorian* again—from the beginning."

"Ritchie only watches programs from the beginning."

"True. Then when we're all set here, probably in the late afternoon, Mrs. Snell can bring the two of you for a visit."

"I'll need vending machine money. Ritchie won't set foot in hospital unless he's promised Cornettos."

"Of course. So with that being the situation—shall I take you home? You can sleep a bit more, have breakfast, and get started priming Ritchie for the big reveal."

"All right." Henry didn't much fancy a day of corralling Ritchie, but knew it wouldn't be so bad once it got underway. He enjoyed the *Star Wars* TV programs, and Ritchie was usually good for a mock lightsaber battle. And when they returned to St. Thomas's Hospital, Henry fully intended to snag two Cornettos for himself.

* * *

THE BIG REVEAL, as Tony called it, went off surprisingly well. Ritchie had enjoyed yet another binge-watch of *The Mandalorian*, repeating key bits of dialogue at times with the precision of a holy man reciting scripture. Naturally, he balked at getting dressed to go out at four o'clock—that wasn't part of his usual routine—and threw a fit in Mrs. Snell's car, kicking the back of her seat all the way to St. Thomas's. But once he was promised Cornettos, steered to the vending machines, and permitted to choose both a vanilla and a chocolate, his mood equalized. When Henry led him into the maternity ward, Ritchie followed contentedly, licking melted ice cream from his fingers.

"Hiya, big brother," Kate said when they entered. "Look what I've got."

She was in bed, hair up in a ponytail, still beaming that maternal smile. Standing beside her, Tony held the carry cot that Kate had ordered from Etsy. It was a near-perfect replica of the flying hover pod used by Grogu, also known as Baby Yoda, in *The Mandalorian*. Despite the concessions the designer had made to infant health and safety, the carry cot looked enough like the hover pod to make Ritchie stop dead and utter, "The Child."

"That's right. The Child is here," Kate said, employing another of the adorable character's aliases. "We're calling him Nicholas. Nicky for short."

"The Child," Ritchie said again in wonder, coming in for a closer examination. Henry suspected his uncle was more fascinated by the replica hover pod than the newborn inside it, but that was all right. It was a start.

When Tony pushed back the blanket to show off baby Nicholas, who Henry was pleased to find looked slightly less red and ugly, Ritchie gazed from the infant to Tony and asked, "Yours?"

And then Tony absolutely floored Henry with a deadpan, "Where I go, he goes."

"Yeah. The Child. Where I go, he goes," Ritchie said excitedly. To him, the Mandalorian's signature declaration was only natural; indeed, if he'd expected any particular reply, that was probably it. But Henry still couldn't believe it. All the times Tony had been in the room while the program was on, ignoring the TV in a variety of ways—looking at his phone, working on his laptop, reading a book—he'd clearly listened to more than Henry ever guessed.

Tony, perhaps reading his expression, winked. And Henry, suddenly feeling very grown-up and in-the-know, winked back.

CHAPTER 25

*B*y the time Kate's official due date rolled around, Nicholas Anthony Hetheridge was twenty-one days old, had spent nineteen of them at home, and was, in his pediatrician's words, "Well on his way." He'd outgrown his apnea monitor, was feeding on schedule, and had even managed to produce a little flaxen blond hair. Tony thought it might darken up as he grew older. As a boy, he'd been platinum blond until he was nine or ten, and then his hair had turned brownish black. As for Nicholas's features, everyone said he looked like Kate, and Tony was pleased to agree with them. Apart from the baby's blue eyes, of course. At present they were a bit paler than Tony's, but in time they might darken up, too.

Inside Wellegrave House, things were humming along more smoothly now that Harvey had returned. He was tanned, rested, and had given up his combover, embracing his baldness with a close crop on the sides that made him look years younger. Mrs. Snell surprised everyone, none more than Tony, by announcing that if the offer was still open, she'd very much enjoy two weeks' vacation at the seaside. He'd driven her to Waterloo Station himself, waving goodbye with a sense of wonder as she disappeared through the glass doors. Then again, was it really so hard to believe that she might bend a little and try a proper vacation for once in her life? Heaven knew he'd evolved, and was evolving still.

The repercussions of Michael Deaver's murderous betrayal of his office, his vocation, and his fellow policemen and women was still being felt throughout the Metropolitan Police Service, and probably would continue to do so for years. Tony coped in a variety of ways, including a temporary hiatus on watching TV news or reading print journalism. The facts of the case, he could bear up to. Internal investigations had been launched. Hugh Pollack had been arrested; his lab company, Queen's Scientific, had collapsed in a riot of emergency conviction appeals and government probes. Meanwhile, inside the Met, a small group of senior detectives was threatening to take early retirement in solidarity with Deaver. They preferred to believe he'd been unfairly hounded and denied due process.

These were painful facts, but bearable. What Tony despised was the sheer glee so many media figures displayed as they twisted the scandal for their personal use. Many TV talking heads and newspaper scolds were having a fine old time of it, using Deaver's infamy to prove their own pet theories about English society—either that Deaver was the epitome of the modern policeman, rotten to the core, or that he was a distinguished public servant, guilty of bending the rules and all but murdered in a rush to judgment. Tony refused to willingly subject himself to either viewpoint. There was too much good in his world for him to waste time chasing caricatures, cynical misrepresentations, and outright lies.

For Parth Chakrabarti, the news that Michael Deaver,

one of the men he'd relentlessly accused of abetting a coverup, was in fact Valeria's murderer and had indeed concealed most of the evidence, came as a shock. The news that Deaver had also been Valeria's lover for ten years, keeping her bundled away in a love nest to rendezvous with her whenever he felt like it, came as a far greater shock. Paul, who broke the news in the presence of Parth, Ken Hussy, Antonio, and Octavia, had described it thus:

"He asked me if Deaver was blackmailing Valeria. I said no, there was no evidence of coercion. He made a sound—I can't describe it. Sort of a gurgle. He asked if Valeria knew Deaver was married. I said yes. He asked why, after ten years, Deaver had turned on her. I said—delicately—that he accused Valeria of infidelity, and she said if he wanted fidelity, he should divorce his wife and marry her. That's when Parth made another sound, grabbed his left arm with his right, and fell over. Wham! Right on his face."

Tony asked, "Did anyone go to him?"

"I rang 999," Paul had said with a shrug. "Octavia and Antonio put their heads together and started talking about solicitors. Apparently Parth had several and they were trying to figure out which one could quickly grant power of attorney. They were still talking about it when the paramedics wheeled Parth away on a gurney. That was all. Oh, except Ken Hussy shook my hand and thanked me for not spilling the beans about his bog hookups with Valeria. I had to wipe my hand off afterward. Sweaty palms—gross."

Parth Chakrabarti survived his heart attack and the stroke that followed three days later, but his reversal of fortune wasn't complete. During his brief but total incapacitation, Antonio had been granted power of attorney and used it to demolish the concrete patio built over Highgate House's old swimming pool. No ground penetrating radar needed—five hours into the job, an ordinary building crew had discovered the remains of Mandy Haystack and Tassos Vlachos. Both had been killed by blunt force trauma to the head. That was Parth—none too subtle.

Even with his vast fortune, Parth was unlikely to escape conviction and imprisonment, unless ill health disposed of him first. Tony had it on very good authority from DC Kincaid that Octavia Chakrabarti had strolled into Parth's posh private hospital room and announced, "Mummy and the pool boy are home at last!" The result had been more doctors, nurses, and a crash cart. Though Octavia had been barred from visiting her father's room again, she'd gone away with a smile on her face.

As for Kate, she was spending plenty of new mummy time with Nicholas, but she was working, too—two or three hours a day, at the computer, on her phone, and via tele-meeting apps like Zoom. Her insight that Orrin Parker's "Happy birthday to you is happy birthday to me" tweet might point to a doppelgänger—in this case, a twin brother—had proved prescient.

Orrin and his identical twin Brent had been placed in care at age two and cycled among various foster families, sometimes together but more often apart. They'd grown up with less of a bond than most twins, seeing one another only sporadically. Few of Brent's friends knew about Orrin, and none of Orrin's friends knew about Brent. While Brent had stayed in Waltham Forest, near his last foster family, Orrin had bounced around London, acquiring boyfriends, draining what he could out of them, reinventing himself, and moving on.

Working on the hypothesis that Orrin had killed Lin Wu Chen—with Brent, dressed in his scrubs and wearing his ID, standing in for him at the hospital to provide an alibi, Kate had dug up sufficient circumstantial evidence to charge Orrin Parker with first-degree murder. Tony worried that the jury would acquit—what Deaver had said about the public expecting unassailable forensic evidence had been true—but the charge alone had provided Deputy Director Xiuying Chen with a measure of closure. Nothing could bring back her son, but at least Orrin Parker had been proved guilty to her satisfaction, whether the justice system upheld that verdict or not.

"Just goes to show," Kate said airily after relaying the news to Tony. She was sitting in a recliner with Nicholas in her arms, who was snoozing after a feeding.

"Goes to show what?"

"That you can learn a lot from Hammer horror movies. My bedrest was time well spent. Take Nicky, will you?"

"Should I? He always wakes the moment you pass him to me."

"I know. It's like your cousin Lucinda Perkins-Jones said. He's not the best sleeper. I'll do it very gently."

The transfer was smooth. Nevertheless, the moment baby Nicholas was in Tony's arms, he gave a sort of half-cry, looked at Tony resentfully, and gave a weak kick to emphasize his unhappiness.

"Sing to him," Kate suggested.

Tony raised his eyebrows.

"Maybe not sing. Talk to him. Tell him about that book you're reading. The one about the Greek."

"Archimedes?"

"That's the one."

"It isn't really about him, because very little about Archimedes is known for certain. It's about science and mathematics in the era of Roman conquest. The law of hydrostatics and—"

"Right. That's the stuff," Kate said, closing her eyes. "I can feel sleep coming on already."

Tony looked down at the child in his arms. Nicholas,

who'd settled a bit while Tony was speaking, kicked again. Apparently he wanted more.

How to begin?

"Once upon a time, in a land called Italy, there was a wise old man named Archimedes. He wanted very much to defend his home, Syracuse, from the invading Roman army. He had the idea of using a claw to defend the city walls against amphibious attack..."

Nicholas's eyes closed. His arms and legs relaxed as his breathing grew slow and regular.

"I'll do my best for you, my little love," Tony said, smiling down at the boy. He waited for another kick or a fretful sound, but his son was fast asleep.

THE END

Lord & Lady Hetheridge will return for future mysteries

ABOUT THE AUTHOR

Emma Jameson is the author of the *New York Times* and *USA Today* bestselling *Lord & Lady Hetheridge Mystery Series*. She also writes the *Jem Jago Mystery Series*, published by Bookouture, and the *Dr. Benjamin Bones Mysteries*.

Ms. Jameson loves to hear from her readers. Look her up on Facebook or Twitter (and sometimes Instagram) and follow her on Bookbub for her semi-weekly book recommendations.

Made in the USA
Columbia, SC
21 February 2022